James jammed the Yellow Boy to his shoulder. He fed round, fired, fed another round, fired. Turning, he sent o more shots at buckskin-clad centaurs. Slugs pock-arked the ground around him. Then his head seemed burst and he fell as if from a great height into a well at wasn't water but a liquid pitch. He feebly tried to ach the surface and was sucked into near nothingness. mly, he was aware of rough hands, of being jostled, of topsy-turvy world with him on his back and painted ages floating in misty ether. Iron fingers gouged his ck. The tip of a knife wavered before his eyes.

Teeth gleamed in a vicious sneer.

This was it, James thought. He tried to resist but he d no strength. His vitality was leaking out his head. e black pitch sucked him down and he was on the rge of going under when a harsh martial blare fell dis-rdant on his ears.

The blackness claimed him.

RIDE TO VALOR

DAVID ROBBINS

A SIGNET BOOK

SIGNET
Published by New American Library, a division of
Penguin Group (USA) Inc., 375 Hudson Street,
New York, New York 10014, USA
Penguin Group (Canada), 90 Eglinton Avenue East, Suite 700, Toronto,
Ontario M4P 2Y3, Canada (a division of Pearson Penguin Canada Inc.)
Penguin Books Ltd., 80 Strand, London WC2R 0RL, England
Penguin Ireland, 25 St. Stephen's Green, Dublin 2,
Ireland (a division of Penguin Books Ltd.)
Penguin Group (Australia), 250 Camberwell Road, Camberwell, Victoria 3124,
Australia (a division of Pearson Australia Group Pty. Ltd.)
Penguin Books India Pvt. Ltd., 11 Community Centre, Panchsheel Park,
New Delhi - 110 017, India
Penguin Group (NZ), 67 Apollo Drive, Rosedale, North Shore 0632,
New Zealand (a division of Pearson New Zealand Ltd.)
Penguin Books (South Africa) (Pty.) Ltd., 24 Sturdee Avenue,
Rosebank, Johannesburg 2196, South Africa

Penguin Books Ltd., Registered Offices:
80 Strand, London WC2R 0RL, England

First published by Signet, an imprint of New American Library,
a division of Penguin Group (USA) Inc.

First Printing, February 2011
10   9   8   7   6   5   4   3   2   1

To Judy, Joshua, and Shane

BEFORE THE WEST

1

His parents named him James Marion Doyle. He was their first and only. His mother doted over him and spent many an hour cradling him in her arms and humming softly while rocking in her chair at the window that overlooked Little Water Street.

His earliest memories were of her. She was always warm and tender and smiling. In those early years she never once spoke harshly to him or hit him.

Of his father he had fewer memories, in large part because his father was gone from before the crack of day until after the streetlamps were lit. Six days a week his father toiled at the Hudson Barrel Company. On the seventh his parents took him to church. They would have a big meal later, their biggest of the week.

James got to know his father hardly at all. So little, in later years he couldn't remember what color his father's eyes had been.

They shared a house with three families. The hallways always smelled of food and tobacco and less pleasant odors. Their rooms were small. In the summer they sweltered and in the winter they were cold, but to him those rooms were heaven.

They lived in the Five Points District. He didn't entirely understand why, but he heard others say it was a bad place to live. The streets were always jammed with people. There was always a lot of noise and commotion. Hawkers sold everything from coal to apples to knives.

One day his mother dressed him in his best clothes and put on her hat and took him to the mercantile. He loved to go there. The bins and shelves were filled with so many delights, he'd gawk in desire and amazement. But that day, along the way, his mother suddenly pulled him close and backed into a doorway and he felt her shiver as if she were cold even though the day was hot.

A group of much older boys was swaggering down the street. Each wore a blue shirt and a high hat. Everyone got out of their way. One man who had his back to them didn't see them and they shoved him aside and laughed. The man had a cane but he didn't use it. He smiled a timid sort of smile.

The group came abreast of the doorway, and James felt his mother's fingers dig so deep into his shoulders, it hurt.

He cried out, and all of them stopped.

"Here's a fine beauty," one said.

"I'd have her," said another.

"None of that," his mother said. She had that tone she used when James misbehaved. It made some of them snicker.

"Tough muff, she is."

One of them with a big belly and a round face came so close that James smelled his sweat.

"How about you and me, then, beauty?"

"Leave us be," his mother said.

Grabbing her arm, he leered and said, "Right here."

James sensed his mother was scared, and he didn't

like that the one with the belly had taken hold of her. "Go away!" he shouted, and pushed.

The other didn't budge. But he did scowl and poke James in the chest. "Will you look at this? Her little protector. Didn't anyone teach you, boy? The Blue Shirts smash gnats." He balled his fist. "Like I'm about to smash you."

James bunched his own fists.

Just then another of the Blue Shirts, who sported a scar on his left cheek, said simply, "No."

"Why not?" the one with the belly demanded. "Do you know them?"

"No."

"Then why shouldn't I, damn it?"

"I said so."

The scarred one spoke so quietly that James barely heard him, yet the one with the belly jerked his arm down and let go.

"I was only playing, Coil. A bit of fun."

"We have somewhere to be," Coil said, and the one with the belly and the rest moved on. Coil looked at James and then at his mother.

"I had a little brother. Looked up to me, he did. It got him killed."

"I'm sorry," James's mother said.

Coil didn't seem to hear her. "The Dead Rabbits gutted him. They didn't care he was only twelve." Coil reached out as if to place his hand on James's arm, but instead he suddenly stepped back. "Sorry about Orlan, missus. He's a bit of a pig."

Then they were alone, and James heard his mother let out a long breath. "Who were they?" he asked.

"A gang."

James's father had warned him about gangs. The Five Points was overrun with them. There were the Slaughterhouses, the Bowery Boys, the Swamp Angels, the Dead Rabbits, and others.

Sometimes at night James heard his parents mention them, but most of the time they talked about money, and how they had too little of it and their dreams of having more. He didn't care about money. He had *them*, and he was happy.

His mother did washing and ironing. People brought baskets of clothes and she'd spend hour after hour with her arms in water up to her elbows scrubbing and wringing, or applying the heavy iron. He helped with what little he could, but mostly he spent his time playing. He had a good life and as young as he was, he knew it was good. He would have liked for it to last forever.

Then came a day that started like any other.

His mother was up first, bustling about making breakfast. James lay in bed half asleep. The occasional clank of a pot or a pan would rouse him and he'd drift off again. Presently James heard the sounds his father made clearing his throat and sinuses, and other sounds James would rather not listen to. Some mornings father came in and pecked him on the head but not this morning. James heard him say he was running late.

After the front door closed, it was always quiet for a while. His mother liked to sit by the window and sip her first tea of the day. Her quiet time, she called it.

A woman brought a basket of clothes to be washed and his mother set to work. He handed her the wet shirts and dresses, and she hung them on the line. He mentioned that he would very much like a kitten.

"Our place is barely big enough for us, son. We don't need any animals besides."

"You'd like a bigger house, wouldn't you?" James asked. He'd heard her say so many times.

"Yes," she admitted, and a wistful expression came over her. "I'd like one with an upstairs and a downstairs, and an extra bedroom for guests, and a yard so I could plant flowers."

"Could we have a pony?" James had wanted one ever since he saw another boy on a pony in the park. He'd pestered his parents to death, but his father always said it was a luxury they couldn't afford.

"A pony for you and a carriage for me," his mother said, and laughed. "Listen to us. Silly, isn't it, James? But a person can dream."

His mother liked to call him James. His father called him Jim. He liked James better.

By early afternoon they were done. His mother was in her rocker, watching the passersby on the street. He was playing with tin soldiers his father had bought for him when there came a knock on the door. He went on playing as his mother rose and asked, "Who is it?"

A man answered, saying he was Mr. Wilbur from the Hudson Barrel Company.

James hardly paid attention. Men from his father's work came to see them now and then. It was nothing new. He heard the buzz of voices and realized there were other men with Mr. Wilbur.

Then his mother screamed.

James would never forget her cry. It stopped his heart in his chest and his breath in his lungs and filled him with his first taste of deep and total terror. He recovered and jumped up in time to see his mother swoon and one of the men catch her. They carried her to the rocker and carefully set her down and Mr. Wilbur went and filled a glass with water.

"What's the matter?" James asked. "What have you done?"

"Hush, boy," one of the men said. His name was Charley, and he was a friend of James's father. "Be still for her sake."

James didn't know what to do. He yearned to run to her, but they were in his way. He saw Mr. Wilbur tilt the glass to her lips. She swallowed and straightened, her blue eyes wide with fright.

"It's not true. It can't be true."

"I'm sorry, Mary," Charley said. "There was nothing any of us could do."

James had never seen his mother so pale. He edged toward her to take her hand but stopped when tears trickled down her cheeks. He had never seen her cry before.

"The team spooked and the load shifted, Mrs. Doyle," Mr. Wilbur said. "Randall was behind the wagon and—" He stopped and sadly shook his head.

"Crushed," another man said, and both Mr. Wilbur and Charley cast harsh looks at him.

"Dear God," his mother said, and bowed her head. "What are we to do?"

Mr. Wilbur patted her arm. "Randall was well thought of. We took up a collection." He reached into a coat pocket and produced bills and coins. "There's nearly fifty dollars here."

"It's the best we could do," Charley said.

"Fifty dollars?" his mother said. As if in a daze, she took the money and placed it in her lap.

Mr. Wilbur patted her some more. "I'm sure you and the boy will do fine. I'm told you are a laundress."

"Fifty dollars," his mother said.

"All the best to you." Mr. Wilbur motioned at the others, and they filed out.

Charley lingered in the doorway. "If there's anything my Sally and me can do, Mary, get word to us."

"Thank you."

The door closed. James hesitated, wanting to go to her but confused and uncertain. She had such a stricken look. He thought she would cry and she did; she covered her face with both hands and sobbed in great racking heaves. It scared him almost as much as her scream. She sobbed and sobbed, and he stood in the shadows until she grew quiet and still, and he asked, "Mama, what's happened to Papa?"

"He's dead."

"Dead?" James had seen dead animals and gone to a funeral for a dead aunt, but he never, ever imagined his father or mother would die.

"Gone, dear. Forever."

James went to her and clasped her hand. "What will we do without him?"

Instead of answering, she burst out sobbing anew.

2

His mother was never the same.

Where before she was always smiling and often laughed and had a sunny disposition, now she never smiled and was often grim. She took in more laundry than ever. She worked so hard that at night she was too exhausted to do more than sit in her chair and stare gloomily at the walls.

James did his best to help all he could. For a while a lot of people came and went and several ladies lent a hand, but they couldn't lend a hand forever and soon it was only his mother and him in their own little world.

One night she lifted him onto her lap on the chair, something she hadn't done since he was small. "I want you to know what's happening. I need you to be brave and it will help you if you know. Do you understand?"

"I think I do."

"I'm doing the best I can, but I can't promise it will be good enough."

"Good enough for what?"

"To keep the life we had. Women don't earn as much as men. I've never thought it fair, but there it is. It would help if we had relatives to help us out, but your father's side of the family never did take to me. They thought he could do better."

"Grandpa and Grandma Doyle?" James got to see them twice a year. They'd bring gifts and tell him that they loved him.

"I was too common for them. They wanted your father to marry up."

James didn't know what that meant, but he decided not to ask.

"I wish my own parents were still alive. The yellow fever took them, as you already know. And I don't have any brothers or sisters." She stopped and closed her eyes and for some reason said softly, "Oh, God."

"Mama?"

She opened them and tenderly touched his chin. "I'm all right. I'll always be all right as long as I have you." She kissed his forehead. "Anyway, I don't want you to worry."

"I'm not," James said.

"We'll make do. It won't be easy, and we'll have to scrimp, but we'll get by." Suddenly she clasped him to her and shuddered. "Oh, my sweet boy. My sweet, sweet boy." She held him awhile and then she set him down. Her eyes were moist. She told him to get ready for bed and went back to rocking and staring at the wall.

James was afraid. He'd lost his father and his mother was acting peculiar. When she took him for infrequent walks, the bustling streets that once fascinated him now seemed a lot less friendly.

His mother lost weight. She didn't keep herself as pretty as she used to. Her hair wasn't always in place and her dresses weren't always as neat. In the evening, she'd open a bottle and sit in her rocker with a glass in her hand.

It was late autumn, the trees stark and bare, when she

sat him at the table one windy night and poured a glass for herself. "I am afraid we have to move."

"Move?" James repeated. This was their home. It had never occurred to him that they might leave it.

"We've used up what little we had saved, and I can't make the rent on my own."

"Move where?" James asked.

"Somewhere cheaper. Don't worry. We'll find a place easy enough. But it probably won't be as nice." She looked around them and her eyes misted.

"I don't want to."

"Now, now."

"I want to stay here."

"Stop," she said. "Don't make it harder than it has to be. I've done the best I can."

"It's not right." James felt his own eyes watering.

"No, it's not," she agreed. "You'll find as you grow older that there's a lot that's not right with this world. Your father and I were able to protect you from what's out there, but now he's gone and there's only so much I can do alone."

"You work so hard."

She smiled wearily. "I do it for us, son. To earn money so we can survive."

"Can I earn money, too?"

"If it comes to that. But I'd rather you were at my side for now. It's more bearable for me with you around." She clasped his hand. "You are my reason for living."

The next day they started looking for a new place. James didn't like any of them. The buildings were too crowded and the rooms were cold and cheerless, and most were in need of repair. Some had no glass in the windows. Others were filthy.

The third day they were met by a portly man who wore an ill-fitting suit and a bowler. He kept smiling at

James's mother in a way that James didn't like. His name was McGill, and he showed them two rooms at the back. Only one had a window that looked out on the grimy wall of another building. There was a small stove and nothing else.

"You'll like it here, ma'am," McGill said. "The nights are quiet, and the people are friendly."

"It needs a good cleaning," his mother said.

"It will make a fine home for you and the wee lad. And if there's ever anything you need, you have only to ask."

"I don't know."

"Yes or no? If you don't want to, there are others who will."

To James's dismay his mother said yes.

She used some of their precious money to hire two men to help move. It took a whole day. The men didn't take the dining room table or his mother's chest of drawers. He was surprised to learn she had sold them.

"It all wouldn't fit," she explained.

Their first night in their new home proved McGill a liar. It wasn't quiet at all. People yelled and cursed and stomped about. Doors were always slamming and children were always crying.

James lay in his bed with his back to the bedlam and hated it. He had an awful feeling. A sense that, as bad as things were, they could get worse. He felt cold all over and pulled his blankets tighter. "Please, God, no," he said, as somewhere in the building a baby bawled.

3

Lost Souls, the street was called. James went out the next morning and stood on the stoop. His mother was ironing. He debated whether to go for a walk around the new neighborhood.

The street was narrow, the flow of people continuous; men in shabby suits, ladies in plain dresses, urchins in need of a washing. Few laughed or smiled and fewer still looked the least bit happy. It made James strangely uneasy. He started to turn to go back in and stopped.

Coming down Lost Souls in a wedge were a dozen or more Blue Shirts. Anyone in their path got quickly out of the way. They hardly noticed, or if they did, they didn't let on. They were somehow apart and different from everyone else.

James felt a tingle of excitement watching them. In the lead was the one with the scar he had seen before. The Blue Shirts went past the stoop, and the one with the scar smiled.

James smiled back. He almost ran after them. He wanted to ask the scarred one what it was like being a Blue Shirt.

The door opened, and his mother's hand fell on his shoulder.

"Here you are! What are you doing outside by yourself?" She didn't let him answer. "If I've told you once, I've told you a dozen times, you're not to step foot out of our apartment without me. Is that understood?"

"Ahhh, Mama."

She pulled him inside and closed the door. "You'll heed me, James Marion. The Five Points is no place for a child to wander about alone. I've lost your father, and I'll not lose you."

That night she lit a candle and put it on the table, and they ate stew and bread with butter and for dessert there was apple pie. They were celebrating, his mother said, their new home.

As she was tucking him in, James asked a question that had been bothering him. He didn't want to bring it up, but he had to know. "Will I go to a new school now?" He had been attending St. John's.

His mother tenderly brushed his cheek. "I'll check into it. To be honest, I've been too busy with the move to think about much else. I'm sorry."

"It's all right," James said. He didn't really want to go. He'd rather stay home with her. To his relief, she didn't mention it the next day or the day after and in a week he figured she had forgotten about it.

For a while they were busy with the laundry. A few weeks passed, and people brought less for her to do. One evening his mother was in her rocking chair and he was playing with his tin soldiers when she remarked out of the blue, "It's getting harder."

James looked up from where he lay on the floor. "What is?"

"To make ends meet. My old customers don't care

to come this far. Some stuck with me for a while out of
courtesy, I expect."

"Can't you find new people with dirty clothes?"

His mother smiled. "I'll certainly try. I'll post notices around. Maybe that will bring them. If not—" She
stopped, and frowned.

"If not what?"

"I'll have to find something else. We can't miss on the
rent. Mr. McGill says he'll overlook it if we're a little
late, but I'd rather not, anyway."

"Do you like him, Mama?"

"Mr. McGill? Why do you ask?"

"I don't know," James said. "He looks at you strange.
If Papa were alive I don't think he would like him."

"Now, now," she said.

More days passed. His mother put up notices, but
only a few people brought laundry. She took to having a
glass of wine with their supper. She had always enjoyed
wine, he remembered, and now she seemed to enjoy it
a lot more. She became quieter than she ever had been.

James wondered why she made only soup for supper. Watery soup, with a few vegetables and sometimes
no meat. For breakfast they had oatmeal but they only
rarely had milk, so he had to have it with water and no
sugar.

One evening there was a knock at the door. James saw
his mother give a start. She squared her shoulders and
smiled and opened it, and it was Mr. McGill, his bowler
in hand.

"How do you do, missus? Sorry to bother you but it's
been a week, and the rent is overdue."

"I know," his mother said, and there was an edge to
her voice that James had never heard, a hint of something he could not quite grasp. "And I'm sorry."

"Do you have it?" McGill asked.

"No, I do not, but I should in a few days. I have more laundry coming."

"Mrs. Doyle," McGill said.

"I'll have it. I promise."

"It's not that. As you know, I only manage the building. The owner doesn't like it when the rent is this late. He might demand I throw you out—"

His mother clutched McGill's arm. "Please. No. Anything but that."

McGill looked at her hand and then at her and his thick lips curled in a smile that somehow wasn't a smile. "Anything, missus?"

"Oh, God," his mother said. She took a deep breath and looked over her shoulder at James. "I need to talk in private with Mr. McGill. Why don't you run out and sit on the stoop? We'll only be a while."

James didn't want to. Something was going on here he didn't understand. But he always did as she asked, so he slipped past and ran down the hall.

Night was falling. All across the Five Points, lights glowed in windows and smoke curled from chimneys. James sat on the bottom step with his hand wrapped around his legs and missed his father more than ever. He tried not to think of his mother and the man with the big belly. He almost wanted to cry, with no idea why. He was so sad that he didn't realize someone had come up to him until a shoe filled his vision. He craned his head back in surprise. "You."

The tall boy with the scar was alone. He leaned against the rail and pushed his high hat back on his head. "Kid," he said.

"You're Coil," James said. "I remember the other boy saying."

"And you would be?"

James told him.

"You have a sharp look about you," Coil said. "I like that. The sharp ones always make the best."

"The best what?"

"Blue Shirts."

"I'm not a Blue Shirt," James said.

Coil sank beside him and leaned back with his elbows on a higher step. "Would you like to be?"

"Me?"

Coil gestured at the dark grimy buildings and the squares of light. "This is the Five Points, boy. It's dog-eat-dog. You can't make it on your own. To survive you need to join a gang and it might as well be us as any of the others. You'll have friends. You'll have money. I'd speak for you if you wanted."

"Speak for me?" James said, unsure what that meant.

"Put you up to join. We're always on the lookout for new blood and I've had my eye on you."

"You have?"

Coil stood. "Think about it. You can find us at the barbershop on Tenth. My uncle owns it and—" Coil stopped.

The front door had opened. Out stepped McGill, buttoning his rumpled jacket. He drew up short and blurted, "Coileanin."

"Fat man," Coil said.

"Don't call me that."

Coil slid a hand behind him. His eyes glittered. "You telling a Blue Shirt what to do?"

McGill shook his head, his fleshy cheeks jiggling. "No. Never. I don't like being called fat, is all."

Coil uttered a bark of contempt. "Do I look like I give a damn what you like, fat man? Maybe I should give a holler. I bet my friends and me can whittle some of that fat off you."

McGill didn't say anything. He slipped past James

and scuttled away down the street as if he had to get somewhere in a great hurry.

"Tub of lard," Coil said under his breath.

"He was afraid of you," James said in awe.

"He was afraid of this," Coil said, and touched his shirt. "When you're a Blue Shirt, you get respect. No one gives us guff, not unless they want to bleed. It's us against them and they damn well know it."

"Them?" James said.

"The rest of the world." Coil hooked his thumbs in his suspenders. "I've got to go. Think about my offer."

"I will," James said.

4

His mother took to drinking more and more. She went all over looking for work to do in addition to her laundry, but there wasn't a lot to be had. It didn't help that there were few jobs for women. She would set out early and not get home until late and have nothing to show for her efforts other than sore feet and fatigue. Then she would feed him sparse fare and sit in her rocking chair with a bottle on the small table next to her and her glass always full.

She had stopped drinking wine and switched to whiskey. James read it on the label. He remembered his father drank whiskey now and then and once told him he shouldn't touch the stuff until he was full grown.

It was several weeks after the incident with McGill that she asked him to come over to the rocker. He sat cross-legged in front of her. He had never seen her so worn. Her cheeks were not as full as they had been and her eyes had dark rings under them. He put his elbows on his knees and his chin in his hands and said, "Mama?"

She sipped and looked down at him. "You should stop calling me that."

"Mama?"

"Didn't you hear me? You're old enough now, you should call me Mother or even Ma. Mama sounds baby-ish."

"But you've always liked me to call you that."

"Not anymore. It reminds me too much of the life we used to have."

"And that's bad?"

"It's not good to think of those days. All it does is bring tears." She downed more whiskey. "We have to have a serious talk."

"What about?"

"You."

James tried to think of anything he might have done wrong. He'd been doing his chores as he should. It kept her in a better mood when she didn't have to ask him again and again to clean or sweep or wash dishes. "What did I do?"

"Nothing. And that's the problem."

"Problem?" James was confused.

She gazed about the room, her face so very sad. "The rent is due in a few days. I have enough this time, thank God. But I might not the next time. Not if I have to do it all alone."

"Work, you mean?"

"Exactly." She nodded and smiled. "You always were a smart one. The truth is, son, this world isn't fair. It's easier for a man than for a woman. For men there are all kinds of jobs. For women there are only a few. There's being a laundress, or a seamstress, or washing dishes, and others, but none pays well. Not enough for a woman by herself to get by."

"What can I do?" James was eager to help. He would do anything to have her happy again.

"You're almost twelve. I see a lot of boys your age with jobs."

"You want me to get one?"

She drained her glass and promptly refilled it and sat back with her eyes pits of misery. "You do know I've tried, don't you? To protect you from the rest of the world? To keep you safe and make things easier for you?"

"I know you love me," James said.

His mother looked away and her throat bobbed. She coughed and drank and sighed. "I hate this. I hate having to ask you to find a job. But unless we have more money coming in, I can't keep up the rent. And McGill made it plain that if we miss the rent a second time we'll be out on the street."

James flushed with anger. "He'll throw us out?"

"He would have to. It's his job. He works for another man who owns this building and the other man doesn't care if I'm a widow barely scraping by. All the other man cares about is his money."

"That's not right," James said.

"No, it's not, but it's how the world is, and there's nothing we can do about it." She paused. "Will you do it? Will you help me and try to find work?"

"Sure, Mama—" James said, and caught himself. "Sure, Mother. Whatever you want."

She bent and put her hand on his head and affectionately tousled his mop of hair. "You've always been a dutiful son. I'll say that for you. I hear other mothers say how much trouble their boys give them, and I give thanks to the Almighty for having a fine son like you."

The very next day James eagerly set out to find employment. He went to a score of merchants and asked if they needed someone to sweep and clean. No one did. He stopped at a stable and asked if they needed someone to clean up after the horses. They didn't. Whenever he saw a "help wanted" sign in a window, he went in and inquired, and each and every time they told him he was too young.

It'd go so, by the middle of the afternoon he was so discouraged he sat on a curb and glumly watched the passersby and wondered how in the world he could help his mother when everything was against him. And then splashes of blue appeared amid the browns and grays and other drab colors, and he sat up. It was half a dozen Blue Shirts. He hadn't seen any of them before. They moved along the street as if they owned it, and everyone gave them a wide berth, even grown men.

James remembered, suddenly. He got to his feet and went in search of the barbershop. A balding middle-aged man was clipping hair for a nicely dressed gentleman who had his head back and his eyes closed. James stood in the doorway waiting for the barber to notice him and finally coughed to get the barber's attention.

"What is it, boy?" the man said as he snipped. "Do you want a haircut?"

"I'm looking for Coil. Are you his uncle?"

The man stopped and turned. He pointed at a narrow hall at the rear. "Go out the back."

That was all he said. James thanked him and hastened through. The latch grated and the door opened into a blaze of sunlight and a small bare lot with a high fence on all sides.

There were Blue Shirts everywhere. Lounging, sitting, leaning against the fence, talking and smiling and laughing. Some were smoking, others were throwing knives and sticking them in the fence. One was hammering long nails into a short club. They all glanced over, and quiet fell.

James wanted to wither into his shoes. Mustering his courage, he said, "I'm looking for Coil if you please."

Some of the Blue Shirts snickered and smirked and

from among them came Orlan, smirking the widest of them all. "If you please?" he mimicked, and put his hands on his hips. "Ain't he polite?"

"I'm looking for Coil," James repeated.

"You found me," Orlan said, "and I don't like you."

"I don't want trouble."

Orlan laughed and raised his voice. "Did you hear that? The brat doesn't want trouble. Yet trouble is what he's in for."

"I'm not a brat," James said. He was scared, but he was also mad. The other outweighed him by a hundred pounds, but he didn't care. "You take that back."

"How about I beat you black-and-blue?" Orlan said, and raised his fists.

James had never been in a fight. Not a real one. He'd wrestled and roughhoused, but he'd never been out to hurt anyone, and no one had been out to hurt him. Orlan hit him in the gut so hard, his whole body exploded with pain, and he doubled over, his head swimming. Orlan gripped the front of his shirt and the next thing he knew, he was flung onto his hands and knees.

James heard gruff laughter. His vision cleared, and he raised his head. He was ringed by Blue Shirts.

"On your feet. I'm not done."

"I just want to see Coil," James said.

"Coil, Coil, Coil," Orlan said in his mincing way. "Sweet on him, are you?"

"What?" James said.

"On your damn feet. You're making me mad and you don't want to be doing that." Without warning he drew back his foot.

James tried to throw himself to one side, but he was too slow. A boot caught him in the ribs and more agony burst in his chest. He was knocked onto his side, and he clutched himself. It took every ounce of will he had not to cry.

"Look at him." Orlan paraded for the others. "A damned sissy boy is what he is."

"Stomp him."

"Beat him good."

"Make him crawl."

Orlan bent so his face was close to James's. "Hear that, brat? They're out for blood. If you're not a Blue Shirt, you're an enemy." He grabbed James's hair. "What will it be first? A black eye or a bloody mouth?"

Deep inside James, something snapped. He had been mad before but never mad like this. Never so furious that he lost control. With an inarticulate snarl of rage and hurt, he swung his right fist and caught Orlan full on the lips. Blood spurted, and Orlan cried out and stepped back, and James heaved up and went after him. He swung in a blind blur, fist after hard fist, hitting Orlan's moon of a face. Cartilage crunched and wet drops spattered him. As in a haze he saw Orlan stagger back, saw scarlet everywhere. He kept on hitting. A blow glanced off his temple. Another seared his side. Orlan had recovered from his initial shock and was fighting back.

James tried to bring the bigger boy down. He was big for his age, but he wasn't big enough. Suddenly his head imploded, and the sky and the ground changed places. He was on his back, overcome by nausea, struggling for breath.

Above him loomed a crimson block of wrath. "Goddamn you," Orlan husked, and spat a gob of blood. "Goddamn if I'm not going to kill you."

"Do it!" someone yipped.

"Cut him!" a second yelled.

Orlan reached behind him and when his hand reappeared, he held a knife. He wagged it so the blade gleamed. His bloody lips curled. "This will teach you to bother the Blue Shirts." He went to lunge but glanced up sharply.

James realized the other boys had gone silent. They were all looking toward the barbershop. He twisted his neck.

Coil filled the doorway, and fire danced in his eyes. When he came toward them, he moved with the menacing grace of a tawny panther. He looked down at James and then at Orlan. "I told you to leave him be."

"I can do as I please," Orlan said.

"I asked him here," Coil said quietly. "To put him up as a Blue Shirt."

"He's not one of us yet. And until he is, he's fair game."

Coil's hand came from behind him, and he was holding a knife of his own. "You did this on purpose. You've pushed and you've pushed and now you'll get your wish."

"Hold on," said a boy who shouldered through the ring. "A Blue never fights a brother Blue."

"Unless it's to challenge the leader," Coil said. "That's what this is about."

The same boy turned to Orlan. "Is this true? You're laying claim?"

"I have the right," Orlan said.

"Any of us does," the boy replied. "But Coileanin has been the best we've ever had. Only a fool would want to take his place."

"I'll remember you said that when I'm on top," Orlan said.

Coil reached down with his free hand and yanked James to his feet. "Out of the way. We'll talk after."

"You're awful confident," Orlan said.

"I'm awful good," Coil answered, and was on the heavier boy in a flash of motion.

Most of the others backed quickly away. Amazement rooted James. He couldn't believe what he was seeing: a real, honest-to-God knife fight.

Coil thrust and Orlan sidestepped. Orlan stabbed and Coil backpedaled. For all his bulk, Orlan had fast hands. But Coil was incredibly quick and it was apparent within seconds that Orlan stood little to no chance. Orlan showed no fear, though, as Coil forced him back. When Orlan had retreated to within a few paces of the fence, he set himself and stubbornly held his ground. He was nicked on the arm. He received a cut on the cheek. Beads of sweat broke out on his face.

"We should stop them," a Blue Shirt said.

"A challenge is to the death," said another.

It hadn't occurred to James that either would die.

A rock caught his eye, and he scooped it up. None of the Blue Shirts were paying attention to him, so it was safe to say they were as surprised as Orlan when James threw the rock with all his strength and it struck Orlan on the side of his head below the ear. Orlan howled and staggered and his knife arm drooped. Instantly, Coil flicked his blade. Orlan howled a second time as blood welled, and his knife landed at his feet.

Everyone froze, Orlan in dread, Coil with his knife poised, the rest of the Blue Shirts in anticipation of the life about to be taken.

"Finish him!" someone hollered, and others echoed his sentiment.

Coil touched the tip of his blade to Orlan's throat.

James's breath caught in his own. He was about to see someone slain. His mother would say it was terrible and he should look away, but he found it exciting, and couldn't.

Orlan was trembling. He poured sweat, and licked his thick lips. "What are you waiting for?" he croaked.

Coil slowly lowered his arm. "I take your life now, some will think I didn't take it fairly." He glanced at James.

"I had to," James said.

"What, then?" another asked. "He challenged you, didn't he?"

"I might be making a mistake, but I choose another punishment," Coil said. "We banish him."

"No," Orlan said.

Coil gestured with his knife. "Take off your shirt. You no longer have the right to wear it. From here on out, you're as much an enemy as the Swamp Angels or the Dead Rabbits."

"Not this," Orlan said, his cuts forgotten as he looked in appeal at the others. "I'd rather die than this."

"Your shirt," Coil said again, his tone brooking no argument, and several of the other boys moved in, knives in their hands.

"You heard him," said a tall boy with flaxen hair.

"You never did know when to keep your big mouth shut, Orlan," remarked a companion with eyes as black as night.

Not a single face mirrored sympathy. Orlan flushed and swore and threw his high hat to the ground. He jerked and tugged at his shirt and peeled it up over his bulk and cast the shirt on the ground, too. "There."

Coil bobbed his head at a gate in the back fence. "You brought this on yourself. Off you go. And keep in mind if you make trouble you won't be spared a second time."

They all watched as Orlan went to the gate and wrenched it open. He turned to glare and for a few seconds his hate-filled eyes lingered on James. Then the gate slammed, and he was gone.

Coil turned. His own features were hard as flint, and there was a savage timbre to his tone as he said, "What in the hell did you think you were doing, throwing that rock?"

"It was because of me," James said. "I had to do something."

"Have I made a mistake about you?" Coil said.

"I didn't want to be to blamed for one of you dying," James said. "Not even him."

"You missed the whole point," Coil said, and cursed.

"What point?" James asked.

It wasn't Coil who answered, it was the flaxen-haired boy.

"Damn you, kid. Orlan has done nothing but make trouble for Coil. But he never pushed it all the way, never gave Coil cause to put an end to him until now."

"And you went and spoiled it," said the black-eyed Blue Shirt. He took a step, a double-edged dagger gleaming in his hand.

"No," Coil said. He sighed and replaced his knife in the sheath at the small of his back. "Listen to me. All of you. Doyle, here, didn't know of the bad blood between Orlan and me. And he didn't want a Blue Shirt to die on his account." He paused. "What's our most important rule?" he said, and pointed at the flaxen-haired boy. "Devlin?"

"We look after our own, always and ever."

"All well and good," said the black-eyed boy. "But he still butted in when he shouldn't."

"He's not one of us yet, Mick," Coil said. "The rules don't apply to him." He looked at all of them. "In a way we should thank him. We've gotten rid of a troublemaker. Orlan would have played his hand sooner or later and I'd rather it was now than someday when my back was turned."

Talk broke out. From the gist, James gathered that most of the Blue Shirts agreed with their leader.

"So now," Coil said. "On to why he's here. I'm putting him up to wear the shirt."

A change came over them. They all looked solemnly at James, taking his measure.

"You speak for him?" Devlin said.

"I do," Coil said.

"You'll teach him the rules?"

"I will."

"You'll learn him all our ways?"

"From first to last."

Devlin nodded and turned to James. "Now you, Doyle. Is it your intention to be a Blue Shirt?"

James hadn't come here for that. He'd remembered Coil saying once that if he was a Blue Shirt, he'd have money, and he'd wanted to ask about it, and maybe then he would join. But now, after all that happened, to say no would be like a slap to their face. He heard himself say, "I do."

"You'll be true to the shirt and all it stands for?"

"I will," James said, although he wasn't sure what that involved.

"You understand that once you are one of us, you are a Blue Shirt until the day you die?"

James hesitated. He hadn't counted on any of this. Finally he said, "I do."

5

James lied to his mother. He told her he was going out to look for work. Each morning he'd be up and dressed and as soon as breakfast was over he was out the door. He'd meet Coil at the lot in back of the barbershop, and off they'd go, usually with five or six others.

The first day, James asked why they had to come, and Coil pointed at a boy named Nally. "Tell him the rule."

"Three or more always unless it can't be helped, *buachaill*," Nally recited.

"Strength in numbers—don't you see?" Mick said.

"You've got to remember always," Coil said, "that once you don the blue, you're fair game for every other gang there is, and anyone else who hates us."

"You're a walking target, is what you are," Devlin said.

"And that's no mistake."

By the end of the first week, James was painfully aware of several things. First, where he thought he knew the Five Points from walks with his mother and father, he didn't know the area at all. His parents had taken him to only certain parts, the better parts, the safer parts, parts that didn't portray a true portrait of life in Five Points.

It was a slum. He'd often heard that word but never fully understood what that implied. A slum was a vile place, reeking of filth and garbage and worse, the buildings in such poor condition that those who lived in them froze in the winter and sweltered in the summer. There were so many people that it was a wonder the buildings didn't burst. It wasn't uncommon to have twenty or more crammed into apartments barely big enough for four.

The landlords didn't care that there was no heat. They didn't care that the walls were paper-thin. Or that cockroaches and bedbugs and rats and other vermin afflicted the tenants. The landlords didn't care about anything except the money they were due.

That was the crux of it, James soon learned. Money, or rather, the lack thereof. In the Five Points poverty reigned. It was the hole into which the city's poor had been poured and left to rot. It was a blight hidden from the well-to-do so that by avoiding Five Points, those with money and means need not be disturbed by the sight of those without.

Crime was rampant. James would never have guessed, so well had his parents protected him, but murder and rape and beatings were epidemic. So was disease. Between the violence and the sickness, it was a feat for a child to outlive childhood.

From Coil, James learned something of the district's history. Five Points had gotten its start decades ago with an influx of Irish fleeing the potato famine and the arrival of blacks tasting their newfound freedom. The two didn't mix well, and blood was spilled. Then the poor of other countries streamed in to what the politicians called a great melting pot, but those who lived there called a terrible hell.

Money became a god, and to earn it people would do anything. Some sold their bodies. Some sold their children into indentured bondage. Some did things more vile.

Supposedly, control of the Five Points rested in the hands of the politicians. But many of the politicians were put up and backed by gangs. As Coil explained it: "Many of the gangs are political. We're not. The councilmen and their cronies are yapping mouths who dole out jobs to the gangs that back them, but we don't need that. We make it on our own."

Each gang controlled a territory. The larger gangs had the biggest slices of the pie, but each protected its own with blood if need be. They took money from businesses for protection, and money from prostitutes for the right to walk their streets, and from footpads and others. Thievery was like the air; it was everywhere.

James's mother and father taught him that stealing was wrong. It bothered him, at first, that the Blue Shirts did so much of it. It bothered him even more when he was informed that he must steal his share.

Coil caught his reaction and said simply, "What?"

"I've never stolen anything," James admitted, at which Mick and others laughed.

"Then it's time you learned how," Coil said, and led him to Chatham Square.

When James was younger his parents often took him there as a treat. There were few open areas in Five Points. Space was too precious to be used for anything but buildings. Chatham Square was where wares were sold and ladies in gaudy dresses paraded and the gangs mixed without bloodshed. It was neutral ground, the one spot in all of Five Points that could make that claim.

James was conscious of furtive stares. Gangs in full dress were always conspicuous. The Blue Shirts had their bright blue, the Bowery Boys had their hats, the Dead Rabbits their rabbit fur, the Swamp Angels their knee-high boots. He felt slightly out of place being with the Blue Shirts but not wearing one. They strolled along an aisle lined by booths. Coil, Devlin, Mick, and the rest had an air about them that made James think of cats looking for mice to play with. Coil leaned against a booth wall and hooked his thumbs in his suspenders and eyed the passersby.

"Pay attention," Mick said.

A well-dressed couple approached, a middle-aged man and woman in fine clothes, walking arm in arm.

"See there," Devlin said, and nudged James. "Come to gawk at the animals, they have."

"The what?"

"At us, damn you," Devlin said curtly. "Look at them close. They're from outside the Points. They're here to sneer and laugh behind our backs."

"They would do that?"

Mick swore and pocked James hard with a finger. "Where the hell have you been? Living under a rock? Those who have look down their noses at those who don't. To them we're filth."

"Or entertainment," Coil said, "which is no better." He suddenly warned, "Quiet now."

The prosperous couple went by, the woman darting a look, her eyes crinkling with amusement.

To James's consternation, Coil grabbed him by the arm and fell in a few paces behind them.

"What are we doing?" James whispered.

"We're about to pick a pocket." Coil grinned and winked. "Be careful you're not shot."

His parents used to warn James about pickpockets. They were common enough. A plague, his father called them. A lot of them were nippers, small boys and girls, quick and fleet of foot. Men that could afford them bought money belts and wore the belts under their shirts so the pickpockets couldn't get at them. Women learned not to carry money in their purses but in small pouches concealed on their person. "But what if we're caught?"

"If we are, it will be just too bad for them." Coil patted the small of his back. He was intently watching the pair while pretending not to. He would turn his head to the side as if admiring wares in a booth, but he never took his eyes off them.

Panic gnawed at James's marrow. Since he was old enough to toddle, his parents had impressed on him that he should always be nice, that he must never, ever hurt anyone, that hurting was bad, that stealing was bad, that to kill was unthinkable, the most heinous of acts. Suddenly he was aware that Coil was staring at him.

"Listen to me, Doyle. I like you. I think you have the makings. But you have to grow up."

"Grow up how?" James said.

"Put away your childish notions. It's you against the rest of the world, and the sooner you get that through your head, the better off you'll be."

"My mother says—"

Coil held up a hand. "Stop right there. I won't mock you for bringing her up as some of the others would. Mother's boy, they'd say. My own mother was a fine lady, and I have fond memories of her." He resumed watching the couple. "But we have to cut the apron strings. They make us weak and in this world the weak are eaten by the strong."

"I don't want to be weak," James said.

"Then pay attention. You're to distract them and I'll do the lifting."

James liked Coil. He liked him a whole lot. Everything his parents ever taught him went against what they were about to do, but he would do it anyway, if only so he could go on being Coil's friend. "What do you want of me?"

"Up ahead of them is an apple barrel by a stall. Do you see it?"

"Yes."

"When I tell you, you're to run past them, laughing and acting like you're having a good time. Pretend not to see the barrel and run right into it and push it over. Then run like hell and make your way back to the others and I'll join you."

"That's all?" James said. He thought he would have to do something a lot worse.

"It's enough. Get ready."

The aisle was crowded with people. James focused on the barrel. He could do this. He *would* do this. He wouldn't let Coil down.

"If the man who sells the apples comes after you, give him the slip or he'll thrash you."

"I understand," James said, fear clutching at his chest. He didn't know if he could outrun a grown man.

"Get ready."

The well-to-do couple were almost to the stall.

"Now," Coil said.

James burst into motion. He weaved around a portly fellow and ran past the couple, laughing as gaily as he could, even though to him his laugh sounded false. He pretended not to see the barrel and slammed into it running full-out. He'd thought it would go right over, but it was a lot heaver than he expected and he bounced as if he had struck a wall, pain shooting up his arms and chest. The barrel tilted and for a harrowing instant he feared it would right itself, but over it went with a loud thump and apples rolled every which way.

"Hey, you!"

The angry shout reminded James he wasn't supposed to stop. He went to run just as a heavy hand fell on his shoulder. A sharp twist and he was free and flying. He dodged around two girls and flew. The fruit vendor was swearing.

James laughed, this time for real. He ran until he judged he was safe and then crossed to a different aisle and back to where the rest were waiting. He was surprised to find Coil already there.

Coil smiled and clapped him on the back and said, "You did right fine."

The others were smiling too, Mick and Devlin and the rest. They were all holding money.

"We've split it the usual way," Coil said. "It's always an even share, except the pair who do it get more." He held out his hand. "This is yours."

James stared at the coins, gleaming bright in the sun.

"Go on. Take them. You earned them."

James held out both hands. "How much is it?"

"Five dollars. That bastard had pretty near fifty in his poke."

James rubbed the coins and held a gold piece up so it sparkled. He couldn't believe it. Five dollars was more than he'd ever had in his whole life. It was more than his parents usually had; he remembered how his father was always saying that they were lucky to have a dollar to spare. "God Almighty," he breathed.

Coil nudged him and grinned and winked. "Feels good, doesn't it?"

"Yes," James admitted. It confused him. They had done a bad deed, yet he felt very good.

"You'll never want for money as a Blue Shirt. We look after our own. Don't we, boys?"

"That we do," Devlin said.

"One for all," Mick declared.

Coil clapped James and laughed. "What do you think of being a Blue Shirt now?"

"I want it more than anything," James said.

6

It didn't happen overnight.

James had to prove himself.

Coil taught him how to pick pockets and lift purses. He practiced day after day until he became adept at slipping his hand into a jacket or pants without his mark feeling a thing. The secret was to do it fast and use the tips of his fingers instead of his whole hand. He learned how to swipe a purse from a woman. Two quick cuts and the deed was done.

Stealing from general stores and mercantiles was ridiculously easy. They waited until the owner or the clerk was looking the other way and scooped the item into an inside pocket or under their shirt or jacket.

James took to it all like a duck to water, with one exception. Some of the Blue Shirts were not above a little burglary now and again.

Devlin was fondest of it. His trick was to swap his blue shirt for an ordinary shirt and trail a well-dressed couple to their home. Once their lights went out, he'd wait until he was confident they were asleep, break in, and make off with whatever struck his fancy.

James went with him once and only once. They

strolled about the market until Devlin spied a likely couple in expensive clothes. The pair hardly ever looked behind them, which made shadowing them to their house ridiculously easy.

James and Devlin sat on a bench on a nearby street corner until an hour before sundown.

"The secret to being good at this," Devlin instructed him as a teacher might a school pupil, "is to never leave anything to chance. Come on. We'll stake a stroll and look for the best way in."

They made several circuits of the yard. A hedge screened three sides and through a gap they spotted a large dog on a chain.

"We'll never get inside," James said. "That mongrel will bark and give us away."

"Not if we treat it nice," Devlin said with a grin, and led James to a butcher shop where Devlin bought half a pound of raw meat.

By the time they got back, night had fallen.

The lamps in the house went out about ten thirty.

Devlin waited another hour, then nudged James and said, "It's been long enough. Are you up for some excitement, my fine lad?"

"So long as it doesn't get us shot," James said.

Devlin chuckled but James didn't find it so amusing.

"First the beastie."

They crept along the hedge, James filled with dread that the animal would spot them and bark loud enough to wake the dead. When Devlin stopped, he stopped.

Awash in pale starlight, the dog was dozing with its chin on its forepaws.

Devlin put a finger to his lips. Drawing his knife, he cut a strip of meat and threw it at the dog. It plopped onto the ground half a foot from the animal's face. Instantly, the dog was on its feet and rumbling in its chest.

It caught the scent of the meat, sniffed at it a few times, and wolfed the meat down in a single swallow.

Devlin cut off a bigger piece and tossed it, as well. The dog didn't even growl. It pounced and chewed. Boldly rising, Devlin went to within a few yards and tossed the rest of the meat. He didn't wait to see what the dog would do but turned and beckoned James. Together they ran to the deep shadow along the bottom floor. Devlin went to each of the windows. All on the near side were latched. They went around the corner to the back. Devlin pushed on the first, but it wouldn't budge. He had the same luck with the second. Then they came to the next and Devlin grinned when it slid up.

James wasn't nearly as happy. Picking pockets was crime enough. This was worse. Judges were a lot harder on burglars.

If they were caught— He wouldn't let himself think about the consequences.

Devlin hiked a leg and slid over and in. Swallowing, James followed him. They were in a dark room that smelled of tobacco. Darkling shapes suggested furniture. He reached out to Devlin, but Devlin wasn't there. Panic welled, and James fought it down. It was an empty room, was all. Nothing to be afraid of.

A whisper from Devlin drew him to a corner and a large desk. A match flared, and Devlin lit a lamp. He began to rummage through the drawers, searching quickly but quietly.

Picking up a letter opener, Devlin held it out to him.

Unsure what he was supposed to do with it, James whispered, "Do you want me to open a letter with it?"

"Simpleton," Devlin whispered, and laughed. "It's made of silver." He bent to other drawers.

James glanced at the doorway to a dark hall beyond. Devlin wasn't making much noise, but *any* noise was too much as far as he was concerned. Burglary didn't strike him as particularly smart, and he would be damned if he would ever do it again.

Devlin moved to a cabinet with a glass front. On display inside were swords in exquisite scabbards. He turned the latch, but the cabinet wouldn't open. "I bet we could get a lot for one of these."

"Hurry," James urged. It was probably his imagination, but he thought he'd heard a sound.

"They're on the second floor and sound asleep. Quit your fretting."

There it was again, the faint sound James thought he'd heard. He cocked his head and strained his ears and was about convinced it was nothing when a shape filled the doorway.

"Don't move a muscle, you scoundrels!"

James's heart leaped into his throat.

Bundled in a thick robe, the man of the house was pointing a pistol at them. He was bald and ruddy with anger and so broad of girth that the robe seemed more like a tent. "I mean it. Move and I will shoot." The click of the hammer was proof he meant it.

"How do you do, sir?" Devlin said cheerfully. "Lovely weather we've been having, eh?"

"What?" the man said in bewilderment.

"We called on you earlier, but you weren't to home, so we came back to see if you would be interested," Devlin told him.

"What are you babbling about?" the man demanded.

"We're here to collect for the Orphans Fund. How much would you care to give?"

"Orphans Fund?" the man repeated, his confusion almost comical. The pistol dipped a few inches.

Devlin whirled and bellowed, "Out the window!" In a long bound he was at the nearest and without slowing he threw his arms over his head and neck and hurtled himself at the glass. With a loud crash the pane shattered and Devlin disappeared over the sill.

Both James and the man of the house were speechless with amazement. James recovered first, and pumped his legs. He wasn't quite to the window when the pistol cracked. Something buzzed his ear and then he dived and cleared the jagged slivers and came down hard on his shoulder. Broken glass crunched under him. Pain shot up his arm and he felt a wet sensation. Before he could rise a hand gripped him and shoved him toward the street.

"Run, damn you! Run!"

James didn't need prompting. He was more afraid than he had ever been.

The man was at the window. He hollered, and the pistol cracked once more.

James and Devlin pounded around the hedge. The dog commenced to bark and now the man was swearing up a storm.

James had an impulse to giggle and only contained himself with an effort.

"Damn the luck," Devlin said. "I really wanted one of those swords."

They reached the street. The few people out and about turned and stared.

James was afraid that someone would try to stop them, but no one did. They fled past an old woman and a young couple.

At the next intersection they turned left and went halfway down the block.

Finally Devlin stopped. "This should be far enough."

"The police," James said between pants. "They'll be after us."

"Don't you know anything?" Devlin said. "It will

take an hour for them to show and all they'll do is make a report. By then we'll be back in Five Points."

"It can't be this easy."

"You were thinking the sky would open and lightning would strike you dead?"

James looked at the stars and let out a long breath in heartfelt relief. A stab of pain and a wet drop dribbling down his arm warned it was premature. "I'm bleeding."

"Let's have a look," Devlin said, and steered him to a streetlamp. "Why, it's no more than a scratch." He chuckled and clapped James on the back. "What do you say? Want to do it again tomorrow?"

"I'll stick with the mercantiles and picking pockets," James said.

"Where's the fun in that?"

James wasn't doing it for the fun. He stole and stole, and it got so that one evening Coil cautioned him not to be so reckless.

"I'm building a nest egg," James explained.

"What for?" Coil asked. "There's always more money to be had. None of us ever saves a cent."

James glanced about to be sure none of the others could hear. "It's for my mother."

The strangest expression came over Coil.

"She works so hard yet she can hardly make ends meet," James said. "I want to help her."

"Damn, Doyle," Coil said.

"What?"

"You might be the best of all of us, deep down where it counts."

Often James was out until past midnight. One night he snuck back into his bedroom through his window, as usual. He moved quietly to the bed and was pulling back the quilt when his room flared with light.

"Where have you been?" his mother demanded. Her

hair was disheveled and she had dark spots under her eyes.

"I went for a walk."

"At this time of night? Tell me the truth."

James had known this moment would come. He'd been sneaking out for weeks now with her none the wiser, but it couldn't last forever. "Go to bed."

"How dare you speak to me like that! I'm the parent here. You will answer my question."

"No, Mother," James said. "I won't."

She gasped, and tears filled her eyes. "I can't believe what I'm hearing."

"I'm tired. I'd like to go to sleep."

"You're too young to be out this late."

James sat and began untying his shoes. "You're the one who told me I needed to find work."

She took a step and her face brightened. "You have a job? Really? Why didn't you tell me?"

"I wanted to surprise you."

"Oh, my sweet, sweet boy." She came and placed her palm on his cheek. "This is great news. You can help with the rent. You can help with the groceries." She bent and kissed him on the forehead. "I can't tell you how happy this makes me."

The smell of liquor on her breath was strong. James glanced away. "I have something for you," he said. He slid off the bed and onto his hands and knees on the floor.

"What are you doing?"

James reached up under the bed and brought out a leather poke. He jingled it and gave it to her.

"What's this?"

"Fifty-two dollars."

"How much?" She loosened the drawstring and up-ended it over his bed. Out spilled a waterfall of gold and silver and copper. "Dear God."

"It's yours." James had intended to save a full hundred and then give it to her.

She picked up some of the coins and held them as if they were fragile. "Where did you get these?"

"I told you. I have a job." James sat on the bed and finished removing his shoes.

His mother sifted the coins still on the quilt. "What do you do that you earn so much?"

"I work for a man," James said vaguely.

"Who?" she pressed him. "Doing what?"

James said the first thing that popped into his head. "At a barbershop. I sweep the floor and whatnot."

"You're lying to me again. No one would pay this much for you to sweep a floor. How did you really get it?"

"Go to bed," James said. He lay on his side with his back to her.

"I demand an answer, young man."

"Don't we need it?"

"We are always short of money. You know that."

"Don't you want it?"

"Yes, I do, but I want honest money. Look me in the eye and tell me you earned this honestly."

James rolled over. He looked her in the eye. "I earned it honestly."

Disbelief and need fought a brief battle and need won. Smiling, she kissed him on the cheek. "I'm sorry. I shouldn't have doubted you. Your father and I raised you to be good and decent."

"Yes," James said, "you did."

She put the coins in the poke and jingled them and laughed. "It's a miracle. I was so very afraid we couldn't make the next rent and now you go and do this. You're the most wonderful son in the world." She spun in a circle. "You've made me so happy, son. You have no idea."

"Yes," James said. "I do."

7

———·—————

Three and a half years went by.

It was a bright Saturday afternoon. The square was jammed. Down an aisle strode a dozen Blue Shirts, wolves among sheep.

At their head was Coil, tall and menacing. Flanking him were Devlin and Mick on one side, James Doyle on the other.

James had grown. He'd gained more than a foot in height and packed on muscle. His thumbs were hooked in his suspenders and his swagger matched the others'. He gave pretty girls saucy stares and glared at any man who dared look at the Blue Shirts defiantly. There was nothing boyish about him. He wore a knife in a sheath under his shirt at the small of his back and had a derringer in his right boot and a dagger in his left.

"So, what will it be today, lads?" Mick said. "I wouldn't mind a visit to Patrick's."

"The best tavern anywhere," Flanagan remarked.

"You'd live there if you could and get falling-down drunk every night," Devlin said, grinning.

At a booth that sold small squares of cake, Coil stopped and bought one. Others followed his example.

They moved to the middle of the square and Coil sat on a bench and the rest clustered around. He took his first bite and chewed. "The Italians are moving in on us."

All eyes were fixed on him.

"What have you heard?" Doyle asked.

"It's the Florentines," Coil said. "They're trying to take over the south end."

"Them again," Mick said, and swore.

"Damned foreigners," Sweeney said.

"We can't allow it," Coil told them. "Any weakness, and the Boweries and the Rabbits and the Slaughterhouses will think they can move in on us, too."

"You have a plan?"

"Doyle does. I've had him spying around."

"He's good at that," Mick said.

"He's a sly one—that's for certain," Maquire said.

James put a foot on the bench and his arm on his leg. "The Florentines have taken rooms in the back of a tenement on Purgatory Street. They had an old woman rent the rooms for them, and they use an alley to slip in and out."

"What do they wear?" Flynn asked.

Coil answered. "They fancy black. They like small caps and polished shoes. They're fond of stilettos." He nodded at Doyle. "Tell the rest of it."

"The Florentines are big on protection. They've gone to every business on Purgatory. Ten percent is theirs, and if the owner won't pay, they do the usual. Three owners have been beaten and another cut up." Doyle paused. "They also warn them not to get word to us."

"So they know it's our territory," Mick said.

"Here's how it will be," Coil said. "We hit them hard at their rooms on Purgatory. And we make it final."

"Final how?" Devlin asked.

"Doyle and me have been talking," Coil said. "We

don't nip this now, we're on a downward slope. The other gangs will come at us from all sides. We'll be stretched so thin we'll be wiped out. So my plan is to wipe *them* out."

"*All* the Florentines?" Sweeney said.

"All those on Purgatory Street. It's ours. We need to send a message. Move in on us and you pay."

"How many are we talking?" Maquire wanted to know.

"Doyle says there are ten to twenty in those rooms at any one time."

"And we're to kill them all?" Mick grinned, and slapped his leg. "Now, that will be a fight."

"Do you know what you're saying?" Maquire said to Coil. He was the second oldest and respected for his judgment. "The rags will be all over it."

"We'll be famous!" Mick exclaimed.

"We'll be in prison or dead," Maquire said. "The police look the other way over a lot, but they won't over this. Not when it will be so public."

"The police won't give a damn so long as it's only Florentines who die. Remember that. No bystanders are to be stuck or hit or snuffed. Spread the word. We want to get in and out and get on with our lives."

"May the saints preserve us," Maquire said.

"Someone has to," Sweeney said, and laughed.

James came to the door and hesitated. He hated to come home and did it rarely. He also hated having to change his clothes each time. But he had hid the truth for so long, he couldn't see the need to bare all. Squaring his shoulders, he used his key and went in and past the parlor, hoping to reach his bedroom without either of them noticing.

Bunton was on the settee, the inevitable beer in his

hand, his obscene gut trying to rip his shirt's buttons. "Hold on there, boy."

James stopped and regarded him as he might a pile of dog droppings. "What?"

"Where have you been?"

"None of your damn business."

Bunton scowled and poked a finger at him. "I'm your father, ain't I?"

"You sure as hell aren't." James barely held his loathing in check.

"Stepfather, then," Bunton said. "And that gives me the right to ask."

"Ask all you want," James said. "But you're nothing to me. A slug, is all."

Bunton made as if to rise off the settee, but apparently it was too much bother and he sank back. "I won't be talked to like that in my own home."

"*Your* home?" James said, itching to draw his knife. He might change his shirt, but he never went unarmed. "This was ours before ever you latched on to my mother."

"Latched?" Bunton said. "You make me sound like a damned leech."

"I couldn't have put it better."

His mother came out of the kitchen humming to herself. She wore an apron and was wiping her hands, and on seeing him she squealed and rushed to enfold him in her arms. "James! James! It's been so long." She gripped his shoulders and held him at arm's length. "Let me look at you. You seem in good health."

"I'm fine," James said. The reek of liquor was so potent she might as well be a distillery.

"Why do you stay away so long? Don't you love your dear mama anymore?" She hugged him. "I miss you so much sometimes, it hurts."

James disentangled himself and went down the hall to his room. It had the musty smell of disuse, and dust was everywhere. He opened the closet.

"I've respected your wishes and stayed out like you asked," she said from the doorway.

"I didn't ask you," James said as he picked up his carpetbag and placed it on the bed. "I told *him* to stay out."

"Why do you hate him so?"

James didn't answer. He took down a pair of pants.

"He's been good to me. And Lord, you know how lonely I was before I met him."

"You still do laundry," James said. "You work yourself to the bone." He shoved the pants into the bag. "What does he do?"

"He works now and then."

"When the moon is blue," James said, and grabbed another pair of pants.

She leaned against the jamb and fiddled with the tiny buttons on her dress. "I have something to ask you."

"I stay with friends," James said.

"It's not that," she said, and wrung her hands. "Then again, maybe it is. Your friends, I mean."

James looked at her.

She coughed and shifted her weight. "Mrs. Fogarty told me she saw you the other day. At least she thought it was you, but I told her it couldn't be." She drew in a breath. "She said you were with a bunch of young men. She said—" His mother stopped and then got it out in a rush. "She said they were Blue Shirts."

"Did she, now?"

"Is it true? It can't be. You wouldn't join a gang. I warned you about them, didn't I?"

"Many times."

"Look me in the face and tell me you haven't. Swear

by all that's holy so I can tell that nasty Mrs. Fogarty to stop spreading her lies."

James looked her in the eye. "I'm not a Blue Shirt."

She let out a breath and grinned and giggled. "I knew it. I knew it as surely as I'm standing here. I told her she was mistaken. I told her it had to be someone else."

James resumed packing.

"What are you doing?"

"Taking the last of my things." James opened a drawer and found socks.

"Whatever for? You don't need to move out completely." She looked around the small room. "I kind of like it that you keep things here. I know I'll always see you again."

James was reaching for a rolled-up pair of socks but stopped. He stared at her, then closed the drawer. "You're right. I don't really need to take any of this. I'll keep it here."

"Thank you," she said.

James started to go past her, but she clasped his wrist.

"You're not leaving, are you? You just got here. Stay for supper. I have beef and potatoes."

"Can't," James said.

"Please." She pressed him to her bosom and kissed his neck. "I miss you so much. For your old ma, can't you stay just this one night?"

"Can't," James said again, more gruffly than he intended.

He kissed her cheek and hurried down the hall and glared at Bunton as he went past the parlor. Then he was out of the apartment and sucking in drafts of air. Composing himself, he turned to the stairs. He climbed two flights and marked the doors until he came to the third on the right. He knocked and said, "Mrs. Fogarty?"

"Be right with you."

He looked both ways to be sure the hallway was empty and drew his knife.

The latch rasped, and a small gray-haired woman in a drab dress crooked her long neck. "Yes? What do you want, young man?" She blinked in the surprise of recognition. "Why, James Doyle? Is that you?"

"Yes, it is, ma'am. Is your husband to home?"

"No, he's off buying tobacco. Was it him you want to see?"

"You," James said, and clamped his free hand on her throat and was inside before she could collect her wits. Kicking the door shut, he slammed her to the floor and pressed his knife to her throat. "I'll make this brief. If you ever again tell my mother you saw me anywhere, if you talk to her about me at all, I'll come back and slit you from ear to ear. Do you understand me?"

Terror rendered the old woman mute and paralyzed her limbs.

"Blink once for yes," James said.

Mrs. Fogarty blinked.

James nodded and straightened and slid the knife into its sheath. "Good day to you, then," he said with a smile, and left her there on the floor.

8

————•————

Purgatory Street was like any other in Five Points: narrow, dark, reeking of odors, heavy with foot, horse, and wagon traffic during the day. After dark the legions of the night emerged. All over Five Points, the groggeries, gambling dens, and dance halls did booming business. Painted ladies sashayed in tight dresses. Revelers had high old times. Footpads hugged the shadows.

The Blue Shirts converged from different directions. They came in small groups so as not to arouse the suspicions of the police and met in a small park a few blocks from the tenement.

This close to the border of their territory, they moved on cat's feet. They gathered under a maple, and when Coil called for attention, they knelt or squatted or sat in a half-moon. James was in the front row with Mick and Devlin.

"You all know why we're here," Coil began. "The Florentines have overstepped and it must be made right." He began to pace, his hands clasped behind his back. "They are always in their rooms by ten, which gives us an hour yet."

"We outnumber them four to one," Mick said. "It will be a cakewalk."

"Don't take them lightly," Coil warned.

"They're Italians," Flanagan said.

Coil put his hands on his hips. "Damn you. I mean it. They're good with those stilettos of theirs, and they have guns, besides."

Sweeney pulled his revolver and patted it. "So do we."

Coil said with some exasperation, "Just do as I say and we'll get through this with little loss." He went over his plan one more time, ending with "We'll be long gone before the fire spreads. No one will ever connect us with it."

"About that," Devlin said. "Are we sure we can get everyone else out? I'd hate to think of any wee ones burned alive because of us."

"We're not animals," Coil said. "I gave the job to you, so you tell me if we're sure or not."

"As soon as the Florentines are dead and we've set the fire, me and five others will go through the building yelling at the top of our lungs. That's all it should take."

James figured so, too. The buildings were old and fire was universally dreaded. A mere whiff of smoke was sometimes enough to empty a place.

"You have it worked out fine, Coil," Flynn said.

"I hope so." Their leader turned to James. "All right, then. Off you go. Be careful not to be seen."

James liked being their spy. He had a reputation for being the slyest and sneakiest of them all. Rising, he hurried from the park to an alley and down the alley to a street that flanked the rear of the tenement. He made sure to stay in the shadows where his blue shirt was almost black. The few people who noticed him didn't give him a second look.

The tenement sat on a corner. It reared five stories.

The windows to the apartments the Florentines had taken were lit up and silhouettes flitted across the shades. None of the Florentines was outside.

James retraced his steps. The others were anxiously waiting for his report. "They're in there, all right."

"We have them, then," Mick said.

"Cocky will get you killed," Coil warned.

The Blue Shirts broke into small groups and approached the tenement from the front and the back.

James was with Coil's group. They were almost to the rear of the building when the unexpected occurred. A pair of dark-haired rakes in suits were on the steps, smoking and talking. They had not been there before. One gave a startled look, and the pair ran inside yelling in Italian.

"Hell," Coil said, and drew his pocket pistol. Raising an arm, he bawled, "On them, boys! And the devil take the hindmost!"

The Blue Shirts rushed the tenement. In a blue tide, they swept up the steps into a narrow hall. The press of their numbers created a jam. James nearly stumbled when someone pushed him, but then he was in and ahead were the apartments the Florentines occupied. One of the doors opened and a head popped out and ducked back again. The door was slammed practically in their faces.

"Get back!" Coil warned.

James flung himself aside just as shots boomed and holes peppered the door. Maquire and another Blue Shirt fell. They were quickly hustled aside and a square timber from a construction site was brought up. Blue Shirts slammed it into the door again and again, but the door held.

James read dismay on many a face. This wasn't supposed to be. They had counted on gaining quick entry. A volley from inside dropped a Blue Shirt and another immediately took his place at the battering ram.

"Put your backs into it!" Coil shouted.

Once more the timber swung. The door shook and the bottom hinge snapped, but the door didn't buckle. From outside came yells and shots. Blue Shirts were assaulting the windows as well as the doors.

Yet another burst of lead from inside felled another of the ram crew.

"Damn it to hell," Mick raged.

A Blue Shirt named McGee, a huge slab of muscle, let go of the ram, drew himself back, and threw himself at the door shoulder-first. Down it crashed. Yelling and shrieking, the Blue Shirts streamed into the apartment. James was jostled and nearly knocked down. He leaped over a body: McGee, a bullet hole between his eyes. At them came the Florentines, and James saw with alarm that there were more of their enemies than there were supposed to be, and heavily armed. Revolvers cracked and blades flashed. The influx of Blue Shirts drove the Florentines back but not for long. From an adjoining room poured reinforcements.

Suddenly James was face-to-face with a curly-haired Florentine armed with a stiletto. The Florentine said something in Italian and lunged. James twisted, barely avoiding the thrust. He struck with his knife, slicing to the hilt in the Florentine's ribs. The Florentine cried out and pitched forward. It happened so fast that James couldn't get out of the way. He tried to catch the man and lower him, but his left leg sustained a bone-jarring blow and the next he knew, he was flat on his back with the Florentine on top.

Around him bedlam raged. It was steel on steel and fist to fist, with lead thrown by those who had guns. Oaths blistered the air.

James saw Flynn take a stiletto in the back. He saw Devlin shove the muzzle of a pocket pistol into the face of a Florentine and squeeze the trigger. And then he saw a lamp knocked over and the whale oil splash onto the floor and the wall. Flames immediately flared, growing swiftly, fingers of red and orange that became writhing sheets.

James pushed the body off and made it to his knees just as someone shouted, "Fire! Fire!"

Most of the combatants seemed not to hear. Mick was fighting two Florentines at once. Sweeney staggered out of the melee clutching his throat, which was cut inches deep.

James heaved erect. He was anxious to help his friends. But suddenly roaring flames shot across the ceiling with astounding rapidity even as a second wall was consumed. In the bat of an eye, most of the room was on fire. The bellows of anger and stormy oaths changed to screams of pain and cries of fear. Both sides had to get out of there or they would be burned alive. As if everyone had come to the same conclusion at the same instant, Blue Shirts and Florentines alike abruptly bolted for the doors and windows.

James was near a window. Intense heat on his head and shoulders was incentive to reach it. The room was an inferno when he slid a leg over the sill and dropped. He ran a few yards and stopped to look back.

Either the fire had spread to other rooms with incredible quickness or fires had started independently in the adjoining apartments, because smoke was curling from the windows of all three the Florentines rented, and from windows above theirs, as well.

James gave a start. A Florentine was right next to him, staring aghast at the fire, the same as him. He looked around and saw Blue Shirts mingled with Florentines, the fight forgotten. From up and down the street people were converging. "Fire! Fire! Fire!" rose from multiple throats. Whistles shrilled, the police or maybe a fire bri-

gade. James suddenly felt conspicuous. He turned to
flee and was frozen in place by the most horrific cry
he'd ever heard, a keening scream from the floor above
the Florentines' apartments, the wail of a woman in
excruciating pain. A curtain was flung aside, and there,
framed in the window, was a sight James would never
forget for as long as he lived: an old woman, aflame.
Her dress was on fire from hem to neck and her hair
was burning, as well. She struck the glass but it wouldn't
break. She turned and must have grabbed a chair because it came flying through the window with a shattering crash. And then she did that which made James
catch his breath in his throat. She dived out the window
headfirst. As if in slow motion, he saw her blazing figure
arc down. Onlookers screamed and scattered from under her. There was the most appalling crunch, and the
woman was still.

James ran. Fear coursed through him. Not a fear
of the Florentines or the fire but a nameless fear that
seared him to his marrow and made him want to put as
many miles as he could between himself and the burning tenement. He slowed at the intersection to look back
and was sorry he did.

The building was going up like a tinderbox. Flames
were leaping, vaulting, racing up the sides and from floor
to floor.

Rooms became fiery ovens in the bat of an eye and
those in them became torches. A cacophony of shrieks
and screeches and wails pierced the night.

James couldn't stand to see any more. He fled to the
park. Under a maple he stopped and leaned against it to
catch his breath. Although he was blocks away, he could
still hear the bedlam and smell the smoke. He sucked in
deep breaths and closed his eyes, and when he opened
them, a figure appeared out of the murk.

James grabbed for his knife and then recognized who it was. "Coil!"

"Doyle. Good to see you made it out in one piece." Coil's shirt was smeared red in spots. He propped a hand against the same tree.

"What went wrong?" James said.

"Everything."

"We had it well planned—"

Coil shook his head. "We thought we did but we were fooling ourselves."

"How many did we lose?"

"I wouldn't know, and it doesn't matter."

"How can you say that?" James asked, appalled at how callous Coil was being.

"We have a more important worry." Coil looked over his shoulder. "The whole city will be out for our heads."

"What? Why?"

"They'll want a scapegoat."

"Who will?"

"Think, damn it. The politicians. When they hear that two gangs were involved, they'll blame the Florentines and us. They'll send extra police into the Five Points to catch as many of the Blue Shirts as they can."

"We can hide until it blows over."

Coil gave an emphatic shake of his head. "This won't be the usual roust. It could mean the gallows for those of us as are caught."

"They'd hang us over an accident?"

"They won't care how the fire started. Trust me on this. It will be hunting season on Blue Shirts and Florentines."

A faint scream reached them.

"Was that a little girl?" James asked.

"A lot will die," Coil said softly. "A whole hell of a lot."

"What do we do?"

"I'm leaving the city." Coil straightened. "I suggest you do the same."

James was stunned. "Where will you go? What will you do? And what about our brothers in blue? Mick and Devlin and Sweeney and everyone?"

"Them that are alive would be smart to do as I am." Coil tensed. "Did you hear that?"

All James heard were distant shouts and screams. He was about to say so when feet drummed—a lot of feet. A large body of people appeared, some thirty to fifty strong, from the direction of the tenement. They were shouting back and forth. He thought he caught the words "Blue Shirts." "Who are they?" he wondered.

"Run," Coil said, and pushed him.

"What? Why?"

"It's a mob out for our blood." Coil burst into motion, flying toward the far side of the park as if his feet were winged.

Confused, James followed. There were a lot of questions he wanted to ask.

Behind him, a man rumbled like a bull.

"There're two of them now! After them, men!"

"Get those Blue Shirts!"

There was more but James didn't listen. He ran full-out. New Yorkers were not above acts of vigilantism when they were incensed, as had happened recently on the docks when a man beat and robbed a woman and was chased down by enraged citizens. By the time the police got there, the thief had been strung from a street post, as dead as dead could be.

Coil had pulled ahead.

James glanced back and was disconcerted to discover several of the mob gaining.

"Murdering bastards!"

"Stop where you are!"

James wasn't about to. He weaved through trees and came to a flat grassy area and ran as he had never run before. He was almost to more trees when inspiration struck. A low limb hove out of the darkness, and he sprang. It was the work of seconds to pull himself up.

Under him streamed dark shapes.

Afraid one of the mob would look up and spot him, James scarcely breathed. Within moments they were past and he was alone.

From out of the dark came a yell. "Here's one!"

"Get him!"

A scuffle ensued, harsh curses and a flurry of blows.

James thought the mob had caught Coil, and he was about to go to Coil's aid when the noises stopped.

"I guess we gave him what for!" someone gloated.

"We shouldn't stay. The police might come."

"Scatter!" a man urged. "They'll blame us even though we were in the right."

Only when all furtive movement ceased did James hang by his arms and drop. He moved warily, so busy watching for lingerers that he nearly tripped over a sprawled form. It was a Blue Shirt. Dropping to his knees, he rolled it over. He was both relieved and horror-struck. Relieved that it wasn't Coil but horror-struck that Flanagan had met his death in so gruesome a manner.

James got out of there, stripping off his shirt as he went. If Coil was right, the entire city would be after them. There had been crackdowns on the gangs before, but this might be the worst ever.

If he stayed he might be hanged.

What was he to do?

INTO THE WEST

9

———— · ————

The death toll was one hundred and sixty-nine men, women, and children. Four of the children were infants. Another eighty-four people had been so severely burned, they needed to be rushed to hospitals. An additional thirty-nine sustained what were described in the newspapers as "minor burns."

Three fire companies joined to fight the conflagration. They had been able to contain it to the tenement but at the cost of two firemen.

It was all the newspapers had talked about for weeks.

Especially after the mayor declared an investigation into the cause. Certain rumors, he said, led him to believe it was more than a bumped lamp or an overheated iron. Those rumors were in the form of witnesses who reported a gang fight had broken out shortly before the fire began. Then there was the battered body of a dead Blue Shirt found in Mulberry Park.

The investigation was quick. It established beyond any shadow of doubt that the Blue Shirts and the Florentines were to blame.

The city was outraged. The police were ordered to arrest Blue Shirts and Florentines on sight. Anyone suspected of being a Blue Shirt or Florentine was brought in for questioning. Nineteen gang members were put behind bars.

Public sentiment was so incensed that the newspapers were saying those responsible should receive the death penalty.

James lay low in his small apartment on Gramercy Street. He tried to find his friends, but they had scattered to the four winds. He could get by for a while on his own. He had some money saved.

On a cold and blustery morning, James decided to visit his mother. He dressed in a cotton shirt and a bulky coat. Buttoned up, his hands in his pockets, a woolen cap pulled low over his brow, he made his way to her apartment.

As usual Bunton's bulk overflowed the settee, a bottle beside him. "Well, look who it is," he said, sneering.

James ignored him and went to the kitchen, but his mother wasn't there. Nor did she answer when he knocked on her bedroom door. He returned to the parlor. "Where is she?"

"Off to deliver laundry," Bunton said. "She's a hard worker, that woman."

"Too bad the same can't be said about you," James said before he could stop himself.

Bunton's ugly face became uglier with resentment. "You shouldn't talk to me like that, boy. You don't want to make me mad."

James turned to go.

"Not when you're worth so much money."

James looked at him and gripped the pistol in his pocket. "Money?"

"I know you're a Blue Shirt. Your mother told me what that old biddy upstairs had said, and I did some checking around." Bunton raised the bottle. Some of the whiskey dribbled down his chin. "I know about the fire, too, and all those people who died on account of you."

James waited.

"Nothing to say, boy? You're always looking down your nose at me when you're not any better." Bunton sneered at him. "Heard about the reward? Fifty dollars to anyone who can point out a Blue Shirt or one of those others."

James walked over. He drew his pistol and pointed it. "Is it worth dying for?"

Bunton did the last thing James expected. He laughed.

"Listen to you. Trying to act the tough. What are you going to do? Shoot the man your mother cares for? I think not, a mother's boy like you."

"You miserable lout—" James began, but got no further.

Bunton levered his bulk off the settee and swung the bottle. James tried to duck, but it caught him across the temple. Pain exploded and he swayed. Bunton raised the bottle to smash it over his head and he staggered back, collided with the table, and fell.

Pouncing, Bunton drove a knee into his gut. "Got you now, boy."

James punched him in the throat. Bunton jerked back and gurgled. James punched him a second time. Bunton dropped the bottle and clutched his neck, gasping noisily for breath. James pointed the pistol, but instead of firing he slammed it against Bunton's head. Bunton tottered.

James made it to his feet. A red haze filled his vision. In pure rage he hit Bunton again and again and again and would have gone on hitting him if the feel of wet drops on his hand hadn't snapped him out of himself. He looked at what he had done. Quickly, he felt for a pulse. There was one, weak but steady.

James straightened. He should shoot him. Bunton was bound to go to the police. But Bunton had been right. His mother did care for the slug. And it would be doubly devastating if her son did him in.

James wheeled and left. For once luck was with him and he didn't run into his mother on the way out. His emotions in turmoil, he walked aimlessly for nearly an hour before he bent his steps to his apartment. In grim determination he packed his bag.

He was at the end of his block when he happened to glance back and saw uniformed officers entering his building.

James had never been on a train. He bought his ticket and sat in the last seat next to the window with his bag in his lap. Coileanin had been right. He had to get out of New York, but he had no idea where to go. He figured a city would be best. Any city. He was accustomed to city life and liked it. His ticket would take him to Philadelphia, but after that, where? Philadelphia was too close to New York for him to feel safe. He thought of all the cities he'd ever heard about. Chicago might be good. It was big enough he could lose himself. Use a new name, and no one would ever suspect. Or maybe somewhere farther.

James remembered hearing that New Orleans was lively. A man who had his hair cut at the barbershop came from there and used to talk a lot about the fine food and the nightlife. James also remembered hearing about St. Louis. The Gateway to the West, it was called, a bustling beehive with, as the newspapers grandly put it, "opportunity for all."

The door at the front end of the car opened and in came two policemen. One had his hand on his truncheon. They moved slowly down the aisle, studying each passenger.

James looked out the window, his skin prickling. He took a gamble. He could pretend not to notice them or he could do what he did, namely, turn and say politely, "Good day to you, Officers."

The policeman with his hand on the truncheon acknowledged the greeting with a bob of his chin. Then they were past and out the rear door.

James let out a breath of relief. It was short-lived. The train was delayed nearly half an hour, every second an eternity of suspense. Finally, with a lurch and a rumble, it was under way. At Baltimore he switched to the Baltimore and Ohio Railroad. Later on, to the Ohio and Mississippi Railroad. He enjoyed watching the scenery roll by, mile after mile of farmland and woods dotted by occasional towns and hamlets. It was his first glimpse of life outside New York City, and he soaked it in.

The rest of the world, he realized, was little like the world he had known. For starters, people were more civil. In New York he'd gotten used to people being surly and sour. It never occurred to him that elsewhere people might actually be nice. He lost count of the farmers and their wives who bid him a hello and women who bestowed smiles rather than fearful glances. It came to him just how much his blue shirt had set him apart from everyone else.

He was also surprised by how little vice he saw. In Five Points, it was as common as sin. Drinking, gambling, prostitution went on twenty-four hours of every day. The truth be told, he'd reveled in it, the same as the rest of the Blue Shirts. He drank. He gambled. He had tried to take up smoking, but it didn't agree with him.

But from what he saw from the train, vice outside New York appeared to be as rare as virtue in a Five Points whorehouse. The few layovers he had, he strolled about towns as clean and wholesome as fresh-made bread.

Finally, James arrived at his destination. He had chosen St. Louis. Situated on the west bank of the Mississippi River, the city was puny compared to New York,
but it was a thriving river hub with over one hundred
and sixty thousand souls. And when it came to hustle
and bustle, St. Louis wasn't second to anyone.

His first day, James took a cheap room along the waterfront. That night he visited a tavern and had his first
taste of liquor since leaving Five Points. It went down
smooth.

So smooth, the next day his head pounded and he lay
abed until noon. Then he went on a tour.

St. Louis was two worlds joined by the common seam
of the river. Along the Mississippi were countless docks
for steamboats and other craft. Saloons, grog shops, and
taverns were as common as fleas on a city rat. So were
dance halls and houses where gentlemen consorted with
ladies in private chambers.

Above the waterfront flourished another society entirely. Culture was its byword. Money was its god. Its
temples were theaters and music halls. That there were
a lot of people who were well-to-do was testified to by
the many mansions.

James strolled about, feeling much as he had as a boy
when his mother took him to his first mercantile. Everywhere there was something new, something different.
The river and the boats and ships particularly fascinated
him. The huge steamboats with their giant wheels churn-
ing sent tingles down his spine.

On his fourth day James looked for work. Finding
a job in that great bustling hub of commerce wouldn't
be hard, he figured, and he was proved right. That afternoon he was hired to load flatboats bound for New
Orleans. It involved a lot of lifting and carrying, but he
was young and vigorous and liked the work. It didn't

pay much, however, and within a month he was loading steamboats. It wasn't much of a change, but it paid
better.

Months trickled by and became a year. James packed
on more muscle and grew a couple more inches. He was
content with his life if not happy. He almost forgot about
his old life and New York.

Then he killed a man.

10

His favorite tavern was called the Keelhaul. It was right on the water. River rats, gamblers, and other rowdies packed the place every night.

James usually showed up within an hour after he was done with work for the day. He'd order food and rum to wash it down, then would sit in on a game of cards or sometimes dice or talk with acquaintances.

On this night, he joined a poker game and soon won several hands. He had a sense he was on a winning streak and bet big on a full house. To his delight, the only player who hadn't folded had only a straight. James chuckled and commenced to rake in his winnings.

The man who lost—a river rat known as Twitch—riffled the cards and scowled. "That makes how many you've won, there, mister?"

"I haven't kept count," James admitted. He began to stack his chips.

"I have," Twitch said. He had a string mustache and a pointed chin. "That was four in a row."

"Lady Luck is with me tonight."

"Something is."

James glanced up. He didn't like Twitch much, and

he definitely didn't care for Twitch's tone. "If you have something to say, out with it."

"Could be you make your own luck."

James bristled. That was the same as saying he cheated. He stopped stacking and leaned his forearms on the table. "I don't like the sound of that."

"Me, either," said an older man called Harper. "You dealt the last hand, Twitch. If anyone was bottom-dealing, it was you."

Some of the others laughed, but Twitch didn't find it amusing.

"Stay out of this, you old goat. What do you know of cards, anyway?" Twitch's beady eyes bored into James. "How about you let us have a look up your sleeves?"

"How about you go to hell?"

Twitch had drunk a lot. He always had. And the more he drank, the more hotheaded he became. Now he smacked a hand on the table and snarled, "No one talks to me like that."

"I just did."

"Calm down, Twitch," Harper said.

"What did I tell you?" Suddenly rising, the river rat came around the table. "I'll check your sleeves my own self."

James pushed back his chair. He was wearing a bulky coat and had his pistol in a pocket. He also had his knife in a sheath at the small of his back. He supposed he shouldn't carry them, but old habits were hard to shake off, and besides, most men in St. Louis went about armed in one way or another, with knives, daggers, sword canes, guns, you name it. "I don't want trouble."

Twitch grinned. "Tucking tail, are you?" he said louder than need be for the benefit of those around them.

"From a runt like you?" James shook his head. "I'd never live it down."

A few chuckles and laughs didn't improve Twitch's disposition. He put a hand on a knife at his hip. "Show us there's only skin under there."

"How about I show you this?" James said, and came up out of his chair unleashing an uppercut that started with his fist down near his knee. His knuckles cracked hard on Twitch's chin, and Twitch's feet left the floor and he crashed onto the table, spilling cards and chips every which way. Twitch lay there and didn't move and James turned away, thinking the river rat was unconscious. It felt as if he had broken his hand. He flexed his fingers a few times, and it hurt like hell.

"Watch out!" Harper yelled.

Twitch came up off the table with his knife out, the blade flashing.

James winced at a sharp sting in his arm. He'd been cut. He backpedaled while sliding his hand under his coat and palming his own blade. As it flashed clear, customers began shouting.

"Give them room!"

"Make way! Make way!"

"Someone fetch the police!"

James hoped that last suggestion wasn't carried out. The St. Louis police were a new department and eager to prove themselves by washing the city clean of crime. The only problem, crime was rampant, as bad as or worse than New York City.

Twitch came at him in a crouch, flicking his knife from one hand to the other. "I'm going to carve you into bits and pieces."

Twitch came in low and fast and almost opened James's gut. James retreated, gaining space, and when Twitch lunged, he sliced at the river rat's throat, only to have Twitch leap out of his reach.

James concentrated on the cold steel in Twitch's hand.

Twitch stabbed at his chest and James skipped aside. He didn't see a chair. He tripped over it and stumbled. Twitch, seeing his chance, sprang—just as James flailed his arms to recover his balance. James saw his knife go in to the hilt. Twitch cried out, and then they were on the floor. Twitch wasn't moving. James pushed and got partway to his feet, shock setting in at what he had done.

That was when a revolver muzzle filled his vision and a man wearing a badge cocked the hammer. "Hold it right there. You're under arrest."

11

James had never been in jail. Among the Blue Shirts, jail had been a joke, so few of them had ever been arrested. The jail in St. Louis was cleaner than he had expected and run so orderly that disturbances were few. He told them he didn't have the money for a lawyer even though he did have a stash in his room. The next day he was taken from the cell to a small room with a table and chairs and told to sit and wait. Presently a mousy man with spectacles entered and introduced himself as Timothy Peabody.

"I'll represent you if you'll have me," Peabody said as he sat, nearly dropping the papers he was carrying in the process. He rearranged them and began flipping through until he found those he wanted and pulled them out. "Ah. Here we go. Now let's see, Mr. Doyle. You come from Chicago, you say, and you've only been in St. Louis a short while. No family?"

James shook his head.

"Ummmm. Well, it's nice to have their support, but if you don't, you don't." Peabody pushed his spectacles higher on his nose. "I've read the police report, and I'm afraid it doesn't look good."

"I didn't kill him on purpose," James said.

"So you claim. But you see—"

"And he started it," James interrupted. "Ask anyone who was there."

"There's the crux," Peabody said.

"The what?"

"The factor this case will hinge on. You don't have a criminal record, which is good. You are gainfully employed, which is good. The bartender at the Keelhaul, though, told the police you come in there practically every night and stay late, which is bad."

"Why bad?" James said. "Lots of people do that."

"Those who like to drink and gamble, yes," Peabody said. "Habits some of our judges take a dim view of. And it's the judge, when all is said and done, who will ultimately decide your fate." He cleared his throat. "Now, as I was saying, the crux of this case is the witnesses. Some agree with your assertion that— What was his name?" Peabody turned a paper over. "Here it is. Horace Twitch. Some witnesses say that Mr. Twitch was in fact the aggressor. Others, however, say that you started the altercation—"

"What?" James blurted. "They're lying."

"What reason would they have?"

"I don't know."

"Perhaps they are, but it's more probable they're telling the truth as they perceive it."

"How's that again?" James was irritated by the man's big words.

"No two individuals ever see the same event the same way. You would think they would but they don't. In your case, some of the witnesses think you were at fault and others say you weren't and they could all be telling the truth."

"You're confusing me," James said. "What does all this mean?"

Peabody sighed. "It *means* this isn't a cut-and-dry case. It *means* that if we let this go to a jury, there is a very real chance you will find yourself hanged."

"God," James said.

"Exactly. Which is why I recommend we don't let it get that far. I suggest we plead guilty and throw ourselves on the mercy of the court."

"Both of us or just me?"

Peabody sat back and stared. "Are you trying to be funny, young man? Because I'm not amused. When I say ourselves, obviously I mean you." He clasped his hands. "I'm trying to help you here. I'm trying to put up the best defense I can. To get you the best terms I can. In short, not to get you sentenced to death. Do you appreciate that?"

"Sure."

"Good. Then we plead guilty. Not to murder in the first degree but to a lesser charge. Manslaughter, say. Specifically, involuntary manslaughter." Peabody held up a hand when James went to speak. "Permit me to continue. All will be made clear." He paused. "Involuntary manslaughter means you killed the man but you didn't intend to do it, which—"

"That's what happened," James said. "It was an accident. He came at me. I was defending myself."

"Calm down, sir. As I have been saying, that may well be the truth. But the law doesn't deal in truth."

"What does it deal in?"

"The law."

James was more confused than ever, and it must have shown.

"Listen, Mr. Doyle. You're young yet. There's a lot you don't understand. Most people think that laws are on the books to protect them and see that the truth always prevails. That's not it at all. Our laws are there to see that justice is done, which isn't the same thing."

"I have no idea in hell what you're talking about," James confessed.

Peabody made a slit of his thin lips. "Cases are rarely open-and-shut. There is nearly always conflicting testimony, as in your instance. Nearly all the time, the party accused pleads innocent even when they are guilty as can be. Do you see where that puts the criminal justice system?"

"No."

"Pay attention. How are we, the lawyers and judges and whoever, to sort through the maze of truths and untruths with any reliability? We're not the Almighty, Mr. Doyle. We're not infallible. So laws are passed to see to it that everyone is accorded the fairest treatment possible under these conditions. That's the true concept of justice, Mr. Doyle. Do you understand now?"

"No."

Peabody drummed his fingers. "In any event, it's beside the point. The important thing is that we do what's best for you. As I've said, I recommend pleading guilty to involuntary manslaughter and throwing yourself on the mercy of the court."

"So the judge would decide what to do with me?"

"Affirmative."

"What exactly could he decide to do?" James wanted to know.

"The judge will take into consideration all of the facts and render a verdict based on his assessment and experience."

"Talk to me like a normal person would."

"I can't predict what the ruling will be," Peabody said testily. "The judge decides at his own discretion. He has a number of options. He could dismiss the charge, although I very much doubt it. I've never, ever seen a case like this where the accused was let off. He could sentence you to prison. For how long would depend on his evaluation of your character and your intentions at the time."

"Could he still sentence me to hang?"

Peabody coughed and looked down at the table and then back at James. "I won't lie to you. We could throw ourselves on the mercy of the court and there won't be any mercy. Yes, you could still be hanged."

"Hell," James said.

12

A flame of hope was kindled in James's breast when he heard the name of the judge: Sullivan. Then he was brought into court and he saw the judge's stern face and heard his hard voice, and the flame was smothered.

Lawyer Peabody and a lawyer for the city went through their rituals. Judge Sullivan listened with no expression, and when they were done, he commanded James to rise and startled James by having him come take the stand. James glanced at Peabody, and Peabody motioned for him to get up there.

James was nervous as could be. He didn't want to be hanged, and he was afraid he'd say something wrong and that would be that.

The judge looked down on him as if from a lofty height and showed emotion for the first time. He actually smiled. "I want you to tell me in your own words exactly what happened that night."

James licked his lips and related it as best he remembered. He didn't lie once, that he could think of.

"Hmmmm," Judge Sullivan said. "And now I'll tell you why I had you do that, given that your attorney had already pled you to involuntary manslaughter."

James waited, tense with dread.

"I like to get a sense of the people I sentence," Judge Sullivan said. "I like to know, are they good or are they bad? Does a man steal because he likes to or does he steal because he has no money to put food on the table for his family? Does a woman sell her body because she's a Jezebel or because she couldn't find any other way to make a living? Do you understand?"

"I think so, sir," James said.

Judge Sullivan studied him. "My sense of you is that you're not a bad apple, young man."

"Thank you, sir."

"I'm not done. You're not bad inside, at least not yet. That you frequent the Keelhaul isn't a good sign. You live on the wild side, and that's not wise. But you haven't gone so bad that you'd kill a man over a trifle like cards."

James wanted to say that no, he wouldn't, but he didn't dare interrupt.

"On that basis alone I'm inclined to be lenient," Judge Sullivan said.

James almost whooped for joy.

"But you *did* kill a man, intentional or not. And I can't let that pass."

There was a strange roaring in James's ears, as of his blood racing through his veins.

"It wouldn't be just for me to impose the maximum penalty and sentence you to the gallows. Nor would it be just for me to simply let you go. I must find a middle ground, a balance of the scales of justice, if you will. Do you understand that as well?"

"I guess so," James said quietly.

Judge Sullivan loomed larger. "There must be no guesswork here, son. You must understand fully the gravity of the charge and why you must be punished according to the rule of law."

"The rule of law," James repeated, for want of anything better he could think of.

"Precisely. We are a nation of laws. Law is the glue that holds civilized society together. Without laws we would be no better than the barbarians of olden times. And we wouldn't want that, would we?"

James thought of his wild and carefree years as a Blue Shirt. "No, sir."

"I've had cases like yours before," Judge Sullivan said. "Where the accused was a good person but had committed a heinous crime. I always try to give them the benefit of the doubt and offer them a chance to redeem themselves."

"Redeem?" James said.

"Make something of yourself. Prove to me and the rest of the world that I've done the right thing."

"Prove how, Your Honor?" James asked. Peabody had told him to call the judge that and he just now remembered.

Judge Sullivan smiled, apparently pleased by James's interest. "By doing something worthwhile with your life. But keep in mind, I'm not forcing this on you. You'll have a choice to make. It will be your decision."

"What will?"

The judge drew himself up and squared his shoulders and said formally, "James Marion Doyle, I hereby sentence you as follows: Either you serve seven years in a penitentiary—"

Unable to stop himself, James exclaimed, "Seven years in *prison*?"

Sullivan acted as if he hadn't heard. "Or you will enlist in the United States Army and serve out a regular enlistment of five years."

The last thing James would ever do was be a soldier. He had no interest in it, none whatsoever. Unfortunately, based on the tales he'd heard, prison was vastly worse.

"No need to make up your mind right this moment," Judge Sullivan was saying. "You can consult with your attorney and have him give me your decision within the next twenty-four hours." Sullivan glanced at Peabody. "No more than twenty-four, you hear?"

"Yes, Your Honor."

Sullivan offered a kindly smile to James. "Think about it long and hard, son. You'll see I'm being fair. Once your enlistment is up you're free to do as you please. Stay in the army or be discharged and become a civilian again. Now, that's not so terrible, is it?"

James clamped his jaws tight to keep from saying that it was terrible as hell.

"All right, then," Judge Sullivan said. "Take him away, bailiff. And, Mr. Doyle, try not to look so glum. It's not the end of the world, after all."

It sure felt like the end of the world to James.

13

Topeka, Kansas

If James were to make a list of the places he never figured to visit, Topeka would have been at the top. It
wasn't that he'd heard bad things about Topeka. He
hadn't heard any good things, either. But Topeka was
where the army sent him, to a camp a mile or so from the
city. Calling it that, to his way of thinking, was stretching
things. Topeka's population was barely five thousand, a
drop in a bucket compared to the ocean of humanity in
New York City. But here he was, with no way out. Judge
Sullivan had warned him that if he deserted he would be
hunted down and sent straight to prison.

"You get only this one chance," the judge had said.
"Make good use of it."

But *God*, it was awful. James was used to city life.
He wasn't a country boy. The rolling green prairie was
a whole new world. It lent the illusion that it went on
forever. And everywhere there was grass. Grass, grass,
and more grass, as many blades of greens as there were
grains of sand on the Atlantic shore.

The morning he arrived he was handed a blanket and

told he would receive his equipment, whatever that was, in a few days.

That night he had to sleep on the ground with nothing to keep him warm except the blanket and his coat, and well before morning his teeth were chattering.

Water came from the Kansas River, named after an Indian tribe, or so he was told. The recruits had to tote it themselves and the buckets were heavy.

The army fed them two meals a day. The morning meal was crackers, bacon and coffee. The crackers were tasteless and the bacon was greasy, but James liked the coffee; it was hot and black and strong enough to jolt him awake.

Now and then other recruits talked to him, but he wasn't in the mood to be friendly and soon he was left pretty much alone.

James learned that he was being mustered into a company, and that the company would soon vote on its officers. He didn't want any part of the nonsense. He didn't care who the officers were. A captain, a first lieutenant, and a second lieutenant were chosen, to the cheers of many of the men.

It was shortly after the vote that James found out he had been mustered into D Troop of the Fourteenth Volunteer Cavalry. He laughed on hearing it, and said to himself, "Volunteer, my ass."

He was assigned to guard duty and posted along the river. For several hours he walked back and forth, feeling like a fool.

They hadn't given him a weapon. Not that there was much danger.

The hostiles, common knowledge had it, wouldn't dare attack Topeka. He was to keep recruits from sneaking off for a night of liquor and fun. A treat he wouldn't mind himself, but he remembered the judge.

The next day was Sunday. The whole camp attended

the services. James wouldn't have minded a priest so much, but it was a preacher who thundered to the sky that they must bend their knee to God. Later, they were given Bibles. James was at a loss with what to do with his.

That afternoon, people came from Topeka to visit, many in carriages and wagons and some on horseback. It was quite the crowd. James took them to be relatives of the recruits until he overheard a remark to the effect that many were townsfolk or farmers with no ties to anyone. He didn't know what to make of it and couldn't be bothered to ask.

James tried to avoid them, but suddenly a woman and a girl were in front of him, smiling. The girl offered her hand.

"How do you do?" she said sweetly.

James's tongue clove to his mouth. She was about his age, and beautiful: eyes as blue as the Kansas sky, smooth cheeks and cherry lips, and hair like spun gold. He shook, and the warmth of her palm sent a spark shooting up his arm.

"Cat got your tongue?" she teased.

"Now, now, Margaret. Be polite. This young man is making a noble sacrifice and the least we can do is treat him with respect."

"He doesn't look so noble, Ma," Margaret said.

"Now, now."

"He looks handsome."

James felt a burning on his cheeks. "What do you want?" he demanded.

The mother offered her hand. She had on a flowered dress and a bonnet. "I'm Mrs. Craydon. We come often to show our support for the soldiers."

"That's nice," James said.

"Is there anything you would like? Cookies? A pie? We'll bring you one next Sunday."

"You'd do that for someone you don't even know?"

"You're doing something for us, young man," Mrs. Craydon said. "Think of it as us returning the favor."

"What am I doing for you?"

Mrs. Craydon acted surprised by the question. "Why, you're serving your country in a time of need. You're defending the frontier with your life and protecting people like Margaret and me."

James gazed about and noticed other mothers and daughters in bright dresses and bonnets and a few with parasols. "Is that why so many ladies are here?"

"You make it sound piddling," Mrs. Craydon said.

"No," James said quickly. "I didn't mean it to. It's a fine thing you're doing, missus."

Mrs. Craydon brightened. "Why, thank you. What do we call you, by the way?"

"Doyle, ma'am," James said, and then remembered. "Private Doyle, if you please."

"Well, Private Doyle, you are the perfect gentleman. Isn't he the perfect gentleman, Margaret?"

"And handsome," Margaret said.

"So, would you like us to visit you next week?" Mrs. Craydon asked. "And if so, will it be cookies or a pie?"

James was dazzled at how Margaret's blue eye sparkled. "A pie would be nice."

The next day his army life commenced in earnest. The recruits were issued their horse gear, as some called it: a rope, a bridle, a saddle blanket, and saddle. James stared at his pile and scratched his head, wondering what in hell the judge had flung him into. Back in New York he had nothing to do with horses except to watch out for their piles in the street. Horses were everywhere, but the Blue Shirts didn't own any, and besides, most people in Five Points used their own legs to get around.

Squatting, he touched the saddle. It was alien to him.

The only part he knew was the saddle horn. Oh, and the stirrups. The saddle blanket was easy enough to figure out. So was the contraption that he was to slip over the horse's head. He picked up the rope, surprised at how heavy and stiff it was. "What am I supposed to do with this?"

A shadow blocked out the sun, and James glanced up. A huge block of a recruit was holding a bridle and grinning like a kid at Christmas.

"Ain't these something? They give us all this, and we don't have to pay for it."

"They're something," James said.

The big recruit chuckled. "Joining this here army was the smartest thing I ever done." He offered a callused hand as big as a ham. "I'm Dorf."

James stood and held out his own. A vise clamped on his fingers. "Doyle."

"You're not from hereabouts, are you?"

"Chicago," James lied. He had been lying about where he was from since he left New York,

"A city boy," Dorf said, and nodded. "Took you to be. I'm a local, myself. My pa has a farm about twenty miles yonder." He pointed. "Him and Ma weren't tickled about me enlisting, but I told them I had it to do."

"You did?" James said.

Dorf looked around as if afraid someone would overhear him and then bent and whispered, "Don't ever tell them or it will break their hearts, but I don't much like farm life."

"You don't?"

Dorf shook his head. "My pa would be shocked but cows bore me. All they do is eat and shit. They are dumb as stumps, and there's only so much dumb I can take."

"The only thing I know about cows is they taste good."

Dorf erupted in giant peals of mirth. He slapped his thick thigh and said, "That was a good one. I like how they taste, too, especially with a heap of salt. The fat's the best. So juicy, I can't ever get enough." He smiled and walked away.

James turned back to his pile. That was the first talk he'd had with any of the recruits since he joined. Short as it was, it made him dislike being so alone. He was bending to examine the saddle more closely when there was a thud next to him and another saddle and saddle blanket and bridle were next to his own.

"I'm back," Dorf said.

"So you are."

"Since we're going to be pards, we should stick together."

"Pards?"

Dorf's smile disappeared and a hurt look came over him. "You don't want to be partners? I don't have one yet, and I figured you looked likely."

"I don't even know what a partner does," James said.

"Gosh. City boys don't know much, do they?" Dorf showed his big teeth in a grin. "A pard is a friend, is all." He thrust out his hand again. "What do you say?"

James considered that hand and what shaking it would mean, and he shook. "Pards we are."

Dorf laughed and clapped him on the shoulder. "This is a great day. Ain't this a great day? And the afternoon ain't even here yet." He suddenly grew serious. "I know a couple of other fellows who might like to join up with us. We can stick together like some of the others do."

"Have our own little gang," James said by way of a jest.

"Oh, no," Dorf said. "Gangs are mostly outlaws. You don't call anybody a gang out here unless they are bad men, and we're not bad men."

"What do we call ourselves, then?"

Dorf regarded him as if he were the most brainless person on the planet. "Pards."

James smiled.

The big farm boy went off again and when he returned he had two others in tow. Farm boys, like him, only nowhere near his bulk. One was short and thin and had strange hair in that it grew thicker in some spots on his head than in others. His name was Newcomb, and he was shy. The other was about Doyle's size but with more muscle from hours behind a plow. His grip was almost as strong as Dorf's. Daniel Richard Cormac was how he introduced himself.

"Pleased to make your acquaintance, Dan," James said.

"No. Not Dan or Daniel or Richard or Rich or Dick even," the husky young man responded. "Call me Cormac or don't call me anything. I never was fond of those others."

Doyle understood. "As you wish."

Dorf nudged Cormac. "Tell him what it means."

"Stop it," Cormac said.

"Go on. Tell him. It's a keen name. You should be proud of it."

"I am."

"Then tell him."

Cormac looked at James and rolled his yes. "It means a man who rides chariots."

"Rides what?" James asked.

It was Dorf who excitedly answered, "You know. Those old itty-bitty wagons with no backs that those Roman fellows rode? You know the Romans, don't you? They wore skirts and carried swords."

James had only the vaguest of notions what a Roman was, or a chariot, for that matter.

"My full last name is Dorfenbacher," Dorf revealed. "My pa says it means people from the foresty hills, or some such, which I thought was funny since we live on the prairie and there ain't hardly any trees." He gestured at their fourth partner. "Newcomb's name means farmer. Ain't that something? His name means what he is."

"I'm a soldier now," Newcomb said quietly.

"Why does any of this matter?" James said.

"My ma always says that our names are a part of us," Dorf told him. "They're important."

"To me a name is just a name."

"That's not true. A name can tell you about a person or about a place." Dorf pointed at where the top of the statehouse was visible in the distance. "Take Topeka. It's the capital of all of Kansas, you know. But I bet you don't know what it means, you being from back East and all. It's an Injun name. A lot of places around here have Injun names. I reckon those who named them couldn't come up with any white words."

James was curious despite himself. "So, what does Topeka mean?"

Dorf stood straight as if making a grand pronouncement. "Where good potatoes grow."

14

The army issued them horses. They weren't allowed to pick. Their names were called, and each stepped forward and took the next animal in a string.

James was nervous as hell. He still wasn't entirely comfortable wearing a uniform, and he didn't like his boots at all. They didn't fit well. His feet always felt pinched. Dorf had told him the leather would loosen after a while and they would be comfortable as could be. "Your feet will feel like kittens in a pair of slippers," Dorf claimed.

Whatever that meant. Now James stepped to the front of the line and heard the captain call his name and stepped to the string. He was supposed to slip the bridle over his horse and lead it back, but he had never used a bridle before. He thought he'd had it figured out, but the horse bobbed its head and he realized he was trying to put the bridle on the wrong way. He quickly did it right and started back, half expecting to hear laughter.

Those who had already picked were admiring their animals. James stared at his in a sort of daze. The enormity of his new responsibility was sinking in. He was responsible for this creature. He was to feed it, groom it, take good care of it. As the sergeant told the com-

pany, "There are two things a soldier must always keep
in good order: his carbine and his horse. Both can save
your life. You need to get to know your horse as good as
you do yourself. Treat it well, and when the arrows are
flying, you'll be glad you did."

Dorf was running a hand along the back of his animal
and saying over and over, "Ain't this something? Ain't
this something?" He looked at James and laughed. "A
free horse. This army beats all." He cocked his head.
"Why ain't you getting acquainted? That's a fine bay.
Don't just stand there. Show him he's your friend."

"A bay?" James said.

Dorf, Cormac, and Newcomb looked at one another,
and Cormac said, "City boy." All three laughed.

"What?"

Dorf came over and draped his big arm across
James's shoulders. "Horses come in colors. There're
bays and buckskins and piebalds and sorrels and duns
and more. See how yours is kind of reddish? But it has a
black mane and a black tail? That's a bay."

"I just thought a horse was a horse."

"You said the same thing about names," Dorf reminded him. "What is it about you city boys that you see
the world around you but you don't know what you're
seeing?"

James soon learned that horses were a lot like people. Each had its own temperament. Some were gentle.
Others were ornery or outright mean. They bucked or
bit or fought the bridle. A few couldn't be ridden at all.
The army weeded out most of the troublesome ones, but
there was an incident a few afternoons later when the
company was practicing how to move in formation. A
horse kept giving a trooper trouble. He was trying to get
it under control when it reared, throwing him. He broke
his wrist in the fall.

The next day they were issued carbines. Spencers, with a seven-round magazine. They were also given twenty cartridges and straps by which they could sling their carbines over their backs.

Dorf actually giggled when the sergeant gave him his. "This army is just like St. Nick."

Targets were set up. Each man was allowed three shots.

James surprised himself. He'd never fired a rifle or a carbine, but after the sergeant showed him how to line up the rear sight with the front sight and instructed him in how to steady his aim by holding his breath, he hit the bull's-eye once and came close with his other two. That was a lot better than a lot of the others did. He felt a terrific pride.

Someone was bold enough to raise a hand and ask as they were forming up afterward, "Why were we only allowed three, Sergeant?"

"Cartridges cost money, Private Brown," Sergeant Heston answered.

"Surely that's not all the practice we're going to get, Sarge?"

"Were it up to me, each of you would shoot a hundred rounds and even that wouldn't be enough," Sergeant Heston answered. "But the army keeps a tight budget."

"I bet the Indians practice more than we do," Private Brown remarked.

"From when they are old enough to draw back a bow-string," Sergeant Heston said. "I've seen warriors put arrows into men while riding at a full gallop. So yes, for the most part they are better shots and better riders. Don't ever take them lightly or you'll regret it."

"What a thing to say to us," Dorf whispered. "Injuns don't scare me none."

They sure scared James.

15

That evening Sergeant Heston came to the tent James was sharing with his new friends and informed him that the captain wanted to see him.

"What about?" James asked. He had been trying his best, but he was painfully aware of his shortcomings.

"Don't you mean, 'What about, *Sergeant*?'"

James repeated the question properly.

"We'll let him tell you."

James matched the sergeant's brisk stride. Heston was highly regarded by the men. A career soldier, the sergeant did everything better than everyone else. Dorf idolized the man.

The captain's tent was larger than those for the enlisted men, with a flap that was tied open. Inside were a table and chairs. James was disconcerted to find not just Captain Pemberton but Lieutenant Finch and Second Lieutenant Myers.

"At ease, Private." Captain Pemberton had a paper in front of him and was reading it. He slowly sat back and thoughtfully regarded Doyle. "How does it feel to kill?"

A bolt of apprehension shot through James and he swallowed, hard. "Sir?"

"I said to relax, soldier." Pemberton smiled and tapped the paper. "I have your history right here. You killed a man in St. Louis. In self-defense, I understand." He paused. "Were there any others?"

"Sir?"

"Have you killed anyone else?"

James was struck speechless. He imagined the army throwing him out and Judge Sullivan throwing him in prison.

"I asked you a question, Private."

"Must I really say?"

"It's important."

James was light-headed. Already he could hear the prison door slamming shut in his face. Out of the corner of his eye, he saw Sergeant Heston start to take a step toward him, but Captain Pemberton waved him back.

"Is there something the matter, Private Doyle?" Lieutenant Finch asked.

"I don't want to be thrown out."

"What?"

"I don't want to be thrown out of the army, sir."

Second Lieutenant Myers laughed. "Thrown out of the army for killing? Have you any idea what we do for a living, Private?"

Captain Pemberton motioned and Second Lieutenant Myers sobered. Pemberton leaned back and folded his hands in his lap. "There seems to be a misunderstanding here. But it would help me, greatly, Private Doyle, if you would give me an honest answer."

"An honest one, sir? And it won't get me thrown out?"

"No."

James steeled himself. "Very well, then, sir. The answer is yes."

"How many?"

"At least one, sir."

Pemberton waited as if to hear more and when James stayed quiet he turned to the two lieutenants. "What do you think?"

"Two is more than any of the others," Finch said.

"Two is as many as me, and I dearly crave to do in more" was Myers's reply

Captain Pemberton stared at James. "Yes. You should do fine. The others will take you as an example."

"Sir?" James said in complete confusion.

"As Lieutenant Myers alluded to a few moments ago, we're soldiers. We took an oath to defend the United States of America from any and all enemies. To that end we must sometimes kill."

James nodded vigorously. "I understand that much, sir."

"Unfortunately, Private Doyle, killing isn't a skill like riding or shooting. Those we can teach. The ability to take another's life has to come from inside us. And it's not an ability a lot of men have. We drill them and drill them, but we can't instill in their hearts and in their minds the ability to calmly squeeze the trigger when the moment of truth comes."

"Calmly, sir?"

Pemberton was warming to the subject. He nodded and said, "During and after the Civil War, studies were conducted. They found that in the heat of battle a lot of men reacted poorly. Some were so scared they ran. Others lost their heads and kept on firing even though their weapons were empty. Still others went berserk and rashly exposed themselves to enemy bullets. So you can see why staying calm in combat is so important."

"Yes, sir."

"They found that, as the saying has it, experience is the best teacher. Those who had killed were the calmest about killing again. Once you've done it, once you've gone over that hurdle, it becomes easier."

James disagreed. It hadn't been easy for him in the fight with the Florentines and it hadn't been easy for him with that river rat.

"Which brings us to you," Captain Pemberton said. "By your own admission you have taken two lives. You are over a hurdle most of the men have yet to face. In addition, Sergeant Heston tells us that you were in the top third at target practice today. Your riding ability is poor, but that can be improved. As for the rest, you do as well as most of the recruits. All in all I'd say you're the ideal candidate."

"Candidate, sir?" James wished he could guess where this was leading.

"We have to pick several and for my money you'll do nicely. Congratulations, Corporal."

"Sir?"

"You are *Corporal* Doyle now. You've been promoted. It means an increase in pay. More importantly, you're a link in the chain of command. A crucial link, I might add, between the sergeant and those under him." Captain Pemberton smiled.

"Anything to say?"

James said the first thing that came into his head. "I'll be damned, sir."

16

James sat on a grassy knoll and gazed off across the Kansas prairie and did some thinking. The most serious thinking he had done in a long time. He wasn't used to it. When he was little, he'd felt his way through everything. Then his father died, and he *had* to think about that, but no matter how hard he had thought about it he couldn't understand why it had happened.

Why were people born only to die? Where was the sense in Five Points? In some people being so poor while others lived in luxury? In a slum where it was dog-eat-dog and people did whatever they must to survive? He'd finally stopped thinking about it because it made no damn sense.

As a Blue Shirt, he hadn't had to think much at all except to stay one step ahead of those who'd do him harm. He'd been as clever as anyone at not being caught, but it didn't involve much thinking. It just seemed to come to him.

In St. Louis he'd lived for his nights of drinking and gambling and sometimes a woman when he felt the need. Not much thinking was called for and he liked it that way.

Now here he was, a cavalryman. He hadn't wanted to be one. Once again life forced him into something against his will. Life did that a lot. A person was going along minding his own business and Life walked up and said, "A fine day to you!" and kicked him in the teeth.

He'd figured to serve his hitch and get the hell out. He had no interest in the army. His whole concern was to stay alive. But now something good had happened, really good, as he saw it, and he needed to think what to do.

James touched the two bars he'd sewn onto his uniform. Unlike a lot of the men, he was good at sewing. He had his mother to thank. She'd taught him how as a boy.

He was a corporal now. To some that might not be much, but to him it was a lot. He had made something of himself. Accidentally, to be sure, but a corporal was better than a private, and it had occurred to him that if he did well enough, if he applied himself, he might even make sergeant.

So here he was, sitting in the grass and thinking on whether he should reconsider this army business and take it more seriously.

James looked down at himself. He liked the uniform, the color of it, and the feel of it. He'd never owned boots and unlike a lot of the others, he rather enjoyed polishing them until they shone. He swung the Spencer carbine from behind his back and stared at it. Such a grand weapon. He never in his life imagined he'd have a rifle of any kind. Maybe it wasn't his, strictly, but the army entrusted him with it, and that was enough.

The army. It wasn't the hell he'd expected. The work wasn't all that hard. At first he hadn't liked getting rousted out of bed so early, but now he was used to it. The officers were decent enough. The bossing around they did they had to do because they were in charge, so he didn't resent it as much as he might. And now as a corporal he got to do a wee bit of bossing around himself. He grinned at that.

Yes, James Marion Doyle, he told himself in his head, you've lucked into something here. Maybe he should make the most of it. The first step would be to learn to ride better. It was god-awful stupid for a cavalryman to ride as poorly as he did. He would work at it.

Coming to a decision, he got up, swung the carbine behind him, brushed himself off, and walked back. Finding Sergeant Heston wasn't difficult; he listened for the bellows. The sergeant was tearing into a sloppily dressed recruit. James waited, and when the recruit withered and slunk off, he said boldly, "Sergeant, a word with you, if you please."

"What is it, Corporal Doyle?"

James was suddenly nervous. "I just wanted you to know that I'll try to be the best corporal I can be."

Heston arched an eyebrow. "Well, now," he said, and he almost smiled. "Like those bars, do you?"

James touched them as he had out on the knoll. "They mean more to me than I thought they would," he admitted.

Sergeant Heston clasped his hands behind his back and nodded. "That's good to hear." He pursed his lips and rocked on his heels. "I'll give you some advice if you care to listen."

"I'm all ears, Sergeant."

"You're not a bad soldier, Doyle. You're not a great one, but you're not bad." Heston held up a hand when Doyle went to speak. "Stick to the basics. They're simple enough. Always carry out orders to the letter. Always put the welfare of the men before anything. And never try to be a hero."

"Sergeant?"

"What confuses you? That hero part? Sooner or later we'll go up against the red devils we're being sent to subdue. When that happens, do your duty. Keep a cool head. Don't be reckless. Don't jump into danger when there's no need. I've seen too many your age who thought that courage was enough to see them through and it's not."

"It isn't?"

"Doyle, anyone can be brave. All it takes is guts. Or as the captain might say, the will not to run when the arrows are flying. But to keep a calm head, there's the trick. Stay calm and do your duty and you might last long enough to become like me." Heston smiled.

"I'd like that, Sergeant."

Heston coughed and said, "Well, then. Our visitors will be here soon and I have things to attend to. If there's nothing else?"

"Visitors?"

"Have you forgotten, Doyle? It's Sunday. We're about to be swarmed with petticoats."

"Oh. That's right." James had forgotten, what with his new bars and all.

"A last word of advice," Sergeant Heston said, and grinned and winked. "A man must always remember what's important in this life."

"Petticoats are important, Sergeant?"

"They sure as hell are."

17

James had had her on his mind all week. At night when he lay on his back staring at the top of the tent, he would see her golden tresses and her blue eyes and red lips and he would yearn in a way he had never yearned before.

James had known more than a few painted ladies back in Five Points. Ladies who liked a frolic. Ladies who didn't expect a man to stick around after.

In St. Louis there were a few he fancied. He'd treat them to drinks and sometimes a meal, and he'd then get to it and be on with his life. He never wanted anything more. He never desired a home and kids and all of that. But when he thought about *her*, he sometimes daydreamed about the two of them with a house and a family. What was happening to him? he wondered. He'd only just met the girl, only ever seen her once and barely talked to her, and here he was, dreaming of the two of them together forever. It was silly.

Yet it wasn't so silly that he wasn't among the many troopers waiting for the carriages and wagons to arrive. It wasn't so silly that he hadn't polished his boots. It wasn't so silly that he hadn't gone to the river and picked a handful of flowers and now had them secreted under his shirt.

The visitors arrived and spread among the soldiers. James craned his neck, checking each wagon and carriage, but didn't see her. He moved about, searching without trying to appear too eager. He didn't spot her anywhere. He had convinced himself she hadn't come and was mentally calling himself all sorts of names for being so childish when a hand fell lightly on his arm from behind.

"*Here* you are, Private Doyle. Land sakes, we've been looking all over for you."

James turned and his heart leaped into his throat. Mother and daughter were finely dressed and both had parasols over their shoulders.

Mrs. Craydon grinned and said, "Did you forget about us?"

"Oh, no, never," James said. "I was searching for you my own self." He couldn't take his eyes off Margaret. She was staring at the ground, and holding a pie. He tried to greet her and his throat wouldn't work. It was stuck, somehow.

Coughing, he forced out "It's a pleasure to see you again, ma'am. Both of you."

"Why, thank you," Mrs. Craydon said. "I'll tell you what. It's such a gorgeous day, why don't we go sit by the river and treat ourselves to what we brought?"

"That would be grand." James was careful not to brush against them or touch them since he had heard that was how gentlemen behaved. "And it's not Private Doyle anymore, ma'am."

"It's not?"

With considerable pride, James touched the inverted V. "It's Corporal Doyle now."

"Why, so it is," Mrs. Craydon declared. "You've been

promoted already? How marvelous. Isn't it marvelous, Margaret? Take a look, will you? Congratulate the boy."

Margaret dutifully raised her head. Her blue eyes glimmered as James remembered and her lips were ripe strawberries. "Congratulations," she said softly.

"Thank you."

"Coming down with something, are you?" Mrs. Craydon asked.

"Ma'am?"

"Your voice. You sound kind of hoarse."

"Oh, no, ma'am. It must be the dust."

A lot of others were already along the river. James picked a spot where the bank sloped to the water's edge. The ladies tucked their legs under them and gracefully sat. He perched next to the mother, but he would really rather sit next to Margaret.

Mrs. Craydon had a big bag. From it she took a pink blanket, which she spread on the grass. She set small plates out along with forks and a knife.

"You've thought of everything, ma'am," James said.

"Well, we can't have the ants getting in our food, now, can we?" Mrs. Craydon chuckled.

"I suppose not."

Mrs. Craydon sat back with her arms across her knees. "You have the pie, Margaret. Why don't you do the honors?"

Margaret placed the pie in the middle of the blanket and picked up the knife. "Apple."

"I beg your pardon," James said.

"It's apple," Margaret said so softly he could hardly hear her. "I hope you like it."

"My mother used to bake apple pies when I was little. I liked them a lot."

Mrs. Craydon wriggled and grinned. "Margaret made this one herself. I offered to help but she wouldn't have it. Said she had to bake it for you with her own two hands."

James's skin grew warm as if with a heat rash. "She did that just for me?"

"Yes, indeed," Mrs. Craydon confirmed with an emphatic nod. "That girl about shooed me out of the kitchen." ·

"Oh, Ma," Margaret said. She was blushing.

"If I am lying, may the good Lord strike me dead."

Margaret cut the pie in half and then into quarters and then cut it again. She used the knife to pry a slice out and placed it on a plate and handed the plate to her mother.

"What are you doing, child?"

"Ladies first," Margaret said. "That's what you've always taught me."

"No, no, no. In most circumstances. But we brought the pie for Pri— I'm sorry, for Corporal Doyle. So by rights the first slice should go to him."

Margaret's hands shifted and held the plate toward James, her face averted. "Corporal Doyle."

"Thank you," James said, and nearly dropped the plate accepting it. He quickly put it on his lap.

"Don't forget to give him a fork," Mrs. Craydon said.

They sat eating in the green grass with butterflies flitting about and the river flowing serenely past.

"Isn't this nice?" Mrs. Craydon said.

"I've never known anything nicer," James agreed. He was looking at Margaret when he said it.

The pie was delicious. James ate every last speck to show Margaret how much he liked it.

Mrs. Craydon finished hers, deposited her plate on the blanket, and unexpectedly stood. "If you'll excuse me I'll be back in a bit."

"Ma'am?" James said in some surprise.

"I have people I'd like to give my regards. Would you sit here with Margaret until I get back? I wouldn't care to leave her without a chaperone, what with all these other young men around." Without waiting for an answer, Mrs. Craydon twirled her parasol and walked off.

James was flabbergasted. He didn't even know what a chaperone was. What was he supposed to do? To cover his consternation he said, "The pie was delicious, ma'am."

"Please don't," Margaret said.

"Ma'am?"

"Call my mother ma'am but not me. Call me Margaret. Or Marge. Or the ones I like best, which are Peggy or Peg. But don't ever call me ma'am. It makes me sound old."

"I'm sorry," James said. "I was being polite."

"You do that well," she said, and smiled.

"Peg," James said.

"What?"

"Nothing. I was just trying how it sounded."

"Oh." Peg leaned back and gazed at the sky. "She did that on purpose, you know."

"Did what?"

"She left us alone so we could talk."

"That was nice of her."

Peggy looked at him. She looked him right in the eye and asked, "What do you think of me, Corporal Doyle?"

"James. If I can call you Peg, you can call me James. That's only right."

"What do you think of me, James?"

James was unsure what he should say, so he hedged by answering, "I don't really know you."

"All right, then. Let me put it another way. Do you find me at all pretty?"

James was taken aback. Was this the shy girl of just a few minutes ago? "I think you're pretty as can be."

"Tell the truth," Peg said. "I know I'm not a beauty. Oh, my hair is nice enough, and everyone says I have nice eyes. But my nose is too long and my ears are too big, and I am more plump than most girls my age, although you can't really tell that, can you?"

"Why are you telling me all this?" James asked in extreme puzzlement.

"I'm being honest with you and I'd like for you to be honest with me." Peg sat up. "I'll ask you again. Do you find me at all pretty?"

"I've never met anyone prettier."

"I don't know how that can be, but all right." Peg glanced about them. "Slide closer."

"What?"

"Are you hard of hearing? Sit closer to me so we can talk without anyone hearing." Peg patted the grass beside her. "We need to work this out before she comes back."

If there was ever a time in his whole life when James was more confused, he couldn't think of it. He slid over and immediately felt the warmth of her body through his uniform. It was like sitting next to the sun. "Work out what?"

"Us."

"Peg," he said, and took a deep breath, "I have no idea what you're talking about."

Peggy studied his face, and nodded. "Lordy, you're handsome."

"You said that the last time."

"And you haven't gotten ugly since, so it's still true. Maybe other girls wouldn't agree, but to me you're as handsome as can be."

"Well, now," James said.

"Listen," Peg said, and glanced around again. "You know why we're here, don't you? All the mothers and their daughters?"

"To thank us for defending the frontier."

"There's that, yes. But for some of us there's more. Some of the mothers bring their daughters to find them husbands. Or possible husbands, I should say."

"They do?"

"God in heaven, how did you make corporal? Ma and me have been here half a dozen times, but I didn't see anyone who interested me until I saw you."

"Well, now."

"Why do you keep saying that?"

"I can't think of anything else."

"All right. I think you're handsome and you think I'm pretty. Is that enough for you to court me? Would you even like to?"

"Where did your shyness get to?" James bluntly asked. This was moving too fast. He needed to ponder on exactly what he did want.

"Confound it, James. Pay attention. I was raised on a farm in the middle of nowhere, and I hate it. I don't want to be a farmer's wife. A soldier's wife, now, that would be different. There are no fields to plow and cows to milk. It's more ladylike. And I'd like that. So I talked my ma into bringing me to these affairs, and I've been looking for a man to take me out of the life I hate and that man can be you if you want it to be. We have to start somewhere, so what I'm saying is you can court me. Write to me, visit me. And if you come to like me and I come to like you, then if you're of a mind, you can ask for my hand and I will gladly give it to you."

She said it so fast that James was a minute absorbing it all. "You make it sound like we're starting up a business."

"So?"

"Shouldn't there be some romance somewhere?"

Peggy's shy look returned. "That has to come natural. If the attraction is real, it will. You'll have more than you'll know what to do with, I promise."

James coughed.

"For now we need to start it off right." Peg adjusted her bonnet and smoothed her dress. "James Marion Doyle, do you want to court me?"

Thinking that Sergeant Heston would be proud of him, James grinned and said, "I sure do."

18

The weeks became a routine of training for six days and Peg's visits on Sundays.

James and his tent mates spent hours every evening talking and joking. He got to know them well. Dorf, for all his size and immense strength, was a kid at heart. Cormac was a rock and the best soldier of any of them. Newcomb had a breadth of knowledge far exceeding James's own. James wondered how that could be since Newcomb spent his whole life on a small farm and then one day he discovered the answer. Newcomb liked to read and devoured everything in print he got his hands on.

To James it was nice to have friends again. He'd been in a gang for so long, the life of a loner didn't suit him. One evening as he was about to turn in before lights out, he gazed about the tent. He really liked these men and they liked him. One for all, as Newcomb was always saying. Friends through thick and thin. It was a good feeling.

He had a lot more good feelings on Sundays. All week he looked forward to Peg's coming, and each Sunday when he first caught sight of her, he'd feel a special warmth. Her mother always came to chaperone but then would considerately leave them alone for long spells. Those were the times he enjoyed the most. Peg was as much a friend as Dorf and Cormac and New-comb, and so much more. Her smile meant the world to him, and he loved to hear her laugh. She told him all about how it was for her growing up, and he learned more about women from her than he had from anyone, even his mother.

Peg was delightfully feminine. She loved when he gave her flowers. She liked to go for strolls along the river, and when no one was looking, she would hold his hand and walk so close their bodies brushed.

It got so, James couldn't get enough of her. At night he'd toss and turn and think of her and break out in a sweat. He didn't put a word to his yearning until one bright and gorgeous day when they were walking on the riverbank and out of the blue she looked at him and asked a question that startled him even though it shouldn't have.

"Do you ever think you'll love me, James Marion?"

She liked to call him that. Usually, he'd noticed, when she brought up something important. He looked at her, trying to read her feelings in her face. "What kind of thing is that to ask?"

"Seeing as how you're courting me, I'd say a natural one."

"All this time, I should think it would be obvious."

"Nothing is ever obvious. And since rumor has it the companies will be moving out soon—"

"What have your heard?" James interrupted. Rumors were always going through camp, but nothing had ever come of them.

Peg was uncommonly serious. "That orders have come down and all of you will be heading off on a campaign. I can't say if it's true, but if it is I'll miss you and I'd like to know now that you'll miss me."

"I'll miss you more than anything."

Peg stopped and faced him. "My question still stands. Do you ever think you'll love me?"

James tried to speak, but his throat wouldn't work. He coughed and watched a fish jump out in the water and coughed again. "I think I already do."

"You think?"

"I've never been in love before, so I have nothing to compare it to. But I feel for you as I've never felt for anyone." James stopped.

"You can say the words. And if you won't, I will." Peg leaned in and her lips touched his ear. "I love you, James Marion Doyle."

James tingled all over and grew light in the head. Yet at the same time his every sense was acute. He felt the warmth of the sun on his skin, smelled the lilac scent of her perfume, saw into her eyes as if into the depths of life itself. He barely heard himself say, "I love you, too."

Peg kissed him.

To James it was miraculous. He'd kissed women before, a lot of women, but none had ever affected him as this did. A bolt cleaved him in half, and his heart jumped and everything that he was seemed finer than it had ever been. He wished the moment would last forever.

Peg looked at him expectantly.

James figured she wanted him to kiss her, so he did and would have kissed her some more except she put a finger to his lips and laughed.

"I'm like cookies, am I?"

"Sorry?"

"I've talked to my ma and my pa and they have no objections to us taking the next step."

"The next what?"

"Think, James Marion. What comes after the court-

ing? I grant you that most courtships last longer, but we
don't have that luxury, do we?"

James was baffled by what she was alluding to. He
needed a clue, so he said, "No, we don't."

"Not when there's no telling when you'll be back. It
could be months," Peg said sadly. "I say we make it of-
ficial. We become engaged."

"Engaged?" James repeated.

"Yes. Some couples do that. I pledge to become yours
and you pledge to become mine. I'll wear your ring
proudly and stay true until you return, and after that,
well . . ." Peg stopped and smiled and blushed.

James would gladly buy her the moon and the stars, if
he was permitted. "I'd have to buy a ring. What if I can't
get into Topeka before we head out?"

"We'll hope for the best. Now say it outright. I want
to hear you."

"Say what?"

"Honestly, James Marion."

"Oh." James's mouth was suddenly dry. He took a
deep breath and got it out. "Would you like to become
engaged, Peggy Craydon?"

"I thought you would never ask."

19

Topeka was young and still being put together. A lot of the buildings sat apart so that you had to do a lot of walking to get around. Back in New York the buildings were jammed so close that the streets were narrow canyons and you couldn't see from one to the next. Here, James could stand in the middle of a street and gaze out over the expanse of prairie to the horizon.

His friends came with him. He had confided what he was doing and they were eager to help him pick. That, and to get into Topeka, was rare treat.

It was Dorf who said James should go up to Sergeant Heston and just ask. "What harm can it do? The worst he'll say is no."

But Heston had said yes and now here they were, taking in the sights before they got down to it.

The statehouse was the talk of the territory. It dwarfed everything else. When James stood at the base of one of the giant columns and craned his neck to see the top, the column seemed to go on forever. A lot of folks were unhappy with it. Money squandered, they complained. That didn't stop the politicians from squandering it, though.

Topeka had a few wealthy citizens and another of the sights was an L-shaped mansion.

Dorf insisted on visiting one of the churches. Stained-glass windows and a high steeple made it stand out. He insisted they go in, too. They stood at the back, grateful for the coolness, in a quiet so deep they could hear themselves breathing.

"I miss going to church regular," Dorf said, and his voice seemed to boom.

It had been years since James was in a house of worship. His mother and father used to take him, but after his father died she went less and less and finally stopped altogether. He turned his hat in his hands and was glad when Dorf led them back out.

"Can we get to it now?" James impatiently asked.

Cormac grinned and nudged Newcomb. "Sounds to me like someone has it bad."

"That he does," Newcomb agreed.

The general store bustled with people, if six could be called a bustle. On hearing what James was after, the proprietor led them to a glass case. It held two dozen rings: misses' rings, baby rings, rolled gold–plated rings and gold-filled rings, and silver rings.

The proprietor was watching James. "You're Irish, aren't you? I could special-order a Claddagh if you were of a mind."

James remembered that his father had given his mother a traditional Irish engagement ring, and she treasured it above all others. "How long would it take to get here?"

"Oh, usually in under a month but sometimes it takes more."

"Too long." James tapped the glass. "I'd like to see the one with the heart."

The proprietor opened the case and set it on top.

"The band is gold and the heart is a ruby. Any young woman would be proud to wear it."

James gingerly picked it up and held it so the ruby caught the sunlight. "How much?"

"Fifty cents. And that's as low as you'll find one like it anywhere."

"That's not true," Cormac said. "I saw one for thirty cents in Kansas City, and the ruby was bigger."

The man glared at him and then smiled at James. "Your friend is mistaken. No one could possibly charge that little for a ring of this quality."

"I don't know," James said. But he really didn't have much choice. D Troop could be sent off into the wilds any day now.

"Tell you what I'll do," the man said. "Just for you I'll lower the price to forty-five cents."

"Make it forty," Cormac said.

"Listen, my young friend," the proprietor said stiffly. "That merchant in Kansas City doesn't have the extra expenses I do. Shipping, for instance. That alone adds pennies and cuts into my profit. Forty-five cents is a fair offer."

"I'll take it," James said.

"A wise decision." The man reached under the counter and brought out a sheet of paper. "Now I'll need your name and her ring size and in a few weeks you can pick it up."

"What?" James said.

"Rings come in sizes like most everything else. I need to know your lady's so we can have the ring adjusted to fit."

James almost slapped his forehead. He had forgotten about the size business. "I don't how big her fingers are."

"Oh, my," the man said. "Can you guess?"

James debated. He might get it wrong and have to go

through this whole thing again. "No, and I don't have time to have it fitted, anyway."

The proprietor gnawed on his lip. "How about this idea? You take it with you and buy a gold chain for her to wear it around her neck. The chain is only ten cents. Later, at her or your convenience, you can have the fitting done."

"The chain should be five cents," Cormac said, "him buying it because you can't fit it for him here and now."

The man shot Cormac another irritated look. "Very well. Five cents, because I have a generous nature."

"And you'll wrap them for him?" Cormac said.

James had never been so nervous about paying for anything in his life. The enormity was sinking in. Giving that ring to Peg was the same as saying he was willing to be hers, now and forever.

The amazing thing was, he didn't mind one bit.

20

D Troop was gathered near the river. Captain Pemberton stood with his hands behind his back and somberly regarded them. Pemberton was flanked by Lieutenant Finch and Second Lieutenant Myers.

Pemberton began. "I don't believe in keeping my command in the dark. No purpose is served by uncertainty and camp gossip. As many of you have no doubt heard, we have been ordered into the field. We leave the day after tomorrow. It's customary for departing troops to parade through Topeka and Colonel Exeter informs me we will follow the custom."

The captain paused to let them absorb the news.

Dorf poked James with an elbow and whispered, "About damn time."

"Don't be in such an all-fired hurry to take an arrow," Newcomb said.

Captain Pemberton cleared his throat. "You'll naturally be anxious to know where we are bound. A rumor has it that we're being sent to Arizona to fight the Apaches. The rumor is wrong. Our orders are for us to head west and north across the plains and to subdue any hostiles we come across."

Several troopers let out whoops and yips.

"Ours is no easy task," Captain Pemberton said. "The hostiles are formidable fighters."

Behind him, Second Lieutenant Myers smirked.

Captain Pemberton went on. "Washington has tried to talk reason, and the Indians won't listen. They refuse to be put on a reservation even though it's for their own good. We're left with no choice but to take the field and round them up against their will."

From among the men someone hollered, "We'll teach the red heathens, sir!"

Others laughed.

Second Lieutenant Myers smiled and nodded.

Raising a hand, Captain Pemberton instilled silence. "I must warn you. It's a mistake to take them too lightly. While we are in the field, you must always keep your wits about you."

James heard chuckles and remarks to the effect that the Sioux better watch themselves, D Troop was on the way.

The next morning the bugle for reveille woke them at four a.m. Sergeant Heston called the roll. The men tended to their horses and ate a quick breakfast. Their bedding was piled in the company wagon and they were ready to head out by seven but they sat around talking until almost ten. The order was given to form up and D Troop fell in with the other troops.

Topeka gave them a fine send-off. Men and women lined Grand Avenue, the men doffing hats, some of the women waving brightly colored handkerchiefs. Peg was there, her mother at her side. As James came abreast she called his name and touched the ring that hung from her necklace.

James was supposed to ride facing front, but he couldn't resist glancing at her and returning her smile.

"Someone is in love," Dorf joked.

James swore he blushed. He smothered an impulse to twist in the saddle and stare after her and presently they were out of Topeka and off across the prairie.

"At last we're going to kill some redskins," a man happily declared.

"If'n they don't kill us first," said another.

"Quiet back there!" Sergeant Heston bellowed.

James was thinking of Peg—and if he would ever set eyes on her again.

RISE IN THE WEST

21

James thought he had seen a lot of prairie, but he hadn't seen a drop in a bucket. The prairie went on and on, and just when you thought it had to end it went on and on some more.

He could tell north from south and east from west, but he still didn't know where he was. In the middle of nowhere was the best way to describe it, but even nowhere was somewhere to those who lived there. To the Indians it was their home and they knew the land as well as they knew anything.

Few whites knew the plains as well, which was why the army relied on those who did. They were ten days out of Topeka when Colonel Exeter sent for Captain Pemberton. Word had it that they were to stay in camp a few days, waiting for their scouts to arrive. James had learned not to trust rumors, but in this case it was true.

About the middle of the third morning, a party of frontiersmen and Indians came riding hard out of the heat haze and were ushered to the colonel's tent. It wasn't an hour later that Captain Pemberton was sent for, and when he came back one of the frontiersmen and two Indians were with him.

D Troop was abuzz. Some said they were to take part in a campaign against the Kiowa. Others said that they heard the regiment was going to fight the Cheyenne.

As Colonel Exeter revealed in a short speech the next morning, it was both.

The Solomon and Saline valleys were red with blood. Bands of Cheyenne and Kiowa had gone on the rampage, burning farms and killing settlers and attacking wagon trains. Two white women had been taken captive. The army was mustering forces from all quarters to deal with the crisis.

The men of D Troop were keen for revenge. Hunkered around their fires, they vented their emotions.

"Those redskins took white gals, by God," Dorf declared. "That ain't right."

"Who knows what those poor women are going through?" a trooper said.

"We all do. They've been violated," Cormac said.

Shortly before taps Captain Pemberton put in an appearance. With him were the frontiersmen and the two Indians.

Pemberton had the ninety-four men of D Troop gather close around, and introduced the newcomers.

"Men, I'd like you to meet our scout. Some of you may have heard of him. His name is Jack Shard."

The captain introduced the two Crows, too, but hardly anyone heard their names. The troopers were excitedly whispering back and forth about the celebrated Jack Shard. James had never heard of him, but he soon learned the particulars. Shard was barely thirty, but he had packed a lot of living into those years. Born in Illinois, he was brought west by his parents when he was twelve and four years later left an orphan when Blackfeet swept down on their cabin. Shard fled south on horseback with the Blackfeet in pursuit. He eluded them, only to promptly fall into the hands of the Sioux. From the frying pan into the fire, some would say, but the Sioux spared him and for the next eight years he lived as one of them. He even took a Sioux wife. Then something happened and Shard signed on to scout for the army. His quick thinking during the Battle of Beecher Island saved the patrol he had been guiding and earned him a mention in the newspapers and ultimately his own dime novel, *Jack Shard, Scout Supreme, or the Lovers of the Plains.*

To hear the men talk, Shard was Hawkeye and Hercules rolled into one. Shard had killed more Indians than anyone could count. He could outshoot and outride practically everybody, and could drink anyone under the table.

The murmuring became so loud that Captain Pemberton had to impose quiet and impart other news.

"Tomorrow we break away from the main body. Our orders are to sweep the country west and south of Emporia for sign of a small band of Kiowas who have gone on a killing spree and left a bloody swath of death in their wake."

Later James lay on his back and stared at the stars. He wasn't like most of these men, who joined the army to wage war on the red man. He had no personal grudge against Indians. They never did him any harm. But he didn't like all the killing they did, and the other.

His thoughts drifted to Peg. They had only been apart a short while, but he missed her. He wished he was free to marry her and start a home and a family. Five years seemed like forever.

James wasn't the only trooper who didn't sleep well that night. A lot of them tossed and turned or got up and couldn't get back to sleep.

Reveille came too early.

James had rolled up his bedding and thrown it on the wagon and seen to his horse and was sipping a welcomed cup of hot coffee when Sergeant Heston materialized.

"The captain wants to see you, double quick."

"What did I do?" James asked as he hustled after the iron-muscled noncom.

"What did I do, *Sergeant*."

"What did I do, Sergeant?"

"Nothing."

Captain Pemberton was outside his tent. With him were Jack Shard and the two Crows. All three had on buckskins, but the famous scout's were by far the fanciest, with beads and long whangs. Shard wore a broad-brimmed hat, one side curled at a rakish slant. In a holster on his right hip, worn butt-forward, was a pearl-handled revolver. On his left hip was a bowie. His face was wide and handsome, with a thick mustache and short trimmed beard. His eyes were the same green as the prairie grass.

"Here he is, sir," Sergeant Heston announced.

"Ah, Corporal Doyle. At ease." Pemberton motioned at the scout. "You know who this gentleman is, of course."

"Yes, sir," James said, puzzled beyond measure over why they had sent for him.

"Are you ready to ride, Corporal?" Shard asked.

"I was eating breakfast," James said.

Shard grinned. "We can wait a few minutes for you to get done."

"Wait for what, sir?" James said to the captain.

Pemberton folded his hands behind his back, as was his habit. "I need a liaison, Corporal, between the scouts and myself. They will be ranging far afield in search of the hostiles, and messages might have to be sent back and forth. You will carry them."

"Good God, sir," James said.

"What?"

"I mean, why *me*, sir?" James was incredulous. He was hardly the best rider in the troop, and as for finding his way across the unending expanse of prairie alone—he almost shuddered at the prospect.

"Because I picked you," Pemberton said. "Because you happen to be one of the best shots we have and you've taken life before."

More than ever, James regretted that. He noticed that the Crows were amused by his reaction.

Shard didn't find it funny. "Is something the matter, trooper?"

"It's Corporal Doyle," James said. "And yes, I don't think I'm right for this."

"*I* say you are," Captain Pemberton broke in, "and that ends the discussion. You'll be ready to ride in fifteen minutes. Sergeant Heston will issue you extra ammunition. You'll have to account for every cartridge, so don't use them needlessly."

"Something else," Shard said. "Bring one blanket and one blanket only. No pots or pans or anything that will clank and clatter as we ride."

"What will I cook with?" James asked.

"Leave that to us," Shard said.

Captain Pemberton wriggled his fingers. "Off you go, Corporal."

Apprehension ate at James like an acid. Out on the prairie he would be easy pickings for the first war party they came across. The likelihood of his being killed was increased tenfold. He contemplated jumping onto his horse and riding like hell, but deserting would only land him on the gallows with hemp around his neck. He was finishing his coffee when his three friends joined him.

"Good God." Dorf said the same thing James had on hearing the news.

"Lucky dog," Cormac said. "You'll tangle with those butchering devils before we do, I bet."

Newcomb didn't help things by saying, "Don't worry. If anything happens to you, I'll get word to your sweet Peg."

22

Life had thrown James into unusual circumstances, but these weren't to his liking even a wee bit. Here he was, trailing after a noted scout and two stoic Crows, crossing the sea of rolling green in the crisp air of early morning, and wishing he was anywhere but where he was.

Jack Shard rode like a hawk soaring on the wind, his head constantly turning this way and that, his eyes seeking signs that might spell the difference between life and death.

The Crows, James noticed, didn't seem half as alert, but they didn't miss anything. When Shard snapped his head at distant moving sticks that turned out to be antelope, so did they. When Shard saw something on the ground that caused him to draw rein, the Crows saw it, too. They ignored him, which bothered him a little. These were the first Indians he had ever been close to and he would like to get to know them better. All he had had to go on to judge their kind were the terrible tales of mutilation and death he had heard over card games and campfires.

At times the prairie was as flat as a floor and at other times the ground rose in rolling swells like the waves at

the shore. Yellow and white butterflies danced among
the wildflowers. Vultures soared in search of carrion.
Long-eared rabbits fled from them in fantastic leaps.

The sun was at its zenith, and they were in the middle of another long stretch of land as flat as a griddle-
cake when Shard said a few words in what must be the
Crow tongue and came to a stop and the Crows did
likewise.

James was glad. His legs and backside were sore. He
was doing his best to ride well, but he couldn't get the
knack of sitting a saddle as straight and still as Shard
and the Crows.

He imagined that to them he must look like a goose
trying to take wing.

With a fluid quickness that James was to learn was
characteristic of the man, Shard dismounted. He hitched
at his holster and opened his saddlebags and pulled out
a shiny brass tube. "Spyglass," he said. "The secret to being a good scout." He grinned and unfolded it.

The Crows stood with their rifles in the crooks of
their arms.

James brushed dust from his uniform and stretched.
"I still wish you had picked somebody else, sir."

Shard glanced at him. "You gnaw it like a bone, don't
you?"

"Gnaw what?"

"Life." Shard raised the telescope to his right eye and
swept the western horizon and then did the same to the
north and the south. "We're safe enough for the moment," he said, and closed it.

"You're used to this, sir, and I'm not," James said by
way of defending his attitude.

"Don't sir me, Corporal Doyle," Shard said, not un-
kindly. "I don't hold rank. I'm on the army's payroll, but
I'm outside the army. Call me Jonathan, which is my

given name, or call me Jack, which is my nickname, or call me by my last name, but don't call me sir."

"Mr. Shard, then."

"You're Irish," Shard said, and chuckled.

"What did you mean by outside the army?"

"I mean I work for them but I don't have to wear a uniform or drill all damn day or take orders except as they have to do with scouting."

"You like it that way?"

"I am my own man and will not be imposed on," Shard said. "And yes, I like being me more than I would like being you."

"Thanks a lot."

"Don't get me wrong. What you men are doing is necessary. It takes guts to go up against an enemy who is better at living off this land than you will ever be if you lived here a hundred years."

"You sound like you admire them," James observed.

"I do," the scout said. "I admire the hell out of the Indian. All Indians."

"I heard you lived with the Sioux."

Shard was watching a hawk or falcon dive and climb. "They call themselves the Lakota. Even that is not enough, as there are seven tribes. It was the Oglala who took me in when the Blackfeet had run me to a frazzle. Later on I lived with the Crows a spell."

"So you like Indians' ways."

Shard turned. "What are you getting at?"

"I'm trying to understand you, is all," James said. "I've never known a scout and here I am with my life in your hands."

"Ah," Shard said. "You're smarter than most. I might even get to like you."

"I don't see where I'm smarter than anybody," James said.

The scout opened the telescope again and scanned the land to the west and as he did he said, "Most of the— What did Pemberton call them? Liaisons? Most I have to work with don't care much for me and don't like my friends at all. They do as I say and hardly ever talk. You ask questions. You want to know the why of things and that's good."

"It is?"

Shard closed the spyglass and shoved it into his saddlebags. "Most folks, Corporal Doyle—"

"James. You can call me James."

"—most folks, James, go through life with blinders on. They don't see things as they are but as they think they are. And that's bad."

This man wasn't at all as James had expected. "I'm not sure I follow."

"Take the Indians," Shard said. "Most whites hate them. The whites don't know a damn thing about why the Indians live as they do and how the Indians think, but the whites think they do and hate them for thinking things they don't think."

"If you say think one more time, my head will explode."

Shard laughed. "All I'm saying is that when you get to know the Indians like I know the Indians, you find out they're people just like you and me."

James looked at the Crows. "They are?"

"Where are my manners?" Shard said, and placed his hand on one of them. The warrior wore his long black hair loose. At the back of his head a lot of short hairs stuck up, which explained what Shard said next. "The whites call my friend here Cowlick. His real name is *Hissheiaxuhke*. It means Red Fox."

"I'll stick with Cowlick. That other is a tongue twister."

Shard rested his hand on the shoulder of the other Crow, who wore his hair in braids and had an unusually long knife on his left hip. "This here is Two Bears. He has the same name in Crow, only it's *Duupedaxpitchee*."

"Good God."

Shard looked at the Crows. "What should we call our liaison?"

"I have a name already," James said.

"Too soon," Cowlick declared in English.

"Call him Buffalo Shit," Two Bears said.

Laughing, Shard turned to James. "Don't get mad. He likes to poke fun."

"I won't answer to Buffalo Shit," James said.

Two Bears's eyes crinkled and his lips twitched.

"All right," Shard said. "Enough rest for the horses. We have a lot of ground to cover." He reached for his saddle horn, and paused. "And, James. From here on out it will be real dangerous. We can't afford any mistakes, you hear? Not if you want to go on breathing."

"I surely do," James said.

23

They hadn't been under way half an hour when Shard again drew rein, vaulted down, and knelt. Cowlick and Two Bears joined him. They touched the ground and spoke in Crow and then roved about. Eventually Shard stopped and gazed to the south, his expression grim.

"What?" James asked.

"Ten Indians went by late yesterday."

"How do you know it's Indians and not whites?"

"White horses are nearly always shod." Shard thoughtfully tapped his chin. "My guess is it's hostiles making for the Arkansas River country. There's a heap of settlers thereabouts ripe for the slaughter."

"How much killing can ten Indians do?"

"You'd be surprised." Shard mounted and waited for the Crows to climb back on. He looked at James and said, "Do I or don't I?"

"Do you what?" James said.

"Send you back to the column to tell Pemberton or wait until we have more to report." Shard wheeled his dun and tapped his heels. "I reckon we'll wait yet."

James was relieved. He wasn't looking forward to

having to find D Troop in the midst of all that vast emptiness. He'd likely as not get lost and be a laughingstock, or dead.

The scout and the Crows rode with determined purpose, pushing their mounts where before they had gone easy. The tracks were plain enough that even James could follow them.

Presently they were in broken country crisscrossed by gullies with here and there low bluffs. They came on a ribbon of a stream and Shard halted so their horses could drink. He paced, his hand on his pearl-handled revolver.

James was curious. "What kind is that?"

"Eh?" Shard saw where he was looking and patted the pearl grips. "Don't know your guns and you a soldier? It's a Smith and Wesson. Some favor Colts or Remingtons. Me, I'm a Smith and Wesson man."

"It get you killed," Two Bears said, grinning.

Shard didn't respond but James did. "Why do you say a thing like that?"

"It pretty gun," Two Bears said. "Indians like pretty guns. Kill to have one."

The tracks followed the stream and they followed the tracks. It meandered like a drunken snake in endless turns and loops. A charred circle marked where the war party had camped for the night.

Shard didn't stop. He had an urgency about him that was justified by gray tendrils in the southern sky. "Damn," he said on spying them, and rode faster.

James slung his Spencer in front of him and held it there.

Where a gully widened into a hollow stood what was left of a cabin, the logs still smoldering, orange and red spots glowing like infernal eyes.

They reined up and beheld it from a distance and

Jack Shard said, "Settlers shouldn't ought to be out this far. They're asking for trouble." He shucked a Sharps rifle from his saddle scabbard and nodded at the two Crows. Cowlick reined wide to the left and Two Bears wide to the right. "Doyle, you stick with me," Shard said.

James nodded. He hoped the hostiles were long gone. He wasn't ready for Indian fighting.

Jack Shard gigged his dun. He rose in the stirrups a couple of times and once he saw something that made him swear. "Have you got a strong stomach, Irish?"

"I've never had cause to think I didn't."

"You're about to find out."

The first was a boy. He couldn't have been more than twelve. The ruin they'd made of him was the ruin a crazed butcher would make of a cow. His neck was severed to where it was attached by a skin string. His scalp had been peeled back to the middle of his crown, but they hadn't lifted the hair and the underside, speckled red and pink, had been pecked at by birds. The hostiles had amused themselves by cutting the flesh down to the ribs and letting the strips hang.

One look and James had to turn away, his stomach trying to crawl out his throat. He dry heaved and spat the bitterest of bile and breathed. "God Almighty."

"I warned you," Shard said.

The next was the mother. She had been running after the boy but neither got far. She lay in a black pool, the surface shining like patent leather. Her body had drained dry and she was paler than snow. Rigor imprinted a ludicrous smile. They hadn't molested her.

The father had been nailed to what was left of one wall.

His eyes were gone and his nose, a cavity crawling with flies and his mouth, was an insect hotel. They hadn't turned him into a woman, but they had sliced it down the middle. His belly had also been slit and loopy coils hung to his feet and past, as if his intestines were trying to crawl off and escape the carnage.

James heaved, and this time it wasn't dry. He half thought the scout or the Crows would tease him, but they were silent and grim.

Jack Shard was staring at the woman with her afterlife smile. "This is why."

Wiping his sleeve with his mouth, James sucked in deep breaths while looking at anything except the bodies. "Why what?"

"I get asked why I do this," Shard said. "Why, when I lived with Indians and admire them so much, do I hunt them for the army?" He nodded at the woman and at the boy and at the man. "This is why."

"Oh," James said. He hadn't thought to ask.

"It's a bad bunch we're after," Shard said. "Their hate won't let them stop." He pushed his hat back on his head and tiredly rubbed his eyes. "I should send you to tell the captain, but we have to move fast and there could be others."

"Other hostiles?"

The scout nodded. "They like to break into small bands and spread out. They can kill and raze more that way."

"I'd hate to run into them by my lonesome," James admitted.

"By yourself or with the whole troop, it's kill or be killed. They won't show you a lick of mercy."

"I wasn't expecting any," James said.

24

A pair of wagons sat in the glare of the sun, the beds blackened. Both tongues were pointing at the sky as if in supplication. The horses had been taken. Scattered seed for planting had drawn birds to an avian feast. Except for the buzzards, the birds didn't take notice of the bodies.

At the approach of James and the scout and the Crows, the feasters took reluctant wing, squawking and cawing in protest.

"Stay back if you want," Jack Shard said.

"No," James responded. "I'll see it the same as you." He steeled himself, but he was flesh and blood and not made of metal and the first one churned his stomach to where he had to look away.

All told, there were five, four men and a boy. The men had put up a fight. Two Bears found where a hostile had been hit and leaked blood. That must have made the hostiles mad, because the butchery was twice the horror of those at the cabin. The hostiles seemed to have tried to outdo themselves in the ferocity of their mutilating.

Jack Shard didn't linger. At a wave of his arm, they rode to the south, smack on the tracks.

James had been hanging back, but now he brought his mount up next to the dun. "Mind if I ask a question?"

"You're part of this party."

"I suppose it's too much to expect we should have buried those people."

"We don't have the time," Shard said. "The sooner we catch up, the more lives we spare."

"There are ten of them and four of us," James pointed out.

"Fourteen of them."

"What?"

"Did I forget to tell you?" Shard said apologetically. "Four more came in from the west and joined those we've been after."

"Hell," James said. "That's almost four to one. Shouldn't we go get D Troop?"

"You're welcome to but I wouldn't advise it," Shard answered.

"The captain will be mad. He gave specific orders."

"You're mine to do with as I please, and I please to keep you by me for your own sake."

James was grateful and said so. As the afternoon waned his apprehension climbed. He imagined they would burst on the hostiles at any moment, but twilight fell and they still hadn't caught up.

Shard chose a high-walled wash for their camp. Cowlick kindled a small fire. Two Bears took a bow and arrows from out of his rolled-up blanket and disappeared for a while. When he reappeared he was carrying a dead rabbit. He dropped it at James's feet and said, "You skin, Buffalo Shit."

"Don't call me that."

Shard laughed. "Don't take it personal. It's his way."

James stared at the rabbit and confessed, "I've never skinned one before. How do I go about it?"

All three regarded him as they might a new sort of animal with two heads or three legs.

"You've never cut up a rabbit?" Jack Shard said skeptically.

"I've never cut up anything. I was raised in the city."

"That's plumb pitiful. Here. Let me show you."

Shard drew his bowie and gave James a lesson in rabbit carving. First he slit the hind legs down the middle on the inside and then the front legs, and then he cut down the center of the belly from the throat to near the bobbed tail. "Do this right and it's like peeling an orange or one of those bananas."

He demonstrated.

After the hideous slaughter at the wagons and the cabin, James found the rabbit-cutting practically pleasant. He chopped up the meat and Cowlick skewered pieces on sticks.

The aroma set James's mouth to watering. He hadn't eaten all day, and he was famished. He was fit to drool by the time the meat was done and tore into it with relish. Chewing lustily, he said, "I didn't think I'd have much of an appetite after today, but I was wrong."

Jack Shard had his back propped on his saddle and was filling a pipe with tobacco. "We get used to things."

"I'll never get used to *that*," James said. Those butchered bodies would infest his nightmares for weeks and months to come.

To change the subject he said, "I've been meaning to ask you about that dime novel."

Shard groaned.

Two Bears chuckled.

"A friend of mine named Newcomb read it, and he said that in it you shot the eye out of a wolf at half a mile away."

"That was the writer's doing," the scout said. "They exaggerate something awful."

"So you never killed a grizzly with your bare hands?" Shard snorted.

"Or ran a gauntlet of a hundred braves?"

"I'd be chopped to bits."

"Or fell in love with a Pawnee princess?" That was all James could remember.

Shard lost his smile and swallowed some coffee. "I was in love once but she wasn't a Pawnee. She was Oglala. As pretty as a rose and as sweet as sugar. I'd be with her now except she was bit by a rattlesnake while her and some other Oglala gals were picking berries. They tried to save her but the snake bit her in the neck as she was bending down and I guess the venom was too close to her heart."

"I'm sorry," James said.

"It was like having my own cut out."

James was surprised the man would make such an admission.

"Damn all rattlers, anyway," Shard said vehemently.

"I haven't seen any yet."

"You do, give a holler. I have killed close to forty since that day and aim to kill a thousand more." Shard put down his tin cup, opened his saddlebags, and pulled out a bottle. He opened it, poured a little in with his coffee, and held the bottle out. "Want some? It's brandy."

It had been so long since James tasted liquor of any kind, his mouth puckered. But he replied, "No, thanks." It wouldn't do for him to lose his senses with hostiles about.

The Crows, though, were more than happy to pour some into their cups.

Shard raised the bottle to the stars. "To Chickadee," he said, and took a long swig.

"I hope to be married within a year, myself," James mentioned.

"She a good woman?"

James didn't have to think about it. "The best. And honest to the bone."

"Find a woman who sees your faults and wants you anyway, and she's the one," Shard said. "What's her name?"

"Peg."

"To Peg," Shard said, and treated himself to another drink straight from the bottle.

"Don't get drunk on me," James said. "Anything happens to you, I wouldn't last two days."

"The Crows will look after you."

"Would they really?" James said, smiling at Cowlick and Two Bears.

Shard addressed them in their tongue and they looked at James and laughed.

"Any hurt to him," Two Bears said, pointing at Jack Shard, "Buffalo Shit on his own."

25

The next day they didn't come across a single body or spy any smoke until the middle of the afternoon when Shard raised a finger to black specks soaring on the air currents to the southwest. "More buzzards."

Atop a low ridge they lay on their bellies and looked down on a farm. The house had been burned, but the barn was still standing. A body was sprawled in a pool of scarlet near a pump and a man with his britches down around his ankles was crumpled near the outhouse. From the barn came sounds, voices and tiny mews that a stricken kitten might make. Beside the barn were two horses without saddles.

"We're in luck," Shard said. "A pair of them are still here. We need to take at least one alive."

More mewing prickled the hairs at the nape of James's neck.

"What's doing that?"

"Stay here with the horses," Shard said, and snaked down the slope. Cowlick snaked left, Two Bears right.

James glanced over his shoulder at their horses and off across the prairie. Nothing stirred, but that was no guarantee.

He fingered his Spencer and looked down—the scout and the Crows had vanished. He looked for ripples in the high grass, but they might as well be invisible. It was spooky.

The mewing went on. In a tree by the house, a blue jay flitted and shrieked. A cat that might have run the jay off if it was alive lay at the base of the tree, cleaved nearly in two by a tomahawk or a knife.

The sun was warm on James's back. A rock was poking him and he shifted position. He glanced over his shoulder again. The prairie was still empty. When he looked down, Jack Shard was at the barn, sidling toward the front.

Out of the grass reared Two Bears. In quick bounds he was at the scout's side.

Cowlick rose at the rear of the barn.

James tensed.

Shard was at the corner. He went on around, Two Bears right after him. They had their rifles to their shoulders.

This is it, James thought. He saw them duck inside and held his breath, but nothing happened. Seconds pregnant with suspense passed like turtles. Then there was a yip and a shot and a commotion as of men struggling hand to hand and unexpectedly a near-naked painted warrior hurtled out of the barn and flew toward the low ridge.

James kept expecting Shard or Two Bears to fly out in pursuit or for Cowlick to come running, but none of them did and the warrior reached the ridge and sped up it. In a state of mild shock, James marked the swarthy visage and the sleek muscles and especially the bloody tomahawk in the warrior's hand. The hostile was looking back and not up.

James stood. He aimed the Spencer. He would dearly

love to shoot, but Shard had said they needed one alive so he bawled, "Stop where you are!"

The warrior didn't stop; he charged. Uttering a fierce war whoop, he raised the tomahawk.

"Stop, damn you!" James shouted, feeling foolish, and curled his finger to the trigger. He squeezed, thinking the hostile was as good as dead, but in his excitement he'd forgotten to thumb back the hammer.

Screeching, the warrior was on him. James raised the Spencer as the tomahawk arced, and warded off a blow that would have split his skull. He swung the stock at the Indian's face, but the renegade ducked and slashed the tomahawk at his gut. James jerked back and felt the slightest scrape along his shirt. He rammed the stock at the warrior's throat only to have the hostile sidestep. Then his hand was on the wrist holding the tomahawk and the other's hand was on the Spencer. They grappled. James was strong but so was the Indian. They spun one way and then the other. Somewhere someone was hollering. The warrior hooked a foot behind James and pushed. James went down, pulling the hostile after him. They rolled back and forth, the warrior hissing and grunting. James drove a knee up and in but connected with the hostile's thigh.

A deft flip of the warrior's arms and James was on his back. A knee slammed into his belly. The tomahawk swished and scraped his neck.

In the heat of the hostile's hate, his face was clouded with bloodlust.

James got his leg against the warrior's chest, and shoved. The warrior fell back and rolled to regain his feet, but he was at the edge of the slope and his moccasins slipped from under him and he fell. He didn't tumble far. Jack Shard and Two Bears pounced and the grass thrashed and when they stood, they each had an arm.

The warrior was purple with rage. He thrashed and bucked and even tried to bite.

"We have him!" Shard gloated.

His heart hammering, James wheezed between gasps, "Took you long enough."

26

The mewing came from a human throat.

She lay curled on her side in a stall, her knees to her chest and an arm over her face. She wouldn't stop quaking. They hadn't taken knives or tomahawks to her, but her dress was torn and they had done other things.

James stood uncomfortably at the head of the stall while Jack Shard and the Crows bound the captured hostile's wrists and ankles. "Miss?" he said softly but got no response.

The scout came over. He squatted and gently touched her foot. "Ma'am? It's all right now. You're safe."

The mewing finally stopped. A brown eyeball peered at them over the arm and a voice husky with raw emotion said, "Go away."

"Didn't you hear me, ma'am?" Shard said. "You're safe. You can get up if you want."

"I'm tainted."

"You're what?" James said, and Shard cast an annoyed glance at him.

"Tainted," the woman said. "They . . . they . . ." She stopped, unable to say the rest.

Shard said softly, "Lie here and rest. We'll tend to business and let you know when it's time to go."

"I'm not going anywhere," the woman said.

"You can't stay here alone," Shard told her. "Corporal Doyle will escort you to the column. The soldiers will protect and look after you."

"No, they won't do any such thing." The eye dipped under the arm and she resumed her quaking.

Shard motioned for James to step away. "We'll leave her be awhile. For some women, what she's been through is worse than being killed."

Shard went over to the Crows and their prisoner. He addressed the warrior in an Indian tongue. The warrior glared defiantly. Shard addressed him again and the warrior barked a savage reply. "Hold him down," Shard said to the Crows.

The captive fought them, but the Crows were too strong and got him on his back with Cowlick holding down one arm and leg and Two Bears holding down the others. Their combined weight was too much. All the captive could do was growl epithets.

Jack Shard leaned his Sharps against a post and drew his bowie. He said something and held the knife to the sunlight.

"What are you planning to do?" James asked.

"We need information," Shard said.

"You're not going to torture him."

"We need information," Shard said again.

"The army doesn't do things like that," James said.

"We need to know how many there are and any plans they've made," Shard explained. "I've asked nice and this Kiowa won't say, so now I'll ask the hard way."

"It's not right."

"Go watch over the woman." Shard bent to the Kiowa and his bowie descended.

James turned his back. He heard a squishy sound but he didn't look. He moved to the stall the woman was in and leaned against it. He wished he could plug his ears. Funny, he told himself. All those years in Five Points, all the fights he had been in as a Blue Shirt. He thought he was tough. He thought he'd seen everything. But that couldn't compare to this. The blood spilled in a clash with another gang was nothing to the blood spilled in war. This was so much worse, so . . . vile. He swallowed, and was conscious that the woman's brown eye was peering at him over her arm. To take his mind off Shard and the Kiowa, he asked, "Is there anything I can do for you, ma'am?"

"What are they doing to that Injun?"

"Questioning him," James said.

"That one is sticking him. I can see it from here."

"Don't look," James said.

"Would they let me help?"

"Ma'am?"

"Give me a knife. I'll get him to talk. After what he did, I surely will make him."

"It's not fit," James said.

"What ain't? A woman carving on a heathen son of a bitch who violated her? Mister, I'll skin him alive for you and cut out his eyes and chop off any other parts you say."

"Jack Shard is handling it, ma'am."

She raised her head. Her face was smudged and her eyes were almost wild. "Ask him if he'll let me."

"I'd rather not."

"Ask him, consarn you. I have a right. No one has a better right than me."

James used to think he knew people. He turned, and it was as appalling as he had known it would be. That the Kiowa hadn't cried out was a wonderment. Shard was holding a severed finger and letting blood drip on the warrior's face. "The woman wants to know if you'll let her cut on him. She says it's her right."

"Bring her over."

James reached down to help her stand, but she had heard and was on her feet and past him, her face aglow with fierce anticipation.

"What's your name, ma'am?" Shard asked.

"Anderson," she said. "Harriet Anderson. My husband was Samuel Anderson. That's him out by the outhouse." She extended a hand. "Give me that pigsticker and step back, if you would."

"We need information."

"I savvy, mister," Mrs. Anderson said.

"You won't cut the Crows?" Shard said. "They're friends of mine and on the army payroll, same as me."

"It's him who done it to me," Mrs. Anderson said, pointing at the Kiowa. "Him and those others."

"Did any of them say anything to you?"

"Just Injun talk. I didn't understand a lick of it." She impatiently crooked her fingers. "The knife."

Shard reversed his grip and gave it to her, hilt first. "Whatever you do, don't—" He got no further.

With a swift movement, Harriet Anderson thrust the big knife into the Kiowa's belly, stabbing up and in and wrenching. The Kiowa stiffened and blood spurted from his mouth, and he was gone.

"Dang it, ma'am," Shard said, and went to grab her wrist. "You weren't supposed to do that."

Mrs. Anderson jerked back, yanking on the bowie, and stood with the red blade pointed at her own belly and both of her hands on the hilt. "I've been soiled."

"Don't," Shard said.

"I'll never be me again."

"That's foolish talk. No one will ever know."

"I will," she said, and plunged the knife into her body.

Shard lunged, but the blade was all the way in before he could reach her. He looped an arm around her waist and she looked at him with a thin smile and scarlet trickling down her dress.

"I can rest in peace now," she said, and her body melted.

Shard swore and lowered her to the ground and swiped at a patch of blood on his buckskins. "Can't nothing go right today?"

27

The barn buffered them from the night wind. Borne with the wind were the keening yips of coyotes and now and again the ululating howl of a wolf. Other than that it was quiet save for the crackling of their fire. Cowlick had found a piglet wandering in the field and killed it, and the Crows and Jack Shard were eating their fill.

James had no appetite. He had his elbows on his crossed legs and his chin in his hands and was morosely gazing into the flames.

Shard stopped chewing to ask with his mouth full, "What's the matter with you, Doyle? You sick?"

"How can you eat?"

"I'm hungry. You should try some. We don't often get roast pig."

"And Mrs. Anderson?"

"We'd share with her if she was alive, but she ain't. What's your point?"

"It doesn't bother you?" James said. "All the killing? And the other?"

Shard was about to take another bite, but he lowered the chunk of pork. "People have been killing other peo-

ple since there have been people. You never heard of
Cain and Abel?"

"What you did today, what those hostiles did." James
stopped and frowned and shook his head.

"You better get used to it. There's a lot of this goes
on," the scout said. "On both sides."

"Surely not."

"Where have you been keeping yourself? In a hidey-
hole? Don't you remember Chivington?"

"Who?"

"Colonel Chivington and eight hundred bluecoats
attacked a village of mostly women and children and
pretty near wiped them out. Back in 'sixty-four, it was.
Blew them to bits with cannon fire and then bashed out
their brains. Little babies were torn from their mothers'
arms and smashed on the rocks."

James bowed his head.

"They got hold of a chief, White Antelope his name
was. They cut off his nose and ears and scalped him. One
soldier sliced off his nuts and made a tobacco pouch. It
was in all the newspapers."

James hadn't paid much attention to the news back in
Five Points. He hadn't cared one whit about what went
on in the rest of the world.

"When it comes to blame, white and red have plenty
to share," Shard went on. "All the hate is to blame.
Whites hate the red man for being red, and the red man
hates whites for being white."

"White-eyes stupid shits," Two Bears said.

Shard laughed.

Cowlick made a comment in Crow and all three of
them chortled.

James got up and walked from the fire. He breathed
deep of the cool air and listened to a coyote. A shooting star blazed the heavens. He had to stop being so

squeamish, he told himself. He'd been strong enough to survive in Five Points; he could survive this. He *had* to survive it. There was Peg, and their future.

From out of the night came a swift *pat-pat-pat*. He turned, or tried to, and a heavy body slammed into him. The impact knocked him off his feet. He was on his back and a painted warrior was raising a knife before he could collect his wits.

He opened his mouth to shout for help.

A battering ram in the form of Two Bears struck the warrior in the chest and bowled him over. Cowlick was a step behind, and as they had done with the Kiowa, they now did with this one; they pinned him.

A hand was thrust down. James gripped it and Shard pulled him to his feet.

"You all right?"

"I think so," James said, rattled by the abruptness of the attack.

Shard faced their new prisoner. "Ain't this interesting? This one's a Cheyenne, not a Kiowa."

The Crows hauled the warrior to the fire and bound him. The Cheyenne sat with his back straight, his jaw jutting.

James forced himself to observe. He would endure the cutting and the blood and not be a weak sister. Only there wasn't any.

The Cheyenne said something. Cowlick untied the Cheyenne's wrists, which puzzled James until the four of them commenced to communicate in sign language. James had heard of it but never seen it used. Their fingers fairly flying, they were at it for over an hour. Then Cowlick retied the wrists and Jack Shard leaned back.

"It's as I thought."

"Care to enlighten me?" James requested.

"It's a bunch of young bucks out to make a name for

themselves. Kiowa and Cheyenne together. This one was sent back to see what was keeping the pair we caught."

"What will you do with him?"

"Turn him over to Captain Pemberton. Or you will. You're leaving in the morning. I'll send Two Bears along so you can find your way."

"Couldn't I stick with you?"

"You're my liaison, remember? Tell Pemberton there are thirty in this band. They broke into two groups and aim to strike as far south as the Arkansas. Their leader is a Kiowa called Long Knife. I've heard of him. His mother was killed at Sand Creek by that Chivington I was telling you about. Reckon he's out to balance the scales."

"Long Knife," James repeated.

"This one," Shard said, jerking a thumb at the Cheyenne, "is called Lean Wolf. Don't let his hands loose, whatever you do. And at night tie his feet, too."

"He can't do much trussed up," James said.

"You'd be surprised."

James turned in, but sleep was elusive. He'd no sooner drift off than he'd have a nightmare and wake with a start. Once he was being chased by shambling red horrors bristling with knives and tomahawks. Later on it was a spectral woman covered in blood. Dawn broke much too soon. He had his horse saddled and ready before the sun rose.

Lean Wolf had told Shard where his horse was hid and Cowlick had fetched it. Now they undid the rope around his ankles and threw him on. Two Bears fitted a lead rope and mounted his own animal.

"Be mighty careful, you hear, Irish?" Jack Shard cautioned. "I'd hate for anything to happen to you."

"Makes two of us," James said.

28

The sun was a furnace, the prairie blisteringly hot.

A shimmering haze made objects in the distance appear different from what they were. Antelope had six legs instead of four.

A rocky stretch gave the illusion of being a lake.

James was wet with sweat outside and parched inside. He refused to touch his canteen. There was no telling when they would find water.

Two Bears appeared immune to the heat. He rode alertly, not sweating a drop, his rifle across his horse.

It had been three days since they left the farm and Jack Shard. In the evenings they stopped and Two Bears cooked. The Crow always tied Lean Wolf's legs and as an added precaution ran a rope from around Lean Wolf's neck, down his back, to his ankles, so that should Lean Wolf try to wrest free, he'd strangle himself. The first evening, James had asked if that was entirely necessary and Two Bears had looked at him and laughed and said, "Heap big pile Buffalo Shit."

James really didn't like that nickname.

The fourth evening they sat at the fire, James sipping coffee, Two Bears deep in thought about something.

James was mildly surprised when the Crow stirred and stared across the flames at him and asked a question.

"Why you here, Buffalo Shit?"

"Your friend Shard told us to deliver a message and the prisoner to Captain Pemberton."

"No," Two Bears said, and smacked his hand on the prairie grass. "Why you *here*?"

"Why do you want to know?" James responded. In his opinion, his personal life was none of the Crow's business.

"You white. You come fight Indian. Why? You like fight Indian?"

"Oh," James said, and sighed. "No. It's not that. I don't like to fight at all, to tell you the truth. I'd just as soon get along with everybody."

"Yet you here."

"I got into trouble once," James revealed. "A judge made me join the army."

"Judge?" Two Bears said. "What that?"

James briefly explained about the court system and the duties of a judge.

Two Bears considered that, then said, "So him say you do and you do?"

"I didn't have any choice, no." James would have done whatever it took to stay out of prison.

The Crow reflected some more and then asked another surprising question. "You like Injuns?"

"I don't not like them," James said, "provided they're not trying to kill me."

"Many Injuns hate white-eyes."

"I don't hate anyone." James remembered Bunton. "Well, almost anyone. I'd just as soon all whites and all Indians were friends."

"You dreamer," Two Bears said. "But good dream." He half closed his eyes and continued with "My people many enemies. Long time fight. Long time kill. Not kill, we die. You savvy?"

"Your people don't have any choice, either."

"No," Two Bears said. "Coyote say kill, we kill."

"Coyote?"

"Him make Apsaalooke. Once world no land. Only water. Him have duck dive deep—"

James was trying to make sense of it. "What was a duck doing there?" he interrupted.

"Only Coyote, four ducks, in all world. Him have duck bring up dirt. From dirt make land. Make first man, first woman. They first Apsaalooke."

"First what?"

"That name my people."

"But Shard said you are Crows."

"Whites call Crows Crows. My people call Apsaalooke. It mean people of big-beaked bird."

"That duck you were telling me about?"

"Him bravest duck. Other ducks not so brave."

"There wasn't a dove anywhere, was there?"

"No dove, duck," Two Bears said. "Why you ask?"

"Just a story my mother used to tell me when I was little. It had a lot of water and a dove."

"Four ducks," Two Bears said, and held up four fingers.

"Then Coyote make other animals. Make many enemies for Apsaalooke fight."

"Didn't Coyote like your people?"

"Like people much. Make enemies so we fight. Fight make people strong."

"I don't know," James said. "Always making war seems to me a shabby way to live."

"What be shabby?"

"A poor way," James explained. "But then I've no room to talk. My own people, the Irish, are known for having a bit of a temper and loving a donnybrook as much as they love to drink."

"What be donnybrook?"

"A fight," James said. "My people love to fight."

Two Bears smiled. "Your people, my people, much same. Fight good. Make strong."

"Or make you dead," James said, "and I'm not all that fond of the dying part of it."

"No one want die," Two Bears said. "It happen when happen."

The next day they got an early start to take advantage of the cool of morning. It didn't last long. By noon James was sweltering. "Damn, it's hot." He swiped a sleeve across his face.

Two Bears didn't respond. He hadn't said much since they started out.

"Don't you like me, Two Bears?" James asked.

The Crow got that amused look of his. "Why you ask, Buffalo Shit?"

"I'd just like to know. You're the first Indian I've ever really known, and I've grown to like you some."

"We friends, eh?"

"I'd like to think so."

Two Bears was about to reply when he straightened and stared intently to the east. Suddenly drawing rein, he said, "We have trouble, Buffalo Shit."

"It's Corporal Doyle. Thank you." James looked and saw only haze. "What kind of trouble?"

"Enemies come," Two Bears said.

James rose in the stirrups. He squinted against the glare and said, "I don't see anything."

"You white," Two Bears Said. "Whites have eyes like blind mice."

James went on squinting. Just when he thought the Crow must be wrong, figures appeared. Riders, coming in their direction. "Maybe they haven't spotted us and we can slip away."

"We try," Two Bears said without much confidence, and reined to the north.

Their mounts raised dust, but it couldn't be helped. James got a crick in his neck from glancing back. It was a quarter of an hour before he established with certainty that the riders had changed direction. "They're after us."

"Yes," Two Bears said even though it hadn't been a question.

For another thirty minutes they pushed their animals as hard as they dared. Their heat-haze shadows never gained—or lost ground, either.

"This won't end well," James said.

"We fight," Two Bears declared.

"The two of us against how many? Ten? Twenty? I can't tell."

"Eleven," Two Bears said.

"How can you tell that from here?"

"Must find place to fight," Two Bears said.

Before them stretched mile after mile of flat.

"This couldn't have happened at a worse time," James said.

The terrain stayed the same. James was desperate for a bluff or a tract of woodland or anywhere they could hunt cover.

He'd already made up his mind he wouldn't submit meekly. The hostiles might win, but they'd know they had been in a scrape.

"There!" Two Bears exclaimed, and leveled a finger.

James wondered what in hell he was pointing at. There weren't any trees, just more flat. Then the ground broke away in front of them and he hauled on the reins on the lip of a wash. It wasn't much protection, but it would have to do. Descending, he slid down.

Two Bears pulled Lean Wolf off his pinto so hard that the Cheyenne stumbled. Lean Wolf righted himself, but the next moment Two Bears kicked his legs out from under him and began tying his ankles.

James climbed to the top and flattened. The hostiles were still a ways off.

Pebbles rattled, and Two Bears was at his side. "We count coup this day."

"We'll wait until they're right on top of us," James said. "If we drop enough, maybe the rest will make themselves scarce and we can be on our way."

"They fight to death," the Crow said. He opened a pouch and took out cartridges and began feeding them into his Yellow Boy.

"Nice rifle," James said. The Yellow Boy was a Winchester. It had a longer barrel than his Spencer and held more rounds. He'd heard tell Indians favored it.

Two Bears's face lit and he ran his hand over the shiny receiver. "Heap good gun. It why me join army."

"Are you a good shot?"

"Jack Shard better."

The hostiles were close enough that James could make out that while most had bows and arrows, a few had rifles. Dust spewed in their wake in thick coils.

"I never shot an Indian before."

Two Bears stopped loading and looked at him. "You kill them or they kill you."

"It's easy for you, isn't it?"

"To kill enemy?" Two Bears chuckled. "You stupid, Buffalo Shit."

James was tired of being treated like a dunce. "For the last goddamn time, stop calling me that."

"You angry," Two Bears said. "That good."

"Why?"

"It easier kill enemy when mad." The Crow finished

loading and replaced the cartridges he hadn't used in his pouch. He glanced at Lean Wolf, who was grinning up at them in clear delight at their predicament, and said something that caused the Cheyenne to spit and glower.

"What did you say to him?"

"That if me die, him die. Kill him with last breath if have to."

"Let's hope it doesn't come to that," James said. He raised his Spencer, but the war party wasn't quite in range. "God. What did I do to deserve this?"

"You afraid?" Two Bears asked.

James examined his feelings and answered honestly. "No, I don't believe I am. Not a lot, anyway. Mostly I'm upset that I might not get to marry the sweetest girl I've ever met."

"That good, too," Two Bears said.

"How in hell can that be good?"

"It help you kill even better."

29

James was itching to squeeze the trigger when to his surprise the hostiles abruptly stopped just out of rifle range. "What the hell? Why did they do that?"

"They see us," Two Bears said.

"How?" James marveled. Only their eyes and foreheads were exposed. "I couldn't see us from that far out."

"Blind mice." Two Bears chuckled.

James figured the hostiles would charge and pressed his cheek to the Spencer. But all they did was sit there. From the sharp gestures a few were making, he got the idea they were arguing. "What in the world is that about?"

"Maybe some want rush us," Two Bears speculated. "Smart ones say no."

"Why smart?" James asked.

Two Bears indicated the sun, which was on its westward slant. "Smart to wait for almost dark."

James was relieved. That gave them a few hours to think of something. His relief was short-lived, however. Five of the warriors separated from the rest and came toward the wash, spreading out as they advanced. "They're going to attack us, aren't they?"

"Yes." Two Bears chortled and took aim.

"Why are you so happy?"

"Me count coup," the Crow said eagerly.

James was about to say that it was stupid to relish being in a fight for their lives when it hit him; he was being a hypocrite. He had done the same thing as a Blue Shirt. Particularly on that last terrible night when the Blue Shirts fought the Florentines; he'd looked forward to it as much as the rest. "We're a dumb bunch," he said.

"Who dumb?" Two Bears asked without raising his head from the Yellow Boy.

"You. Me. Anyone who thinks killing is grand."

"You not like kill but you in army?" Two Bears laughed. "Maybe bunch not dumb. Maybe you dumb, Buffalo Shit."

"I told you. I didn't have any choice."

"You not have choice now."

Life does that a lot, James thought. He took aim at one of the advancing warriors.

Two of the five had rifles. The others had arrows nocked to bowstrings. All wore war paint and several had paint on their horses, as well.

"Wait yet," Two Bears said.

A bead of sweat trickled from under James's hat and down his cheek. A fly buzzed his face. He slowed his breathing as Sergeant Heston had taught him and forced himself to stay calm.

At a yip from one of the warriors, all five exploded into motion. Two Bears's Yellow Boy banged and one of the hostiles with a rifle flung his arms into the air and pitched from his warhorse. The others swung onto the sides of their animals, hanging by the crook of an arm and an ankle.

"Damn," James said. They would be impossible to hit with so little of them showing.

"Shoot horses," Two Bears said, and fired.

A sorrel squealed and crashed to earth. The rider was flung clear and bounded to his feet. Firing his rifle, he sprinted for the wash.

James had yet to shoot. He shifted the Spencer, centered on the chest of the onrushing warrior, and smoothly stroked the trigger. The warrior's feet came off the ground and he hung suspended for a heartbeat as if transfixed by an unseen spear. James swiveled to aim at a horse that was almost to the wash. He worked the lever, thumbed back the hammer, and involuntarily flinched when a shot kicked dirt into his eyes. He blinked to clear his vision, and the horse was on them. A swarthy form hurtled from its back. James jerked the Spencer to shoot just as a shoulder smashed into him, tumbling him down the incline. His spine slammed hard and his head swam but only for a second. As it cleared he beheld an airborne fury clutching a knife. He jerked the Spencer and fired and tried to roll aside. It felt as if a boulder fell on him. Panic swelled as he imagined the blade biting into his flesh. He heaved and pushed and worked the lever.

The hostile's face was inches from his own. Their eyes met. The other's hate was prodigious. The warrior spoke a single word.

James scrambled to his knees. He didn't realize the hostile had gone limp until he went to shoot. He stared at the body, amazed he was still alive.

The crash of Two Bears's rifle brought him out of himself. He swiveled and saw the Crow go down with two warriors on him. In a whirl of arms and steel, they fell into the wash.

The combatants came to a stop. A hostile reared. He howled and raised his knife to stab Two Bears.

James shot him.

The Crow and the last hostile were grappling and slashing in a blur.

James jacked the Spencer's lever, but he couldn't get a clear shot.

Of a sudden it was over. The hostile collapsed, scarlet pumping.

Two Bears slowly propped an elbow under him, grunting with the effort, and leaned on his arm. "Heap tough redskin," he said.

James ran to the top. By his count there was still one of the five left. He need not have worried. The last lay on his belly, an oozing hole where the left eye had been, a bronzed hand still gripping a bow.

The rest of the war party sat their horses well out on the prairie.

"We did it," James marveled, and smiled and turned. His smile faded.

The front of Two Bears's shirt was dark with blood. The feathered end of an arrow protruded from his side, the feathers slick with red.

"God, no." James bounded down and squatted. "I didn't see you take the arrow."

"Me see," Two Bears said. He laughed and blood trickled from his mouth.

"What can I do?" James anxiously asked, knowing even as he did that the wound was mortal.

Two Bears didn't answer. Instead he stared at the arrow.

His mouth curved in a grin and he touched the tip of a finger to James's cheek. "Buffalo Shit," he said, and died.

30

The sun blazed low on the horizon. Half an hour more and it would set.

James Doyle lay with the Spencer in his hands and the Yellow Boy beside him. Flies by the score were crawling over the bodies and buzzing about. He was constantly swatting at them.

The six hostiles were seated in a circle. Every now and again one or another glanced to the west.

James didn't stand a prayer. He could flee but they would overtake him. It occurred to him that they might try to take him alive so they could torture him. He'd rather die. "God, I hate this." He glanced at Lean Wolf, who to his surprise had lain quietly near the horses all this while.

A peculiar sort of serenity came over him. Since he was damned if he stayed and damned if he went, he accepted the inevitable. Closing his eyes, he rested his chin on his forearm. He was tired. What he wouldn't give for a couple of hours of sleep.

In his mind's eye Peg shimmered, golden and loving-eyed, his ring on the necklace around her neck. They would have been happy together. It figured, he told himself, that here he was on the verge of happiness and he wouldn't live to enjoy it.

"Life," he said sullenly.

A sound came from below.

James snapped his head up. Lean Wolf had moved a little.

He gazed toward the hostiles. They were on their feet and moving to their mounts. It wouldn't be long now.

Again James heard a scraping sound. He spun. Lean Wolf was where he had been. "I'm a damn bundle of nerves," he chided himself.

The hostiles were on their horses. Half reined to the east and brought their animals to a trot. The others rode to the west.

"What the hell?" James said. He didn't for a second believe they were leaving.

A third of the sun had been devoured and the sky had gone from blue to gray.

James was finding it harder to stave off near-numbing fear.

Two Bears had warned him they would attack right before the sun went down. In the muted light of dusk, they'd be a lot harder to hit. He set down the Spencer and picked up the Yellow Boy and then set down the Yellow Boy and picked up the Spencer.

"Stop it, damn you."

James heard yet another scrape but didn't think anything of it. He looked down but not because of it; he was looking at the horses and contemplating riding for his life. That he caught Lean Wolf in the act of stalking toward him with a knife in his hand was pure happenstance. He rolled and brought the Spencer to bear, but Lean Wolf was on him and swatted the barrel as he was squeezing the trigger. The Spencer went off and the slug missed.

Lean Wolf slashed at James's jugular. He turned his neck and felt a sting. Lean Wolf cocked his arm to stab and James smashed the Spencer into Lean Wolf's face. Teeth crunched, and Lean Wolf leaped back, spitting blood. James let go of the Spencer and scooped up the Yellow Boy. It already had a round in the chamber; he fired.

The top of Lean Wolf's head exploded.

Suddenly hooves pounded. Warriors were sweeping down the wash from both directions.

James jammed the Yellow Boy to his shoulder. He fed a round, fired, fed another round, fired. Turning, he sent two more shots at buckskin-clad centaurs. Slugs pockmarked the ground around him. Then his head seemed to burst and he fell as if from a great height into a well that wasn't water but a liquid pitch. He feebly tried to reach the surface and was sucked into near nothingness. Dimly, he was aware of rough hands, of being jostled, of a topsy-turvy world with him on his back and painted visages floating in misty ether. Iron fingers gouged his neck. The tip of a knife wavered before his eyes.

Teeth gleamed in a vicious sneer.

This was it, James thought. He tried to resist but he had no strength. His vitality was leaking out his head. The black pitch sucked him down and he was on the verge of going under when a harsh martial blare fell discordant on his ears.

The blackness claimed him.

31

An uncomfortable itch was James's first sensation. Pain was his second. The pain told him he wasn't dead. A spurt of nausea made him wish he was. He opened his eyes and shut them again.

"He moved!" a familiar voice exclaimed.

"You sure?" someone replied.

"Yes, by God. He's coming around."

"Not so loud, Dorf," said a third. "He's bound to have a headache."

James forced his mouth to move. "God, do I!" A whoop of joy set his head to pounding worse. He blinked, and got his eyes open even if they did water, and looked uncertainly about. He was in a tent on a cot. Hovering over him were his three friends.

"Welcome back, pard," Newcomb said. "You had us worried."

"You've been out for two and a half days," Cormac informed him. "The sawbones said it was fifty-fifty whether you'd pull through."

"Gosh, I'm happy," Dorf declared.

The itching was abominable. James reached up and

found half his head swathed in bandages; the itch came from under them.

"The bullet creased you," Cormac said. "A couple of inches deeper, the doc says, and you wouldn't be here."

"How did you find me?" To James's way of thinking, it had been a miracle.

"You can thank your Maker that the captain heard shots," Cormac said.

"We got there just in time," Dorf said.

Even though he had only been conscious a few minutes, James was growing tired. "What about my horse and my carbine?"

"Your animal is fine and your carbine is under the cot," Dorf said. "The Injuns who were about to kill you skedaddled when they heard the bugle."

"The captain is making you out to be a hero," Newcomb mentioned.

"What are you talking about?"

"We found eight dead redskins not counting the Crow. The captain is going to put in a request for you to get a medal."

"You're joshing."

"As God is my witness," Newcomb said.

"But Two Bears . . . ," James began, and sank in the black well once again.

A warm wetness was spreading down his throat. James coughed, and winced, and attempted to sit up. He tasted broth reminiscent of chicken.

"Whoa, there, hoss," Dorf said, gently pushing on James's shoulder. "You're not to get up. Not for another couple of days." He was perched on a folding stool, a bowl of soup in his lap, a spoon in his other hand.

"You've been feeding me?"

"We have to keep you alive, don't we?" Dorf grinned and dipped the spoon in the bowl. "Cormac and Newcomb and me have been taking turns."

A different sort of warmth spread through James. "You went to all this trouble?"

"What are pards for?" Dorf wagged the spoon. "Open up. You have to eat this whole bowl."

James was famished. He was only half done when profound drowsiness washed over him and it was all he could do to stay awake. "Wait," he said as Dorf raised the spoon to his lips. "What about Jack Shard and Cowlick?"

"The captain sent a patrol out with Lieutenant Finch, but they haven't come back yet." Dorf sighed. "All we do is sit around and wait for something to happen and nothing does. Army life ain't as exciting as they make it out to be."

Images of the hostiles converging on him in the wash sparked James to say, "I've had my fill of exciting for a while. Give me peace and quiet."

He finished eating. Another wave of drowsiness gripped him, and snuggling under his blanket, he let it sweep him away. The last thing he heard was Dorf.

"Doyle? I almost forgot. The captain was in here today and he said that you—"

When next James woke it was night. The tent was dark save for the glow of a lantern hanging from a tent pole. He raised his head to test how much it hurt, and a shadow took on form.

"I was just about to leave."

"Sergeant Heston?" James licked his dry lips. "I sure am thirsty, Sarge."

Heston brought water. He slid the stool next to the

cot and straddled it. "I've been wanting to talk to you, Sergeant Doyle."

James gratefully chugged. He finished and started to lie back down, and stopped. "Wait. What did you just call me?"

"Sergeant Doyle."

"I'm a corporal."

"Not anymore. Captain Pemberton has promoted you. It's called a battlefield promotion. A lot of them were done during the war, and it still is from time to time." Heston smiled. "Congratulations. You've gone from private to sergeant faster than anyone I know."

"It's not right," James said.

"You're promoted and you complain?"

"I didn't do anything to earn it."

Heston folded his arms. "You and that Crow fought a war party all by yourselves. You were outnumbered and nearly lost your life. That's an act of bravery if ever I heard of one."

"Two Bears did as much as me, if not more. He's the one who deserves praise."

"He's dead. You're not." Heston considered a bit, then said, "Whether you agree or not, you deserve this. But it's not just for your sake that the captain gave you the promotion. He did it for the men, as well." Heston held up a hand when James went to speak. "You've become a hero, Doyle. And the men need heroes. A lot of them are young like you. They're green and scared and haven't been tested in a fight. That's where you come in. They hear about someone like you, someone who is one of them and was put to the test and lived through it, and it gives them the courage to face their own test and maybe live a little longer."

"I'm not a hero," James said.

"Have it your way. But word of what you've done

will spread. Not just through our troop but everywhere. A few months from now, the whole army will have heard."

"God, I hope not."

"What harm can it do? It'll open doors, that's for sure. You might think of becoming an officer. There are worse careers."

James lay back and stared at the top of the tent. He was looking forward to the end of his enlistment in five years. To stay in for twenty seemed impossibly long. What would Peg say?

"What I like about you, Doyle, is that you're not a cocky bastard," Sergeant Heston said. "You don't act like you know it all. Which is good, because when it comes to the army, you don't know a thimble's worth. But we'll change that. The captain asked me to make you a personal project, as he called it. I'm to teach you how to be the best soldier you can be."

"So I won't embarrass him over making me a sergeant. I understand," James said.

Heston displayed rare annoyance. "Like hell you do. It's not him he's thinking of. It's the men who will be under you. Sloppy noncoms get their men killed."

"Oh."

"Damn right, 'oh,' " Heston said. "Before I'm through, you'll be able to hold your own, and do it well."

"I suppose I should thank you, then."

"Don't jump for joy." Heston stood. "I thought it best you hear this right away. To put your mind at ease."

"Thank you."

"First lesson," Heston said. "Good sergeants always put their men first. You're their teacher, their nursemaid, their protector. Half our purpose in life is to keep them alive."

"What's the other half?"

"To follow orders as if they were the Ten Commandments. Those two are everything in a nutshell."

"God, I hope I don't mess up."

"For your own sake and the sake of the men," Sergeant Heston said gravely, "I hope so, too."

32

James recovered his strength. His head hurt a lot less, but the army doctor insisted he keep the bandage on for another week to ward off infection.

He was feeling cooped up, and he'd taken to walking about the tent to stretch his legs. One warm evening he was pacing and pondering and the tent flap parted in and in came two visitors.

"Good to see you alive, Doyle."

"Shard!" James impulsively shook the scout's hand. "Same here. I was worried the hostiles had gotten you." He thrust his hand at Cowlick, and the Crow stared at it and then grunted and shook. James sobered and said, "I take it you've heard about Two Bears?"

"Captain Pemberton and Sergeant Heston filled us in," Shard said. "But I'd like to hear it from the horse's mouth."

Reluctantly, James gave a brief account. He concluded with "I'm sorry about Two Bears. He deserves a medal."

"Cowlick and me appreciate that," Shard said. "A lot of whites wouldn't give a rat's ass that he died fighting at their side."

"Isn't that a little harsh?"

"No," Shard said, "it's not. There's enough hate on both sides to choke a mule. If more folks lived in both worlds, like I do, there'd be a lot less."

"I don't hate anybody," James said.

The scout motioned at the Crow. "We noticed that early on. Were you raised religious? All men are your brothers? That sort of thing?"

"My mother went to church a lot," James said. "But no. I learned my lesson the hard way." He hesitated, unsure how much he should reveal. "I was part of something once. It had to do with hate and a lot of innocent people were hurt. Ever since, I've thought that hating people for no reason is stupid."

The scout smiled. "You'd do to ride the river with, Sergeant James Marion Doyle. And we've got a lot of riding tomorrow if you're up to it."

"Us three?"

"All of D Troop. I found where the hostiles are holed up. They look to be there awhile, so if we move fast, we can catch them with their leggings down."

"I'd sure like another crack at them."

"Then talk to Pemberton. He made it sound as if you would be laid up for another month yet."

The moment the scout and the Crow left, James made himself presentable. He stepped from the tent and breathed deep of the cool night air. Seldom had he felt so grateful simply to be alive.

Pemberton, Finch, and Myers were in chairs in front of the captain's tent, drinking coffee. They were so engrossed that James had to clear his throat to get the captain's attention.

"Doyle!" Pemberton exclaimed, and rising, he clapped James on the arm. To the junior officers he said, "Gentlemen, I give you the hero of the hour."

"You did fine, soldier," Lieutenant Finch said.

"I wish it had been me," was Second Lieutenant Myers's comment.

"What are you doing here, Sergeant Doyle?" Captain Pemberton asked. "You're supposed to be on bed rest until I say otherwise."

"I've heard the troop is heading out tomorrow to engage the hostiles. I want to go, sir."

"I'm sorry, son, but no."

"With all respect, sir," James pressed him, "I have as much right as anyone. More, since the hostiles nearly killed me. And I'm fit enough now. I no longer get lightheaded and I can ride." He stopped. "*Please*, sir."

"I can't afford anything to happen to you," Captain Pemberton said.

"Sir?"

"You're worth more to the army alive."

"Does this have anything to do with—" James tried to remember what Sergeant Heston had said. "—me being an inspiration to the men?"

"It has everything to do with it," Pemberton confirmed. "If I have my way, you'll become an inspiration for every soldier on the frontier."

James digested the revelation with unease. "I don't like this, sir. I don't like it even a little bit." He continued in a rush. "I'm a soldier like any other. I don't deserve special treatment. Treat me different, and I'll raise a fuss. I'll go to the colonel or over his head if I have to. But I'm part of D Troop and I'll damn well fight with them. Sir."

The captain was quiet for a while. Finally he said, "You feel strongly about this, I gather."

"As strongly as I've ever felt about anything." James was a little surprised that he did. After all, he'd been forced into enlisting. Why did he care so much about being with his fellow soldiers? He put the question aside for later consideration.

"Very well, then," Captain Pemberton said. "You may rejoin the men."

A spike of elation made James grin.

"However, now that you are a sergeant, your duties have changed. Since you're new at this, I'm assigning you to ride with First Sergeant Heston until further notice. You'll be in his charge, you understand?"

"Yes, sir."

"I'm doing this against my better judgment," Captain Pemberton said. "Don't make me regret my decision, Doyle. Don't go and get yourself killed."

"I'll try not to, sir," James said.

33

When most people east of the Mississippi River thought of Kansas, they imagined flat prairie from one end to the other. They were unaware that Kansas rose in elevation. From a low of seven hundred and thirty feet above sea level in the southeast, the land climbed to its highest point of over four thousand feet in the west.

Beyond lay broken country. Rugged country. It was there, in a wooded tract between two bluffs, that the hostiles had camped. Bisected by a stream, it was an oasis of life and shade.

From a rise nearly three miles away, Jack Shard surveyed the bluffs and the woods with his spyglass. "There's no smoke or any other sign, but they're there."

Captain Pemberton was using glasses of his own. "You're absolutely certain?"

"I'd be a hell of a poor scout if I wasn't."

"Don't take offense," Captain Pemberton said. "They might have left in the time it took us to get here."

James and Sergeant Doyle were a few yards away, attentively awaiting orders.

"I'll ride on down and see," Shard offered. "Cowlick and me."

"And have them spot you and run?" Captain Pemberton shook his head. "Not on your life. They've butchered their last settler. We'll do this by the book."

"There will be upwards of thirty," the scout said. "They won't go down easy."

The captain divided his command. He planned to send Lieutenant Finch to the south with a third of the column and Second Lieutenant Myers to the north with another third.

Sergeant Heston was to accompany Myers. James noticed a slight downturn of the first sergeant's mouth when Pemberton told him.

Carbines were checked. Cinches were checked. Anything that would clatter or jingle was made sure it wouldn't.

Second Lieutenant Myers went down the line, inspecting his men. A trooper with dirt on his Spencer received a rebuke.

Another was taken to task for his slovenly uniform.

James had gotten to know Sergeant Heston well enough that he could tell when Heston was out of sorts. "If you don't mind my asking, Sergeant," he quietly said, "why do you look like you swallowed arsenic?"

"There's a time and a place for dressing down the men," the noncom said. "Right before a battle isn't it."

"Why don't you say something?"

"It's not our duty to second-guess a superior, Doyle. Myers is a bit of a glory hound, but he's a good officer, overall. So long as he doesn't endanger the men, I'll keep my mouth shut and so will you."

Captain Pemberton chose to attack at noon. At the appointed time, Finch and Myers broke from the main body.

Sergeant Heston was behind Myers and James was alongside Heston, his Spencer in front of him.

A degree of dread crept down James's spine. There was a lot that could go wrong. The plan called for them to loop around to the bluff on the north side. They were to quietly work their way around it and into the timber. At the blast of the bugle, the three forces would link up and sweep in, ideally taking the hostiles by surprise and decimating the war party.

"How's your head?" Sergeant Heston asked.

"I'm fine," Doyle said. Other than a twinge now and then, he was his old self.

"If it acts up you're to fall back. Captain's orders."

James would be damned if he would. Especially when his three friends were in Myers's column with him. Twisting, he caught Dorf's eye. Dorf grinned. Cormac and Newcomb were behind Dorf.

"I didn't hear a 'yes' out of you," Sergeant Heston said. "I want your word."

"You have it," James said.

The bluff was a quarter of a mile long. On their side it presented a sheer rock face that couldn't be climbed on foot, let alone on horseback.

James was scanning the rim when he received a shock. He thought he saw a face. It was there and he blinked and it was gone. It didn't reappear. "Sergeant, how easy is it to climb to the top from the other side?"

"I wouldn't know. Why?"

"What if the hostiles have lookouts posted up there?"

"Then we lose the element of surprise and a lot of us will die."

They proceeded at a walk around the bottom of the bluff. Quiet was essential if they were to take the hostile force unawares.

James knew he should concentrate on the matter at hand, but he kept thinking of Peg. He'd never missed anyone so much.

Back when he fled Five Points he had missed his mother for a while but not nearly as much as he thought he would. They'd drifted apart after he became a Blue Shirt, although he never stopped caring for her. How could he? She was his mother.

A lot of the Blue Shirts had girls they were fond of. There had been a couple of girls he liked but not to where he pined to be with them and couldn't stop thinking about them.

A sudden whisper brought James out of himself. Lieutenant Myers and Sergeant Heston had stopped. He drew rein. Behind him, the rest of the men did the same.

Heston moved up next to Myers and the pair consulted in low tones. They were at the point where the bluff curved to the south. From here on they must be doubly careful. Myers motioned and the column advanced.

James was on edge. His previous clashes had taught him how suddenly violence could strike.

Lieutenant Myers stopped at the south end of the bluff. Green woodland spread before them, the contrast of sunlight and shadow lending an aura of menace to the undergrowth. The eyes played goblin tricks.

Quickly, the troopers spread out. If all went according to plan, they would fall into formation with the end of Captain Pemberton's line.

They moved on at the ready. James had Sergeant Heston on his left and a soldier named Carns on his right. Dorf and his other friends were farther down.

James wasn't a woodsman, but it seemed to him that these woods were unnaturally quiet. He didn't hear a single bird, didn't see a single squirrel.

A variety of trees flourished: oaks, a few pines, cottonwoods. Briars had to be skirted, as well as dense thickets where their horses would make too much noise. Fortunately it wasn't autumn or there would be so many fallen leaves, the crunch of heavy hooves would give them away.

To the left of their line, a second line appeared and the two became one. Captain Pemberton was midway down. At that same moment Lieutenant Finch's men should be linking up to the other end of Pemberton's line.

D Troop was in place. The plan was working.

James curled his thumb around the Spencer's hammer. Any moment now they should spot the hostiles. He wasn't the only trooper rigid with anticipation.

The trees thinned. Beyond was a broad open area. Through it flowed the ribbon of water. It was an ideal campsite. Recently used, too, as the blackened circles of campfires testified. But of the makers of those fires, there was no sign.

Captain Pemberton signaled and the line came to a halt.

"Where are they?" Private Carn whispered.

James was wondering the same thing. Their absence, combined with the ominous silence, compounded his unease.

Captain Pemberton signaled and D Troop moved out of the trees into the open. Pemberton stopped and motioned, and Jack Shard and Cowlick climbed down and roved about, reading the sign.

Pemberton broke the silence. "I was afraid of this. They're long gone."

Shard came to a black circle and sank to one knee. He pressed a hand to the charred bits of wood, and stiffened. Suddenly rising, he glanced sharply at the surrounding woods. "Captain, these are still warm."

"Then the hostiles were here just a while ago," Pemberton said.

"Maybe they still are," Jack Shard said. "Maybe we've waltzed into a trap."

The words were barely out of the scout's mouth when the air pealed to war whoops. From out of the woods on all sides burst hostiles. Far more than the twenty to thirty Jack Shard had said they would find.

To James there seemed to be upwards of a hundred. He was one of the first troopers to bang off a shot. Many were in shock. Arrows began to rain and lead to fly, and D Troop retaliated with a ragged volley that sent warriors and horses crashing to the ground. Some of the hostiles stopped but others kept coming.

Captain Pemberton bellowed. The lieutenants and sergeants shouted for the troop to form up, but they weren't give the time.

At a gallop hostiles smashed into their line and men in blue went down.

James jacked the Spencer's lever, curled the hammer, fixed a bead on a buckskin-clad chest, and fired. Next to him Private Carn threw out his arms and shrieked, a feathered shaft through his throat.

Chaos erupted. Troopers and hostiles were intermixed in fierce combat. Guns blasted and arrows whizzed. The din rose to a crescendo of rabid bloodletting. A stocky warrior came at him with a lance raised to hurl and he cored the warrior's brain. Another bore down on him and he narrowly reined aside to keep from being rammed and shot the warrior in the back as the man went past.

Men were screaming, yipping, cursing, dying. Out of the wild melee came tinny notes. It took James a few seconds to realize the bugler was sounding retreat. He saw troopers breaking away and slapped his legs. Fearful of arrows, he bent low over the saddle. A heartbeat later a shaft cleaved the space above his head.

Around him flew troopers. Among them was Dorf, his hat gone, blood on the big farm boy's brow. Newcomb was fiercely lashing his mount.

D Troop burst out of the woods onto the prairie.

Inexplicably, the hostiles weren't giving chase.

The bugler began blowing for them to rally. With a speed born of long practice, the cavalrymen marshaled. Gaps were closed. Carbines were reloaded.

Captain Pemberton and Finch and Myers were in urgent converse. When Sergeant Heston moved to join them, James went along. He had been ordered to stick close to the first sergeant and that was exactly what he would do.

Second Lieutenant Meyers was saying, "... seventeen, at a rough count, sir."

"That leaves us seventy-seven," Captain Pemberton said. "And how many hostiles, would you say?"

"I made it out to be a hundred to a hundred and twenty," Lieutenant Finch said. "We took a high toll. Thirty or more, possibly."

"Damn Shard, anyway," Meyers said.

"We can't blame him." Captain Pemberton looked around. "Where is he? And the Crow?"

Sergeant Heston spoke up. "The last I saw of them, sir, they were cut off and fighting for their lives."

From out of the woods wavered a scream.

"They're torturing the poor devils they took alive." Lieutenant Finch stated the obvious.

"We haven't another moment to waste," Captain Pemberton said. "Fall in. We'll charge through them, wheel, and charge again. With any luck it will break them and they'll scatter."

From a walk their horses were brought to a fast walk, from a fast walk to a trot. By then they were in the trees and their formation was less compact but still in good order. Piercing yips warned they had been spotted. Arrows sailed at them.

Clear and loud rang out Captain Pemberton's "Charrrggge!"

Most of the Indians had dismounted. Some were mutilating soldiers. A lot were gathered around a fallen warrior.

A chief, James suspected.

The command came to fire. James did so, doubtful he hit anything. It was next to impossible to score at a full gallop even with lots of practice. Still, some hostiles fell.

The counterattack disconcerted the Indians. A few stood their ground, but the majority vaulted onto their painted ponies and lit out in all directions.

D Troop swept across the open area, stopped short of the woods, wheeled in perfect order, and thundered down on the hostiles who remained. Another volley crackled and the troopers were past. Once again D Troop wheeled, but this time Captain Pemberton called for them to halt and the bugler sounded the cease-fire.

James was covered in sweat, his uniform more brown with dust than blue. He was ungodly thirsty. His horse pranced and he patted its neck, awaiting orders.

Captain Pemberton didn't waste a second. "Lieutenant Myers, take a sergeant and twenty men and make sure the hostiles are gone while we see to our fallen. They might take it into their heads to circle back and try us again."

"Yes, sir," Myers said briskly.

"Under no circumstances are you to engage them," Captain Pemberton ordered.

"Yes, sir," Myers said, less heartily.

To James's amazement, Myers then pointed at him and said, "I pick Sergeant Doyle, there."

34

James couldn't understand why Second Lieutenant Myers had picked him. Of all the sergeants he had the least experience. He learned the answer shortly after they entered the woods.

"This is a stroke of luck, Doyle," Myers said excitedly. "A chance for us to shine."

"Sir?"

"I pray to God we find hostiles. Nothing leads to a faster promotion than exterminating these vermin. And no one knows that better than you, eh?"

"Sir?" James said again.

"A nice little skirmish will benefit my career greatly," Myers said.

"Begging your pardon, sir," James said, "but the captain ordered us not to engage them."

Myers grinned and winked. "But what if *they* engage *us*? We can't be faulted for defending ourselves."

James didn't like the sound of that. "We only have twenty men," he reminded him.

"Hell," Lieutenant Myers scoffed, "we can lick five times our number. Redskins have no backbone. You saw yourself. They tucked tail and ran."

"It was smart of them," James said. "We caught them by surprise. Sir," he remembered to add.

Myers's face pinched in a scowl. "What the hell is the matter with you? I thought of all the noncoms, you would share my sentiments."

James tried to think of what he had done to give Myers that idea.

"You made sergeant because of one fight. Imagine what another might do for your career."

James glanced over his shoulder at the other troopers. Most were like him, young and almost as green. Only a handful were worth a damn with a carbine. Yet here they were, hunting enemies who could ride rings around them and shoot them from the saddle while doing it. "Sir, I must object."

Lieutenant Myers went on as if he hadn't heard.

"The captain was clear as can be," James said.

"I'm in charge of this patrol and you'll damn well follow *my* orders or I'll have you brought up on charges." Myers muttered something. "And I must say, Sergeant Doyle, that you're a disappointment."

They were on the westward loop of their sweep. A wide swath of pockmarks showed that at least part of the war party had come this way.

Lieutenant Myers bent low and said, "Where's Jack Shard or that Crow when we need them? Can you tell how many hostiles there were?"

No, James couldn't, but judging by the number of tracks, it was a lot. To his consternation, Myers uttered a laugh and reined after them.

James wished First Sergeant Heston was there. Heston had impressed on him that a sergeant's paramount duty was to follow orders, but he doubted the stolid sergeant would agree to this. Heston had also said the welfare of the men came first.

"Look!" Lieutenant Myers exclaimed, and pointed.

A pair of hostiles sat their horses in plain sight a quarter of a mile away.

"Stragglers, by Jupiter," Myers said. "We'll take them prisoner and make them tell us where the rest are heading." He turned and yelled, "At the double, men!"

Reluctantly, James goaded his animal. He didn't like how the pair were just sitting there, or how they continued to sit there as the patrol swept toward them. To him it smelled of a ruse.

Some of the troopers whooped and hollered.

James did as he thought Sergeant Heston would do. He shouted over his shoulder, "That's enough of that!"

Lieutenant Myers was intent on the hostiles. When the two warriors reined to the northwest, he shouted, "After them, men! We can't let them get away."

Swirls of dust rose in the hostiles' wake. They were making for a series of bluffs that reared like giant tombstones.

James held the Spencer close to his side so it didn't flap on the sling. His horse was holding up, but it was tired.

One of the cardinal rules they were taught early on was that a cavalryman's horse was his salvation and to never, ever exhaust their animal unless their lives depended on it.

Lieutenant Myers didn't care about his horse. He didn't care about anything but the two warriors. Now and again he laughed, as if this were great fun.

James had to say it. "This could be a trap!" he shouted, and was again ignored.

The pair of hostiles reached a bluff. They looked back, and James would swear money they were grinning. His every impulse screamed at him that Myers was making a terrible mistake and he should do something.

The next instant it was too late.

From around the bluff poured more hostiles. There had to be sixty, painted furies voicing war whoops and brandishing weapons. Many controlled their horses by their legs, leaving their hands free to let loose shafts or shoot rifles. Whatever else was said about Indians, one fact was undeniable: they were superb riders.

Outnumbered as the troopers were, there was only one sensible recourse: get the hell out of there. But to James's bewilderment, Second Lieutenant Myers waved his revolver and yelled, "Charge, men! At them, I say!"

Through James's head flashed the thought that the man was unhinged. For his own part, he drew rein so abruptly that his animal came to a sliding stop. Automatically, he raised his arm to bring the column to a halt. All but three troopers followed his example. Those three galloped after Lieutenant Myers, heedless of the insanity of his attack.

James reined around. "Retreat, men!" he roared. "To the woods! To the woods!" As he went past each pair, they turned and flew on his heels. James glanced back.

Lieutenant Myers had realized few troopers were with him and drawn rein. His features were a study in baffled rage.

He looked at the onrushing hostiles and common sense finally prevailed. Snapping an order at the three soldiers who had followed him, he wheeled and raced to rejoin James and the others.

James had a new worry. They might make the woods; they might not. It was over a quarter of a mile and their horses were lathered with sweat and at the limits of their endurance. It could be the hostiles would overtake them before they reached cover. He glanced back again. The Indians were rapidly overhauling them. Lieutenant Myers was using his reins and legs with great vigor, but his horse was slowing. The soldiers with him pulled ahead.

The heat, the pounding of hooves, the dust and the sweat, the whoops of their pursuers, James experienced it all with acute clarity, as if his senses were somehow sharper.

A cry drew his gaze.

Lieutenant Myers's horse had stopped. He was hitting it and kicking it, but it was spent, its head drooping low. He yelled for the three troopers to stop, but either they didn't hear him or they pretended they didn't. Myers shifted in the saddle. The hostiles would soon reach him. He did an incredible thing. He calmly dismounted and faced them. Raising his revolver, he took aim and fired, shot after methodical shot. And he scored, too. Several warriors fell headlong. Myers emptied his six-shooter and was reaching for his Spencer when a wave of red avengers crashed over him. One moment he was straight and proud; the next he was down, riddled with arrows.

"God," James said.

The hostiles didn't slow. In their fevered hatred a few let arrows fly too soon and the shafts fell short.

James gauged the distance to the woods and the rapidly lessening distance between the Indians and his men and came to a disheartening conclusion. Shifting, he shouted, "We won't make it! We have to make a stand!" He drew rein, unsure if any of them had heard or if they did they would stop, but when he did, they did. Swiftly, they dismounted.

James didn't know a lot about military tactics. But he did know that their Spencer carbines, with their rapid rate of fire, were the only hope they had. He had three men hold the horses while the rest formed into two rows, the first row on one knee, the second standing.

The troopers who had been with Lieutenant Myers galloped up and swung down. They didn't say a word and scrambled to obey as James ordered them to take positions.

The hostiles were coming on fast.

James called out for the troopers to load and aim and prepare to fire. "At my command!" he bawled, and raised his arm overhead. An odd calm came over him. He supposed he should be filled with fear, but he wasn't. And then there was no time for thought, no time for anything save action.

The Indians were on them.

35

Sergeant Heston had once mentioned that a skilled soldier could fire a Spencer twenty times in a minute. None of the troopers with James, though, was very skilled. Still, while he had never amounted to much at arithmetic, he guessed that with sixteen Spencers, in one minute his men could fire hundreds of rounds.

"Wait for me to say!" James instructed. Every shot must tell.

The warriors were as blind to their peril as Lieutenant Myers had been to his. Or maybe they were used to the army using single-shot rifles and didn't consider James and his men much of a threat.

James let them get so close he could see each dab and streak of war paint. "By rows!" he hollered, and slashing his hand down, he bellowed, "First row, fire!" Eight Spencers crashed in unison. "Reload!" he shouted. "Second row, fire!" Another crash of carbines, and more lead tore into the hostiles. "First row, fire!" He paused. "Second row, fire!"

Indians were down. Horses were down. Others broke right and left, but still arrows streaked and their rifles boomed.

A trooper clutched his chest and fell.

"First row, fire! Second row, fire!"

More hostiles reeled or pitched headlong. Their front ranks had been decimated and confusion was rampant. The blistering storm of lead was unexpected, and devastating.

Wiser heads sought refuge or escape.

Another soldier dropped.

"Front row, fire! Back row, fire!"

Between the gun smoke and the dust, it was growing impossible to see. Horses whinnied and plunged. A warrior on foot came running out of the clouds with his tomahawk raised.

Quick as thought, James shot him.

A painted horse flew past their lines.

"Front row, fire! Back row, fire!"

A cacophony of chaos and death arose, a din so clamorous it hurt the ears.

Then, abruptly, the war whoops ended, the squeals and hoofbeats faded.

James sent two more volleys into the smoke and dust and only then gave the order to cease fire. In the sudden quiet his ears rang. His nose stung from all the smoke and his throat was raw. He worked his Spencer's lever.

The men had their rifles ready to shoot. "Where'd they get to?" a trooper breathlessly asked.

James advanced, swatting at the smoke. He couldn't see more than a few yards. He did hear horses, moving away.

"Do we go after them, sir?" a soldier asked.

Despite the circumstances, James smothered a grin. It was the first time anyone had called him "sir." "We do not, Private. We stay right where we are." Until he was sure the hostiles were gone and they were safe.

But not a minute later a bugle's clarion notes pealed, and out of the woods streamed D Troop.

"They heard the shots and are coming to our rescue!" a man cried for joy.

"A little late," another said.

"Hush, men," James commanded. He was on the lookout for the hostiles. The breeze gusted, thinning the smoke, and he beheld the slaughter he had caused. A dozen horses and almost as many hostiles lay in spreading scarlet pools. Several of the horses were alive and thrashing. None of the Indians moved.

James turned as Captain Pemberton brought D Troop to a halt. Pemberton took in them and their foes with an expression of both relief and incredulity. He dismounted, as did Lieutenant Finch and Sergeant Heston.

"What happened here?" Pemberton demanded. "I told Lieutenant Myers not to engage the enemy. Where is he?" He looked around.

James had to clear his throat to speak. "We were ambushed, sir. The lieutenant was the first to fall." He glanced at the others and some of them nodded or smiled in understanding.

"His body is out there a ways." James pointed.

"Then you rallied the men and made a stand on your own initiative?"

"On my own what, sir?"

"You did this on your own," Captain Pemberton said.

"Yes, sir," James replied. "I couldn't think of anything else to do."

Pemberton glanced at Finch and Finch smiled and shook his head.

Sergeant Heston had gone to the troopers who were down and was examining them. "Two dead here, sir."

"Counting Myers, that makes three."

"I make it to be fourteen hostiles accounted for,"

Lieutenant Finch said. He rose onto his toes and shielded his eyes from the sun. "With more off yonder."

Captain Pemberton turned to James. "Do you have any idea what you've accomplished here?"

"We stayed alive," James said.

FOREVER THE WEST

36

Seven years had gone by since the Battle of the Bluffs, as the fight became known.

Second Lieutenant James Doyle studied his reflection in the mirror. His hair was cropped closer than on that fateful day. He had filled out more, but none of it was fat. He adjusted his hat and rested his hand on the flapped holster to his Colt single-action Army revolver, standard issue since 1874. The Dyer cartridge pouch on his prairie belt held forty cartridges. In addition, there were loops filled with cartridges for his Springfield carbine, which had replaced the Spencer.

Satisfied he would pass muster, James emerged from the bedroom. Their living quarters were small but included a parlor and a kitchen.

Peggy was chopping carrots and humming.

Quietly coming up behind her, James wrapped his arms around her waist and pecked her on the neck. "You're awful cheerful."

"Why wouldn't I be?" Peg grinned and kissed him on the cheek. "Fort Sisseton isn't as bad as everyone made it out to be."

"I was worried you wouldn't like it."

"I'm the wife of a soldier," Peg said lightheartedly. "Where my soldier goes, I go. And not just because I'm in the family way."

"The frontier can be hard," James said.

"But you like it out here. It's in your blood."

James chuckled. "That's a strange thing to say to a boy born and bred in New York City."

"Maybe so," Peg allowed, giving him another kiss. "But somewhere between there and here, you learned to love the West as much as you love me."

"I can't ever care for anything as much as I care for you," James corrected her. He meant it. He hadn't done a lot of smart things in his life, but one of them was marrying her. The other was letting Captain Pemberton convince him to make a career of the military. He tickled her and she giggled.

"Didn't Colonel Maxton send for you?" Peg gave him a playful push. "You better go see what he wants. We only just got here four days ago and you shouldn't keep him waiting."

Fort Sisseton was the northernmost post in Dakota Territory. Situated on a plateau known as Coteau des Prairies, it was one of half a dozen established to control hostile tribes, principally the Sioux, and to safeguard wagon routes to Montana and Idaho.

The site had been well chosen. Thick timber provided lumber, an abundance of clay and lime allowed for the making of bricks, and a lake ensured that the soldiers would never want for water.

James stepped out into the harsh glare of the Dakota sun. Summers here were as hot as on the Kansas prairie. He crossed the parade ground and entered headquarters. The orderly admitted him.

Colonel Maxton wasn't the ideal image of a cavalry officer; he was short and portly and balding. But during the Civil War he'd served competently. Later he was assigned to the frontier.

By his own request, James had heard.

"Have a seat, Lieutenant Doyle." Maxton gestured. "We have a lot to discuss and you might as well be comfortable."

"Thank you, sir," James said as he sank down.

Colonel Maxton tapped papers on his desk. "I've been reading your file. Quite the rise you've had. The commendations. The medal. And then your appointment to West Point. Apparently a Captain Pemberton had a hand in that. He even got your congressman involved. You graduated thirty-fourth in a class of seventy-six, I believe." Maxton consulted the file. "Yes. That's it. As I say, quite the rise."

James shrugged. "I was lucky, sir."

"To the contrary, Lieutenant," Maxton said. "You pulled yourself up by your bootstraps and made something of yourself. No one did it for you. Oh, you had help getting into the academy, but graduating was your doing. Then there's your experience fighting hostiles. You were the acknowledged hero of the Battle of the Bluffs. It says so right here."

"Others were just as heroic."

"Why diminish yourself?" Colonel Maxton asked. "Humility is well and good in a parson, but you're a military man."

James said nothing.

"No one ever advanced their career by being humble, Lieutenant. Be forthright. Be bold. I expect that of my men, especially my officers."

"Yes, sir."

"This post is no place for the timid. The Sioux and the Cheyenne and other tribes are far from contained. At this very moment General Terry and General Custer are out in the field on a campaign to blunt these Indian uprisings once and for all."

"I hope they succeed, sir."

"As do I, Lieutenant," Colonel Maxton said. "Because if they don't there will be hell to pay."

37

There was hell to pay.

Lieutenant Colonel George Armstrong Custer and five of the seven companies of the Seventh Cavalry were wiped out. The overwhelming force of Cheyenne, Lakota, and others tried to do the same to what was left of Custer's command, who were entrenched on high bluffs. Given time they might have succeeded. But word reached them of more bluecoats converging on the Greasy Grass River where they were camped and they hastily tore down their lodges and fled.

James was stunned by the news. He never met Custer. He'd heard about him. Everyone had. Custer was famous not only for his daring during the Civil War but for his flamboyant nature, dashing good looks, and his recent political battle with President Ulysses S. Grant. Custer testified against Grant's brother and a friend of the president's in a scandal involving payoffs, and Grant tried to ruin him. Ironically, Custer had to practically beg to join the very campaign that witnessed his demise.

To James the fate of the Seventh was added proof, not that any was needed, that once beyond the haven of a fort, a cavalryman's life could be as quickly extinguished as the blowing out of a candle. He'd learned that lesson on the brutal plains of Kansas.

Fort Sisseton was abuzz with the news about Custer. Public and political pressure had mounted for the army to, as a newspaper editorialized:

Do something to finally end the Indian problem. For far too long our frontier has been besieged by these red heathens who refuse to give way to the advance of progress and civilization. Their stubborn and witless resistance has led to the loss of untold lives and the destruction of untold property and livestock. Enough, we say! Put an end to it! Put an end to them! Exterminate the vermin as they exterminated Custer. Americans one and all have tolerated this situation long enough. Do you hear us, President Grant? Unleash the army. Throw all the troops you must against the savages and end the red menace now and forever.

James didn't share the same sentiments. Not since that terrible day he fought side by side with Two Bears. He had liked Cowlick, too. Getting to know them had taught him that Indians might be different from whites but they were still people, still human beings, and not the animals they were often portrayed. It had saddened him when Lieutenant Finch found the bodies of Cowlick and Jack Shard.

At the moment James was on his way to an officers' call. As one of the junior officers, he took a seat at the back. He'd met all the rest and rated them as dependable men. Not a Lieutenant Myers in the bunch.

Colonel Maxton stood at the front and cleared his

throat. His hands were behind his back and his demeanor was grave.

"Gentlemen," he began. "You are all aware of Custer and the Little Bighorn. Custer's death has become a lightning rod that has galvanized this nation as never before. The army is mobilizing on a scale not seen since the War Between the States. A concerted campaign is being mounted to put every last Cheyenne and every last Sioux on reservations, and to deal summarily with those who refuse." He paused. "They will submit to our will or we will kill them dead."

Assent rippled among the officers.

"While we are not directly involved, we nonetheless have an important role to play. Emboldened by the victory, bands of renegades are more active than ever. And it is our job, gentlemen, to see that the surrounding territory is spared those depredations. Accordingly we are under new orders to increase our patrols. Hostiles are to be rooted out and engaged."

James noticed the excitement that gleamed on many a face.

"We are, in effect, at war. Should you encounter hostiles, you will show no mercy. Should any of them throw down their arms and surrender, then yes, disarm them and take them into custody. But otherwise you are to do to them as they did to Custer. Is that understood?"

Maxton paused as if waiting for comments, then went on.

"Tomorrow night will be your last night of leisure for a while. Enjoy it. The day after tomorrow all of you are going out into the field. You'll be gone for weeks."

James thought of Peg and how she would take the news.

"I don't need to stress the danger. The Indians have

been made bolder than ever by Custer's defeat. They are out for white blood and won't hesitate to shed yours if you give them the slightest advantage." Maxton looked as grim as death.

"Don't give them that advantage."

38

Peg had spread linen on the table and set out candles. She'd used her best china and not her everyday plates and bowls, and her best silverware.

James stared at the table, wondering what the occasion was. Then it hit him. She had heard patrols were going out in the morning and she was treating him to a special meal. "I'm home," he announced, and sat.

Peg came around the corner, smiling. She had on her newest dress and an apron to protect it from spills. Wiping her hands, she kissed him warmly. "How did the meeting go?"

"You don't know?"

"How could I, dearest? I was here the whole while." She retraced her steps, saying over her shoulder, "I'll have the food out in a minute."

James debated whether to tell her. He decided not to. It might spoil her mood. He compromised with "There's a lot of concern about the Indians, what with Custer's downfall."

"I met his wife once," Peg's voice floated out. "Did I ever mention it? Libby, her name was. Every inch the lady and devoted to her husband. Much as I'm devoted to you."

James took a sip of water. "The Cheyenne and the Sioux did themselves no favors. They defeated Custer but will reap a bitter harvest."

"How do you mean?"

"The public has never been so stirred up against the red man as they are now, and when the public is stirred up, it stirs the politicians to act. Before, the policy was mainly to contain the Indians. Now I'm afraid the army will be much more ruthless."

Peg reappeared carrying a bowl of mashed potatoes. "Haven't we been ruthless enough? Their villages have been attacked, their women and children killed. And don't forget the poor Cherokees and that awful march they were forced to make."

James sat back. "I never realized you were so friendly toward them."

Peg set the bowl down. "I wouldn't go that far. I wish we could live in peace, but we can't."

James dropped the subject. "So, what else is for dinner? Or is it just potatoes?"

"You're about to find out."

The main course included thick beef steaks as well as the potatoes, macaroni, long sauce, and bread. To drink there was coffee for him and tea for her. For dessert she had prepared one of his favorites: sweet-potato pie.

James ate heartily. This would be his last home cooking for a while. He looked at her over the flickering candles and felt an intense welling of affection. Peg was as fine a woman as any man could ask for. That she had chosen him out of all the men in the world never failed to stir him. He smiled and forked more sweet-potato pie into his mouth.

Peg gave a little cough. "Did you enjoy your meal?"

"Do birds have wings?"

"I'm glad you're happy. I'm happy, too, but for a whole other reason. Can you guess what it is?"

James was terrible at guessing her thoughts and moods, but he tried to please her. "Your mother is coming for a visit?"

"No."

"Your sister is coming for a visit?"

"No again."

"You bought a new dress."

"Keep trying."

"You bought a new hat?"

"No."

"New shoes."

"Silly goose."

James drummed his fingers. "This is pointless. I'll never guess. Why don't you come right out and tell me?"

Peg sipped her tea and delicately placed the china cup on the china saucer. "Very well. But I want you to take the news with an open mind. I know we talked about waiting a while, but somctimes it's not up to us."

"What are you—" James stopped. "No," he blurted.

"Yes."

"You're not—"

Peg smiled and nodded. "Yes. I am. I'm pregnant, James. We're going to have our first baby."

James pushed his chair back and came around the table. She rose, and they embraced. He felt the softness of her skin and smelled the lilac in her hair and imagined the new life taking shape inside her. "How long have you known?"

"I was only sure this very day." Peg's smile lit her whole face. "Isn't it wonderful?" She gripped his shoulders. "You must promise me to take extra care of yourself from here on out. Don't take risks unless you absolutely havc to. Agreed?"

"About that," James said.

"I won't take no for an answer. Your baby and I need

you, James Marion Doyle. A woman alone is at a great disadvantage in this world."

James was reminded of his mother, and he almost couldn't bring himself to say, "There's something you should know. I go out on patrol tomorrow."

"You're a cavalryman. That's what you do." Peg looked him in the eye. "It's no different from any other patrol, is it? The element of danger isn't any greater because of that awful Custer business?"

"No," James lied. "It's not."

39

The colonel called it a "get acquainted hour." All the married officers and their wives were on hand in Maxton's quarters to informally welcome James and Peg to Fort Sisseton.

Peg thought it wonderful of the colonel to be so considerate.

James worried that the subject of the impending patrol would come up. He'd spare her the anxiety if he could.

Colonel Maxton brought James and Peg over to a corner where a square-jawed captain and a petite woman with a wealth of curls were enjoying glasses of brandy. James had already met the captain, briefly, but now he was given cause to study the man in earnest.

"Captain Stoneman, Mrs. Harriet Stoneman," the colonel said. "I trust you know Lieutenant Doyle and his lovely wife, Margaret? The four of you should become fast friends, especially as the captain and the lieutenant are going out on patrol together."

Mrs. Stoneman clasped Peg's hand and said, "Oh, how delightful. Yes, let's you and me have tea together every day until our men return."

"I'd like that."

"And don't you worry about your handsome husband," Harriet assured her. "He's in good hands with my Bryce."

"I'm not worried," Peg said.

"Come now," Harriet responded. "No need to pretend around any of the ladies here. We're army wives, young lady. All of us live with fear every day. It's the burden we bear for falling in love with soldiers."

James could have kicked her.

"I have every confidence in my man," Peg said. "He knows I want him to come back to me."

Mrs. Stoneman adopted a maternal manner. "That's well and good but it's not very realistic. I have long been of the opinion that a wife should prepare herself for the very worst. It makes us that much happier when it doesn't come to pass."

"Always keeping the worst in mind would depress me," Peg said.

"That's why it behooves us to keep busy. Busy bees, we should be, the better to take our minds off the perils our men face."

"I think you're upsetting her, my dear," Captain Stoneman said.

"Nonsense. And even if that's so, she must learn to cope. Otherwise the long periods of being alone we must endure would be unbearable."

"I can endure them," Peg said.

"How brave of you to say so," Harriet said. "But with the danger so much greater after that terrible massacre, we need all the support we can get. Which is why I want you to know I'm always here for you, any hour of the day or night."

"So much greater?" Peg said.

"Surely your husband told you? My Bryce would

never dream of keeping anything from me. Our marriage has lasted as long as it has because we are always completely open with each other. I recommend that you and your husband do the same."

"So much greater?" Peg said again, with a meaningful glance at James.

"Honestly, dear. How can it not be? The northern tribes won a great victory, as they see it. It has emboldened them to go on the warpath all along the frontier."

"Have there been reports of hostiles in this area?" Peg inquired.

"We're on the frontier, aren't we?" Harriet rejoined. "The very edge of it, in point of fact. Nowhere is the danger greater, in my estimation."

James was grateful when Captain Stoneman said, "That will be enough. You're scaring the poor girl needlessly. I haven't lost a patrol yet and I don't intend to start."

"There's always a first time," Harriet, incredibly, said.

The rest of the evening was small talk about matters of little consequence. James hoped that his wife had forgotten about Harriet's remarks, but as they strolled under the stars back to their quarters she abruptly stopped.

"Don't ever lie to me again."

"I didn't—"

Peg held up a hand. "I'm not a child and I won't be treated as such. I asked you if you were in more danger than usual and you told me you weren't. You lied, James. Why? Give me one good reason."

"I love you," James said. "Is that reason enough?"

Peg looked away. When she spoke next her voice was husky with emotion. "You wanted to spare my feelings. I appreciate that. But in the future I want the truth and nothing but the truth."

"If that's what you really want."

"Would I say so if I didn't?" Peg hooked her arm in his and leaned her cheek on his shoulder. "The life of an army wife is hard enough. Harriet was right about the absences. They tear at the heartstrings. More so if you play false with me. I deserve better."

James embraced her and kissed her brow. "You are everything to me. I'm sorry if I hurt your feelings. From now on it will be the truth and only the truth."

"So let me hear again from your own lips how dangerous this patrol will be."

"It will be dangerous as can be," James said.

40

Captain Stoneman was at the head of the column, James at his side.

Families and friends turned out to see them off. Peg and Harriet were together. Peg smiled bravely and waved, her other hand on her belly.

The troopers were the usual mix. Most were young and half were immigrants: German, Italian, Irish and one Swiss. Several had been farmers, one a blacksmith, another a cook, yet another a teacher. None had held a firearm before they enlisted. Most were middling riders.

Under James was Sergeant Strake, a third-generation American. His grandfather had come from England to visit the former Colonies and liked them so much he stayed. Strake despised slavery so intensely that when the war broke out, he enlisted. He was at Gettysburg. When the war ended he elected to stay in the army. He was the most competent soldier at Fort Sisseton and James considered it fortunate to have him with their patrol.

The first several days were routine. They saw no trace of Indians, hostile or otherwise. On the fifth day they spied a herd of buffalo, which caused some excitement.

That night around the campfire, Private Plover from New York remarked that he wished the herd had been larger. "I read about some that were a million strong. Wouldn't that be a sight?"

"I reckon only a Yankee would think so," replied Private Howell. He was from Tennessee and one of several at the fort who had served in the Confederate army. "Killin' those critters is the smartest thing we could do."

Plover tilted his head like a bird that had seen a snake. "How can you say such a thing? Buffalo are magnificent."

"Magnificent?" Private Howell said, and snorted. "That's what too much book learnin' will do. Buffalo are nothin' but hairy cows with bigger horns."

Some of the men laughed.

"It's a shame, I say," Private Plover insisted. "We're killing them off just like we're doing to the passenger pigeon and before that the beaver."

"That's the whole point, Yank," Private Howell said.

"I must have missed it."

"We *want* the buffs killed off. In case you ain't heard, Injuns depend on the buffalo like we do cows. The meat is their food. The hides are their robes and their shirts and their lodges and their parfleches. Hell, they even use the bones for awls and hoes and such." He nodded sagely to his fellow troopers. "We wipe out those hairy cows, we wipe out the redskins." To Plover he said, "Why do you think we've been killin' 'em off wholesale?"

James was a few feet away, listening and drinking coffee, and Private Plover spotted him.

"Is that true, sir?"

"General Sheridan and General Sherman think so," James said.

"It doesn't seem right," Private Plover said.

Private Howell snorted. "There ain't no right and

wrong in war. I learned that back in 'sixty-five. Only winnin' counts."

Their route brought them to rolling hills. They were traveling north when, late on a cloudy morning, wisps of smoke betrayed a campfire.

Captain Stoneman sent Sergeant Strake and two troopers to investigate and they were back in half an hour. "What did you find?" he demanded as they came to a stop.

"They used to be hide hunters, sir," Sergeant Strake said.

"Used to be?"

"You'll have to see for yourself, sir."

James had an inkling of what they would find, but it still didn't prepare him.

First they came on two wagons of the sort hide hunters used. Both were empty. But from the bloodstains and the hairs, they had recently been laden with hides. Their teams were missing. Not so their owners. Four white blobs marked where they had met their horrid ends. Their corpses had bloated and swarmed with flies and not a few maggots. All four had been savaged. Tomahawks and knives had rent their torsos and opened their thighs from hip to knee. Their bellies had been slit from sternum to navel. Each corpse had an arrow jutting obscenely from its crotch. All had been scalped.

"God in heaven," one of the younger troopers bleated, and was sick.

James picked a burial detail and oversaw the digging. Plover and Howell were part of it and he happened to be near when they went at it again.

"I'll have nightmares about this for the rest of my life," Private Plover said as he gathered what few rocks there were to cover the shallow graves.

"What do you think of your precious redskins now, Yank?" Private Howell asked.

"I never said they were precious," Plover said. "All I said was that killing off the buffalo is a shame." He gestured at one of the grisly testaments to man's viciousness. "The Indians do terrible things, I grant you. But so do we."

"I agree that we do 'em," Howell said, "but I don't agree they're terrible."

"How can you not?"

"Killin' comes natural. Ain't you ever heard about Cain and Abel?"

"Whatever the excuse, you don't call that terrible?"

"No," Private Howell said. "I call that normal."

As he had done before, Private Plover appealed to James.

"How about you, Lieutenant Doyle? Do you think it's normal for men to murder each other?"

James remembered one of his instructors at West Point saying that if it wasn't for the human urge to kill, there wouldn't be any need for the military and West Point wouldn't exist. "Normal or not, it happens a lot," he said noncommittally.

"That it does, sir," Private Howell declared. "And there's one thing you can be sure of."

"What's that?" Private Plover asked.

"There's goin' to be a whole heap more of it before these Injun wars are done."

41

More days went by. They were deep in the interior, in country few whites had ever set foot in, and of those who did, few made it out again. In country where the red man had lived for untold ages and resented being told by the white man that he couldn't live there anymore. In country where a father-to-be was rightfully anxious about living long enough to be a father.

James tried to keep that thought out of his head, but he wasn't entirely successful. It ate at him although not to where it affected his duties. He was, as Sergeant Heston would say, a good soldier, and he wouldn't let anything interfere with that. He liked being a good soldier.

It surprised him a little although he supposed it shouldn't. After all, he had gone from being a Blue Shirt to a bluecoat, and was it that much of a difference? The gang had worn their own sort of uniform and protected their territory in Five Points from all others. The cavalry had its uniform and protected the territory of the United States from any and all enemies. The gang was about loyalty to one another and to the gang as a whole. A cavalryman was all about loyalty to the men who were serving with him and to the army as a whole. But most of all the Blue Shirts had been a band of brothers, and what was the cavalry if not the same?

On a bright and sunny morning, they came on a nameless small stream and followed its winding course. It brought them to a rise overlooking a wooded lowland and as they sat letting their horses rest, the sound of an axe biting into wood came sharp to their ears on the clear morning air.

"Surely not," Captain Stoneman said, more to himself than to James. "Take four men and go see. And be careful. We've been seeing a lot of sign."

That they had. Mostly in the form of tracks made by unshod horses.

James picked Plover and Howell and two others and advanced along to a break that hid them as they descended and moved into the timber. The woods were thick and dark with shadow. Usually small game was everywhere, but James saw none, a clue that someone had been doing a lot of hunting.

The ring of the axe grew louder.

"Keep your carbines at the ready, men," James advised. He drew his Colt. They made little noise and presently reached a bend in the stream. The trees stopped short of it. Half a dozen horses were hobbled on the bank. Three men were in the water up to their knees, one using a pan and the other two working a small sluice. A fourth man had felled a sapling and was chopping it for firewood.

"They're white, sir," Private Plover whispered, as if James couldn't see that for himself.

"Doesn't mean they'll be friendly," James responded. "When I give a nod, cover them. Don't shoot unless I say to but be ready."

"Shoot a white man, Lieutenant?" Private Plover said.

Private Howell grinned. "You can count on me, sir. I'll shoot anybody."

James gigged his mount out of the woods, and nodded. The axe wielder was the first to see them and froze with the axe in midair. James rode up to him. "Lieutenant James Doyle, United States Army," he said by way of introduction. "Who are you men and what are you doing here?"

The man was scrawny and scruffy and wore homespun faded by long use. His belt was a piece of rope and one of his shoes had a hole in it. "Howdy," he said.

"You can lower the axe," James said.

The man looked at it as if he'd forgotten he was holding it, and did so. "What are you soldier boys doing so far from anywhere?"

"I'll ask the questions, and I already asked one," James said.

"Oh. Sorry." The man nervously shuffled his feet. "I'm Thaddeus Melleck. Those there are my friends. We're prospecting."

"In the middle of Sioux country?"

"We ain't scared of no redskins," Melleck said. "We got us repeaters and we're damn good shots."

"Call them over," James said.

Melleck turned and hollered and the three men stopped working and looked up. They were as taken aback as he had been. As they climbed over the bank, they picked up their rifles, all Winchesters. The biggest of them had shoulders like a bull and no neck to speak of and beady eyes that glittered with annoyance.

"What's this about?" he demanded. "Why are your men pointing their carbines at us?"

"Name," James said.

"Eh? Clinton Burr, as if it's any of your business."

"Are you aware, Mr. Burr, of the recent Indian uprising and the death of General Custer?"

"What's he got to do with us?" Burr said. "As for the savages, we got as much right to be here as they do."

"Technically, yes—" James began.

"What's that fancy talk, technically?" Burr interrupted. "Talk plain."

"Technically," James patiently resumed, "yes, this isn't Indian land. But you are near the Sisseton reservation, which was established back in 'sixty-seven."

"Listen to you," Burr mocked him. "And if we ain't on no reservation, we're not doing anything wrong."

"It's not the Sissetons you have to concern yourself about. Other bands are on the warpath and they might be in this area."

"I ain't scared of no heathens. Now leave us be." Burr went to return to the stream.

"I'm afraid," James said politely, "that we are under orders to escort any civilians we find to safety. You'll accompany us to Fort Sisseton and remain there until the uprising is over."

"Like hell we will."

"Be reasonable, Mr. Burr."

"I'll give you reasonable, damn you," Clinton Burr growled, and jerked his Winchester up.

James was quicker. He pointed his Colt at Burr's face and thumbed back the hammer before Burr could press the stock to his shoulder. "Set that down."

Burr froze, the Winchester only halfway up. "You wouldn't."

"Try me."

"I'm a—what's the word?—civilian. The army doesn't go around shooting civilians."

"You don't shed that rifle, I will sure as hell shoot you," James said. In the leg or in the arm. Burr was right in one regard; the army took a dim view of officers who shot citizens.

"This ain't right," Burr said as he slowly lowered the Winchester to the grass.

"The rest of you do the same."

A heavyset man with dropping jowls said, "We ain't done nothing. You can't threaten us."

Private Howell trained his carbine on the man's belly. "Care to bet, mister?"

Resentfully, the others obeyed. James had Plover climb down and gather up their weapons. He sent another soldier, Private Kearns, to bring the captain and the rest of the patrol. Dismounting, he holstered his Colt and stepped to the bank. The sluice was a simple affair, the pans battered and scraped from a lot of use. "Find any gold?"

"None of your damn business," Burr snapped.

"Oh, hell," said the last of them, a younger man with a shock of red hair and freckles. His pants were too short and stopped inches above his ankles and his shirt was so baggy it could fit two of him. "Why are you and Treywick bein' so contrary?" He turned to James. "No, we ain't found nary any, and them sayin' as how we'd be rich." He added a few choice cusswords.

James chuckled. "Who might you be, firebrand?"

"Chester," the young man with freckles said. "Chester Gilliam. I'm from Arkansas."

"A Southern boy like me!" Private Howell exclaimed. "I like that."

Chester regarded him with interest. "You're Southern and you're a blue belly?"

"Back up a step, cousin," Private Howell said. "For one thing, the war is long over. For another, you're too young to have taken part, so what's it matter? For another, a soldier is a soldier on the inside and not because of the uniform."

"I reckon as how that's true," Chester allowed, and offered a bony hand. "Shake, then, hoss. From here on you and me are friends." He bobbed his head at the stream. "As much success as I've been havin' at this gold business, maybe I should see about wearin' one of those uniforms my own self."

"Have you seen any sign of Indians?" James asked all four of them.

Burr muttered. Treywick's jowls quivered with anger. Melleck poked a toe at the ground.

Chester Gilliam looked at the three of them and did more swearing. "The bunch I am in with," he said with marked disgust. "I can answer that."

"You hush, boy," Burr said.

"I ain't the fruit of your loins, nohow," Chester said. "What harm can it do? You heard him. The army is runnin' us off anyway."

"Don't," Treywick said.

"You two are a pair." Chester pointed at a height across the stream. "You see that hill yonder, Yank? Just last evenin' there was an Injun sittin' there on his paint as bold as you please, watchin' us."

"All he did was watch?"

"For about ten minutes, I'd say it was," Chester said. "Burr wanted to go after him, but Treywick said to leave him be and he'd leave us be."

"He just rode off?"

"Just like that," Chester said, and snapped his fingers.

"Think it was a friendly, sir?" Private Plover asked.

James had no way of knowing. It could have been a Sisseton from the reservation, perhaps on a hunt. But there were also renegades about.

"Of course it was," Burr said. "The Injuns know we're here and leave us be. You should, too."

"I'm following orders," James said.

"You can as easily unfollow them," Burr said. "Don't mention you saw us."

"Too late for that," James said. "Our patrol will be here in about ten minutes. Then I think I'll go look for sign of that Indian you saw."

"No need for that," Chester Gilliam said.

"Why not?"

Chester pointed at the hill. "Because it appears he came back and brought his friends."

James turned.

The top of the hill was covered with warriors.

42

Whether the Indians were hostile or friendly was demonstrated the very next instant as they erupted in war whoops and fierce cries and charged down the hill.

James's men and the prospectors were momentarily stunned by the abruptness of the attack. He wasn't. "Reclaim your weapons and get your horses into the trees," he shouted.

The war party was five hundred yards away and coming on fast, spreading out as they closed. Only a few had rifles and they would wait to shoot so as not to waste lead.

Private Howell and Private Whitten were following his orders. The prospectors were at their horses, fingers flying, removing the hobbles.

James ran to his mount and climbed on. As he was reining around, he saw that Private Plover was agape with fear. "Snap out of it, Private. Into the woods."

"They're coming to kill us."

"Move," James ordered.

"They're really coming to kill us."

James reined closer and cuffed Plover across the cheek. Not hard, but it jarred him.

Plover blinked, and swallowed. "Sorry, sir," he said. He clumsily hauled on his reins and brought his animal around.

James paced him, continually looking back. The war party was still out of range and they gained cover without incident.

His men and the prospectors were apprehensively awaiting his instructions.

"Do we run or do we fight, sir?" Private Howell asked.

"We run," James said. There were too many to fight. They would be overwhelmed and slaughtered. "We fly to Captain Stoneman and I do mean fly." He lashed his reins and jabbed his heels.

The yips and war whoops were louder. The hostiles had reached the stream. It was so narrow and shallow they barely slowed.

James thought of Peg and her condition and promptly put her from his mind. Now wasn't the time. He avoided a tree, vaulted a log. In the years since Kansas he had become an accomplished rider.

The two Southern boys, Howell and Chester Gilliam, rode as if they and their horses were one. James had found that Southern soldiers, by and large, thanks to childhoods spent on farms and in the country, were better riders than recruits from the North. Plover and Whitten were pitiful riders. Burr and Treywick weren't much better. Melleck rode by the novel technique of pressing himself to his mount and clamping his long limbs tight.

It didn't bode well. They needed speed and lots of it or the warriors would overtake them before they reached the patrol.

James prayed that Captain Stoneman heard the din and came at a gallop.

The lowland climbed gradually toward the hills. The undergrowth was a checkerboard of thick and thin so that one moment they were racing and the next they were forced to slow.

It was frustrating, the more so because the cries of their pursuers grew.

They weren't going to make it, James realized, even as an arrow thudded into an oak he was passing.

There was a shriek, and Melleck flung his arms out and pitched from his horse, a shaft sticking from between his shoulders blades.

A tight cluster of saplings loomed. James flew in among them and yelled for the others to stop and dismount. He was off his horse before it stopped moving. The carbine in his hands, he aimed at a bronzed bare chest and squeezed.

Howell and Plover and Whitten and Gilliam were off their horses and firing.

The hostiles broke and sought cover. Within moments it was as if the earth had swallowed them.

James stopped shooting and yelled, "Cease fire! Don't waste ammunition! Only fire when you have a clear target."

The problem with that was that the Indians were too versed in woodcraft to show themselves, and all the while they were closing in.

James looked for the other prospectors, and swore. Burr and Treywick had kept on going. All they cared about were their own hides.

Private Howell suddenly fired. The retort was greeted with a cry of pain, and he laughed. "Like shootin' turkeys at the county fair," he crowed.

A second later Chester Gilliam's rifle spoke and he, too, laughed. "This is a lot more fun than gold huntin'."

Southern boys, James thought.

"I see a bush moving," Private Plover whispered. "Do I shoot, Lieutenant?"

"Only if you see the Indian moving it," James replied. He lowered his voice in case any of the Indians knew English.

"All of you, listen. We're retreating in skirmish order. Flatten and crawl until I say to rise."

"What about our horses, sir?" Plover asked.

"Leave them."

"But the Indians will get them." Plover was so upset he forgot to use "sir."

"We try to ride off, they'll hear us and be on their own horses and after us before we get twenty yards." James sank down and began crawling. When he was sure they wouldn't be seen, he rose and jogged.

Private Whitten was limping.

"Were you hit?" James asked. He didn't see blood.

"No, sir. I twisted my ankle when I jumped from my horse. But don't worry. I'll keep up."

"Good man," James encouraged him.

The woods were silent. James listened for the column but didn't hear them. He wondered if he had gotten turned around in the excitement and was going the wrong way. No, a check of the sun confirmed he was moving in the right direction. He looked over his shoulder—and stopped cold.

Bounding toward them were a dozen painted wolves.

"Behind us!" James warned, and wheeled. "Turn and choose your targets." He sank to a knee and raised his Springfield. A painted face filled his sights and he fired.

An arrow split the air and sliced into Private Whitten's rib cage. He staggered but didn't cry out and brought his carbine to bear.

More arrows flew. The troopers and Chester Gilliam replied with lead. Indians fell. The rest sought cover with remarkable alacrity, so that in the blink of an eye they were gone.

Private Whitten collapsed. James ran to him, knelt, and lifted the young soldier's head onto his leg. Whitten was conscious, his eyelids fluttering. "Hang on," James urged. "We'll get you out of this."

"No, you won't, sir," Whitten said, pink froth flecking his lips. "I'm done for and I know it." He coughed and scarlet bubbled with the pink.

The other privates and Chester Gilliam were behind trees, watching for hostiles.

"Go," Whitten urged. "I'll only get you killed if you stay."

"We're not leaving you," James said. Not while breath remained.

Whitten tried to say something, but all that came out was more blood. He sagged and placed a hand on the shaft in his body. "Do me a favor, would you, Lieutenant?"

"Anything."

"Write to my family in Ohio, would you? Tell them I was thinking of them. Tell them I was a good soldier."

"I will," James promised, hoarsely. He hardly knew Whitten, but the bond of their profession made him feel the loss more deeply than he would otherwise.

"Thank you, sir," Private Whitten said, and died.

James lowered him to the grass. He was loath to leave the body knowing the hostiles might mutilate it. Motioning for silence, he backed away. When he had gone a short distance, he turned and ran, Howell and Plover and Gilliam pumping hard at his heels.

A sharp cry made James think the hostiles had spotted them. He twisted and glimpsed two-legged forms flying with deerlike bounds away from them, not toward them. "They're running off," he said, and stopped.

A rumbling explained why. Hooves pounded and a blue crescent swept from the greenery with the glint of gunmetal in every hand.

Captain Stoneman drew rein and Sergeant Strake bellowed for the men to halt.

"We heard the shooting and the cries," the captain said, scouring the woodland, his pistol cocked. "Where are the hostiles?"

"They heard you coming and wisely fled." James pointed. "I would guess fifteen to twenty are left."

"Stay with them, Sergeant," Stoneman said to Strake. Rising in the stirrups, he gave the command to advance at the ready and the patrol flowed on.

Private Plover leaned against a trunk, his face flushed, his chest heaving. "I don't believe it. We actually lived through that."

"Hell, Yank, that was nothin'," Private Howell said. "I've been in a lot worse scrapes."

"I thought we were dead," Plover said. "As God is my witness I didn't expect to live out the day."

"Where are my so-called partners?" Chester Gilliam asked.

Until that moment James hadn't realized that Burr and Treywick weren't with the troopers. He asked Sergeant Strake where they had gotten to.

"We saw no one, sir. You say they were coming our way? They must have gone in a different direction."

"Or they heard you and hid," James guessed.

"Why would they do that, sir?"

"I can answer that," Chester Gilliam said. "The no-accounts lit out because they don't want you soldier boys taking them away. They think there's gold in these parts and they mean to find it."

"Then they're fools," Sergeant Strake said.

"You'll get no argument from me," Chester said. "I ever see those coyotes again, I aim to give them a piece of my mind."

The vegetation had swallowed the blue line.

James straightened. "Howell, Plover, move out ten feet to either side. Sergeant Strake, you're with me. Stay on your horse. You can see better from up there. Gilliam, you can follow us or stay here."

"Where are we going?" Private Plover anxiously asked.

"Where are we going, *sir*," Sergeant Strake corrected him.

"Have you forgotten Private Whitten?" James said. "We must see to his body and find our horses."

"Why don't we leave that to the captain, sir?"

Sergeant Strake abruptly turned his horse so that it practically pressed Private Plover against a tree. Bending down, he poked Plover in the chest. "Did I just hear you talk back to an officer?"

"I was just—" Plover started to respond, and Strake's thick finger pressed on his throat.

"When an officer tells you to do something, you follow orders. You don't question. You don't complain. You don't suggest a better way. You do as you're damn well told. Do you hear me, Private?"

Plover looked more scared of Strake than he had of the hostiles, if that was possible. "I hear you, Sergeant."

"Good. Because if I ever again hear you do what you just did, I'll make your life as miserable as I can make it." Strake uncurled and swung his horse to James's side. "Sorry about that, sir. It won't happen again. Will it, Private Plover?"

"No, sir. No, sir."

Sergeants, James had sometimes mused, were the glue that held the army together. He made a mental note to buy Strake a drink when they got back. "Let's go."

Just then the woods were rocked by gun blasts and the yowls of renegades.

43

The hostiles had fired shots from the hill as the patrol emerged from the trees. None scored, and with displays of bluster they galloped to the northwest.

Captain Stoneman posted pickets and had the men dismount. The bodies were gathered and hasty burials took place. James oversaw the digging of Private Whitten's grave. After examining the arrow extracted from Whitten's body, Sergeant Strake, who had been on the plains longer than any of them and clashed with several tribes, was of the opinion that the band they had just fought were Sioux.

Within half an hour the patrol was ready to move out again.

James was puzzled that the Indians hadn't taken any of the horses. Then again, they had been busy trying to take life and then preserving their own.

James rode at Stoneman's side. Plenty of tracks and newly churned clods of dirt made it easy for them to stay on the hostiles' trail.

"What do you say, Lieutenant Doyle?" the captain said as they crossed a stretch of plain sprinkled with buffalo wallows. "I'm for following this band to the ends of the earth. Are you with me?"

"It's our duty to bring them to bay."

"That goes without saying," Captain Stoneman said. "But we could follow them for a day or two and give it up as a lost cause and Colonel Maxton would be perfectly pleased."

"Whatever you decide is fine by me," James assured him.

"Don't be so quick to agree," Captain Stoneman said. "When I said we should dog them to the ends of the earth, I meant it. Left free, they'll go on killing and butchering. Settlers, wagons trains, all will suffer. For their sake as well as our own, we must put an end to these hostiles."

"This doesn't have anything to do with Custer, does it, sir?" As James recollected, Stoneman was a great admirer of the colorful officer and had taken the news of Custer's death particularly hard.

"What's wrong with wanting a little revenge?" Stoneman rejoined. "They've brought it down on their own heads. Are you with me or not?"

"So long as it doesn't put the men in more danger than we can handle," James said.

"Oh. You're one of those."

"Sir?"

"It used to be, the army molded hard men for a hard land. These days we mollycoddle recruits and hold their hands for them."

"I don't mollycoddle anyone, sir."

"I'm not finished. So we train them barely enough to get by and send them out in the field where they're barely more than useless. Because of that, certain officers think it best not to expose them to too much danger. I take it you're one of those."

"If they're as useless as you say," James defended himself, "it's up to us to ensure that their shortcomings don't get them killed."

"That's your view. Mine is that by pitting them against the enemy every chance we get, we mold them into the hard men they're supposed to be."

"And a lot of them die in the process, sir."

Captain Stoneman shrugged. "You can't cook eggs without breaking the shells."

"These are men, not eggs."

"Boys, is more apt. And they'll stay that way unless we stop protecting them from becoming men."

James had met other officers who shared Stoneman's view but few so passionate about it. "I repeat, sir," he said. "I'll back whatever you do so long as the men aren't sacrificed."

Stoneman stared at him. "Very well. To the ends of the earth, but daintily." He shook his head. "I mistakenly thought a West Point man would have more fire in his veins."

"I was a soldier before I was accepted at the academy, sir," James said. "One of those mollycoddled recruits who was next to useless."

"Ah. So you feel you share a special bond with the misfits, is that it?"

"I just don't want them killed if we can help it, sir. Is that really so bad?"

"No," Captain Stoneman said, but he didn't sound entirely sincere.

For the rest of that day they only spoke to each other when they had to. James wrestled with his new insight into his fellow officer and how it might impact the patrol. He considered talking to Sergeant Strake, but Strake might tell Stoneman and Stoneman might resent it. So he kept his worries to himself.

On the fourth day after the skirmish, the hostiles bore to the southwest.

"Bound for the Black Hills would be my guess," Captain Stoneman said.

The Black Hills were the heart of Sioux country until recently. Gold had been found, and the government decided to open the Black Hills to settlement and move the Sioux elsewhere. The Sioux didn't want to go.

James spied a score of buzzards in their line of travel. So did Captain Stoneman.

"Maybe the hostiles slaughtered some buffalo and left the remains."

It wasn't buffalo. Two white men had been stripped and tortured. The things done to them reminded James of Kansas. The worst was their faces. Their flesh and their eyes and their noses had been literally scraped away, leaving hideously grinning skulls.

Stoneman encouraged the men to dismount and inspect the bodies. "So you'll appreciate what we're up against," he told them. He nudged a leg with his boot. "I wonder who they were."

"I can answer that," Chester Gilliam said. Squatting, he indicated the tattoo of a ship's anchor on a shoulder. "This here was Treywick, so that heavyset blob must be all that's left of Clinton Burr."

"You're positive?" Captain Stoneman asked.

"Treywick was a sailor in his younger days," Chester said. "He liked to tell sailin' yarns around the fire and showed us that there tattoo more than once." Chester laughed.

"You find the deaths of your friends amusing?"

"Hell. Friends is too strong. They run off when they should have stuck, so I'd say they got what they damn well deserved."

"You're a hard man," Captain Stoneman remarked, and grinned. "I like that."

"It's a hard world," Chester said.

44

Four days later the patrol came on wagon tracks.

"Whoever it is," James said as they examined the ruts, "they shouldn't be here."

"They struck off on their own instead of sticking to the usual trails," Captain Stoneman speculated. "The fools."

"You know how settlers are, sir," Sergeant Strake said. "The grass is always greener where no one else has been."

James gazed to the north where the ruts disappeared into the heat haze and the vast heart of hostile country. "I'm not much of a tracker, but I'd say it's a small wagon train. Ten to twenty wagons, no more."

"I agree, sir," Sergeant Strake said.

Paralleling the tracks were the unshod hoofprints of the war party they were pursuing.

"Our duty is clear," Captain Stoneman said. "We have to save them from themselves. We'll go after them and escort them to the fort and hope to high heaven the hostiles don't attack before we reach them."

Word was passed down the line. With lives at stake, a new grimness came over the troopers. James felt it, himself. The lives of innocent men, women, and children were at stake. They should have known better than to strike off on their own, but the prospect of a new and better life impelled them to put their lives at hazard. Thirst, starvation, hostiles, all took a high toll. Hopes and dreams were crashed to ruin on the jagged rocks of reality.

The patrol rode hard, always mindful of their mounts. Frequent brief rests were called for.

Fortunately there were only about twenty warriors in the war party. They wouldn't go swooping down on the wagon train the moment they saw it. They'd wait to catch the settlers off their guard.

The sun was relentless. Water became a concern. They needed to find some in the next several days or they and their animals would suffer.

Chester Gilliam had taken to riding by James's side, and one afternoon he grinned and said, "So, this is how you blue bellies earn your livin'? Ridin' and fightin'."

"Pretty much," James said. He didn't mention the endless hours of drill and the thousand and one petty jobs around the fort when they weren't out in the field.

"That Howell is right. This army beats all. I could get used to this life right quick."

"It's not all roses," James said drily.

"What life ever is?" The Southerner then related, "Me, I come from poor stock. We never had more than the clothes on our backs. Ma and Pa were powerful fond of one another, so we had us a big family. Eleven kids, and them, livin' in a small cabin in a clearin' in the backwoods." His face lit at the memories. "I miss those days."

"Why'd you leave?"

"Promise not to tell?"

James nodded.

"I got into a lick of trouble and had to light a shuck. There was this feller who wouldn't leave my sister be, so I had to learn him not to."

"Did you kill him?"

"I'm not rightly sure. Ma and Pa were afeared I had, so they told me to make myself scarce. The sheriff of our county was big on hemp socials." Chester looked at him. "You sure you won't blab?"

"I was in trouble a time or two in my younger days," James said.

"Yet here you are. You reckon the army will take me, then?"

"The army isn't all that particular about who enlists, and even less about what the recruits did before they signed up."

"Awful nice of them."

James laughed. "Nice" had nothing to do with it. There was always a shortage of men and officers, and enlistment quotas had to be filled.

That evening the patrol made camp, as usual. After the sun was down, James looked for flickering points of light that would show they were getting close. The empty blackness was unrelieved.

Captain Stoneman came up. "We can't be that far behind. A day or two at the most."

"I could take two men and go on ahead," James proposed. "Ride the whole night through if need be."

"To what end? Three men can't hold the hostiles at bay."

"I could warn the settlers the hostiles are shadowing them," James said. "I doubt they know."

Stoneman pursed his lips in thought. "I doubt they do, either. Very well. Pick your men. Ride your horses into the ground if you have to, but get to them."

James turned.

"And, Doyle," Stoneman said.

"Sir?"

"Try not to be scalped. Your coddling of the men aside, you're a damn good officer."

45

The prairie at night was a different world.

James and the three men with him were ripples of motion in a sea of black. From out of it the wind bore the yips of coyotes and the occasional howls of wolves, and now and then a bleat or a sharp cry told of a meat-eater that would fill its belly.

James rode at gallop despite the perils. Prairie dog towns were common, their burrows treacherous. A horse could easily break a leg and need to be put down.

Every couple of hours James stopped. At their second rest, as he was peering in vain to the north, Private Plover cleared his throat.

"Mind if I ask you a question, Lieutenant?"

"Ask away," James said.

"Why me, sir?"

"Pardon?" James was intent on spotting campfires.

"Why did you pick *me* for this when you had your choice of any of the men?"

"You show promise, Private," James said.

"Me, sir? Are you sure you don't have me confused with someone else? What have I ever done that's shown promise?"

"You did well in the skirmish at the stream."

"Sir, I was scared silly."

"But you held your ground and did what you had to," James praised him.

"It's the only fight I've ever been in."

"And that's one more than most of the men. A couple more and you'll be an old hand at it."

Plover laughed without mirth. "Don't take me wrong, sir, but I could do without the experience."

"This is what that uniform you wear is all about," James said. "You requited yourself well and I'll say so in my report. Keep up as you are and you'll make corporal before the year is out."

"Thank you, sir," Private Plover said, although he didn't sound grateful.

Private Howell had been listening to their exchange.

"That's why you brought him along, Lieutenant, but why'd you bring me?"

"You like to fight."

Howell grinned. "Like you say, it comes with the uniform. And you're right, by God. If there's anything I like more than a good scrape, I've yet to find it."

"Never been with a woman, have you?" Chester Gilliam teased.

"You shouldn't even be here," Private Howell said. "You're not a soldier, so why'd you come?"

"We're pards, ain't we?" Chester replied. "It was right kind of the captain to let me tag along."

"The condition was," James thought it prudent to remind him, "that you follow my orders at all times. I trust you'll be as good as your word?"

"Hell, Yank," Chester said. "A man who doesn't do as he says he will ain't no man at all."

By midnight James was shrugging off fatigue. By two

a.m. a brisk wind had picked up and to the west the sky flared with vivid flashes.

"Lightning, sir," Private Howell said. "There's a storm headin' our way."

No, it was an isolated thunderhead, common on the plains at that time of year, and it passed well to the north of them.

A little later James's horse snorted and bobbed its head, and he drew rein.

The others did the same.

Ahead loomed a vague bulk. James's first thought was that it must be a buffalo and he unlimbered his carbine. Warily, he gigged his horse forward.

The bulk didn't move or make a sound.

"Why, it's a wagon," Chester Gilliam declared.

The sharp-eyed Southerner was right. A prairie schooner, canted at an angle owing to a busted rear wheel, a spare wheel lying on the ground next to it. A jack had been placed under the axle, but the owner got no further. The man lay naked and spread eagle, his scalp and his genitals missing, his eyes empty sockets. The contents of the wagon were scattered about, much of it broken. The canvas top had been cut to ribbons. James almost missed spying a woman on her side on the seat, curled as if in sleep, a broken arrow jutting from her bosom. The Indians hadn't torn off her homespun dress or mutilated her in any way.

"Why didn't the other settlers bury the bodies?" Private Plover wondered.

"Could be they'd gone on ahead," Chester Gilliam said. "Could be this'n here told them to after his wheel broke. Probably didn't want to slow them any and reckoned he'd catch up quick."

That was James's assessment, as well. "The hostiles

saw their chance and took it. Keep your carbines handy, men."

No sooner were the words out of his mouth than the stillness was shattered by war cries and a shot.

"At a trot," James commanded.

They hadn't gone fifty yards when another shot and a chorus of savage whoops were punctuated by a hideous shriek, followed by an ominous silence.

James changed his mind. He slowed to a walk before they were heard.

From up ahead came a commotion followed by a flurry of retreating hoofbeats and then more silence.

"What do you make of it, sir?" Private Plover whispered.

"Not another word," James said.

They went a quarter of a mile and might have ridden past the body if not for Chester Gilliam, who had eyes like a cat. "Over here, Lieutenant," he said, and reined to the right.

The man was dressed in overalls. His long beard was stained with the blood that had gushed from a hole the size of James's fist. He had been scalped.

"Looks to be a farmer, sir," Private Howell said.

"What was he doing here?" Plover asked.

"Sent to see what was keeping the wagon with the broken wheel," was James's hunch. "He blundered into the hostiles and there's the result."

"That could be us if we're not careful," Chester said.

"Don't say things like that," Private Plover criticized. "It's bad luck."

"Spare me your superstitions, Yank. I never was one for rabbit's feet and four-leaf clovers. My pappy swore by 'em, but he never had any great luck nohow."

"Cover me." James dismounted and went through the farmer's pockets. All he found were a few coins, a folding knife, and a small ball of twine. He put them in his saddlebags, saying, "I'll give these to his relatives if he has any." His saddle creaked as he climbed on. "From here on, no talking unless I say. Understood?"

The dark seemed alive with shadows. Twice James nearly drew rein because he thought he saw someone on horseback. But it was a trick of the pale starlight and his imagination.

By James's reckoning dawn was an hour off when he raised his tired eyes to the north and beheld a shimmering orange finger.

"We've found them," he announced, and drew rein.

Private Plover forgot James's earlier order and asked, "Why did we stop, sir?"

"We'll dismount and lead our horses and be as quiet as we can be," James explained. "The hostiles are no doubt watching the camp and we want to sneak in without them knowing."

"And we got to be careful those settlers don't shoot us by mistake," Chester said.

"There's that," James agreed.

46

The seventeen wagons were in a circle, aligned rear to tongue. Horses and oxen were picketed inside the ring to prevent their being run off. James was pleased to see they had taken the precaution but not so pleased that only one man was standing guard. Or, rather, sitting guard, since he was cross-legged by the fire, his elbows on his knees and his chin in his hands, a rifle across his lap.

Frontier protocol called for James to hail the camp, but if he did he'd wake everyone. The old man didn't hear him walk up to the fire and gave a start when he shook him.

"Are you a soldier or am I dreaming?"

"Touch my arm," James said. "I'm real enough."

"Where did you come from? Did you drop out of the sky or sneak up on me like an Injun?"

"Do you see any wings on my back?" James said. "Wake up, old fellow. Your situation is serious."

Shaking himself, the old man stiffly rose. "I'm awake. What do you mean by serious? And who are you? I'm Ezekiel Smith." He rattled on without taking a breath. "My pa and his pa before him were all from Maryland

and I was, too, until my son took it into his head to come west and I tagged along to lend him a hand and have someone to talk to since my Martha passed away nigh seven years now."

James held up a hand. "Save your family history. I'd rather hear how it is with this train in a minute."

"Sure thing." Ezekiel yawned and scratched himself.

James posted the troopers and Gilliam as sentries. "Keep a sharp eye. It's a wonder, given how careless these people are, that the hostiles haven't struck before now."

"When do we get to sleep, sir?" Private Plower asked.

"When I say so. I wouldn't advise doing it while you're keeping watch or you might have your throat slit."

James returned to the fire. The old man had sat back down and added a log.

"Wait until the captain sees you," Ezekiel said. "He'll be happy you came along."

"Captain?" James said.

"Oh, he's not a real captain like you."

"I'm a lieutenant."

"We call him captain on account of he's the wagon boss and that's what some call their wagon bosses. Captain Guttman. We paid him good money to bring us to Oregon Country."

James couldn't believe his ears. "You've only missed it by a thousand miles. I'd say your wagon boss would be better suited making shoes."

"Hey now," Ezekiel said. "It's not his fault. It's ours. We were tired of all the traveling and Peter Dermit suggested we try Montana Territory as it's closer and there's plenty of land to be had."

"Plenty of Indians, too, or didn't you hear about Custer?"

"Oh, we heard," Ezekiel said. "We also heard the

army was rounding all the redskins up and it would be safe to go just about anywhere."

"Where did you hear that?"

"Peter Dermit read it in a newspaper. He knows a lot, that Peter. Captain Guttman says Peter knows more than he thinks he does. The two of them have been squabbling since we left St. Jo."

"Tell me, Ezekiel," James said. "Do you and the others know about the hostiles on your trail?"

"What are you talking about? We haven't seen hide nor hair of Indians this whole trip. You ask me, all those tales people tell are so much hot wind."

"Tell that to the three of you the hostiles have already killed."

Ezekiel stiffened. "You don't mean Sam and his wife, and Aaron Marsh who went to fetch them?"

"If that was their names, I do." James looked at the prairie schooner. "Does every man here have a gun and know how to use it?"

"We all have guns. Captain Guttman made each of us bring one. But as for using them, we can plunk a grouse if it's standing still, but I daresay there's not one of us who would be of much use in a life-or-death fight."

"Wonderful," James said.

Sunrise was breathtaking. Bright splashes of red and pink heralded a golden crown. A few pillowlike cumulus clouds floated serenely overhead, their snow white a contrast to the deepening blue.

Soon the camp was astir, and in no time James was surrounded by curious men, women, and children. He had learned a lot about their journey from Ezekiel Smith, and when a stocky man in a deerskin coat and a wide-brimmed hat strode toward him, he knew from

Ezekiel's account that it was Captain Paul Guttman. They shook, and James explained why he was there.

Guttman possessed a craggy face burned brown by the sun.

Years ago he had made his living as a trapper and now as a guide.

"I'm right sorry to hear about Sam and Minerva, but they wouldn't listen. They insisted we come on ahead and they would catch up." He sadly shook his head. "I've never had so much trouble with a train as I have with this bunch. They're a passel of know-everythings."

"Here, now," a man took exception. Lean as a broom, with a hooked nose and a pointed chin, he was dressed in store-bought clothes and knee-high boots. "You can't blame us for looking out for our own interests."

"Who would you be?" James asked.

"Peter Dermit's the name." Dermit didn't offer his hand. "I'm the leader here."

"He thinks he is," Guttman said.

"Did you hear him?" Dermit asked James. "He's been like this the whole trek. Treats me as if I don't know a buffalo from a badger."

"We should never have left the Oregon Trail," Guttman said. "It was your brainstorm, and now three people are dead on account of it."

"On account of hostiles," Dermit said, bristling. "How dare you blame me, you overstuffed—"

James stepped between them. "That will be enough. I'm in charge now and I won't put up with this squabbling."

Dermit switched his anger from Guttman to James. "See here. Who do you think you are? The army has no authority over us. We're free to do as we please."

"As of this moment, no, you're not," James said.

"What is it you want of us?" Guttman asked.

"We'll sit tight until Captain Stoneman arrives. Hopefully, the hostiles will leave us alone. Then we'll escort you to Fort Sisseton."

"How long must we stay there?" a matron in a bonnet inquired.

"That's up to the army, ma'am," James answered.

"At least tell us if it will be days or weeks."

"Until the uprising is quelled."

"Hellfire," Dermit said. "That could take months. What will we live on in the meantime? The army's generosity?"

"I'm sure Colonel Maxton will see to your needs," James assured them.

Some were clearly displeased. Others didn't appear to mind.

To judge by Dermit's clenched fists and the twitching of his jaw, he was the most upset of all. "We can't allow this," he addressed his fellow travelers. "Summer doesn't last forever. This far north, the cold weather comes early. We need to find a place to settle and start on our cabins with all dispatch."

"I don't see what else we can do," a man said. "It's the army."

"We can stand up to them," Dermit said. "We can refuse to go with this man and his superior. The loss of our friends aside, the Indians haven't attacked our train. We're too many for them and they're afraid of our guns."

"I don't know," another man said.

Dermit raised his voice. "Who is with me? Who will stand up for our rights with force if we have to?"

Private Howell and Private Plover were observing the proceedings from opposite ends of the camp. James motioned and they came on the run and stood at attention.

"Sir?" Howell said.

James pointed at Peter Dermit. "Take this man to his wagon and see that he stays there."

Howell reached for Dermit's arm, but Dermit jerked away.

"Now, you just hold on. You can't just come in here and treat us like criminals. You have no jurisdiction."

James touched his insignia. "This is all the jurisdiction I need. You can go quietly or I can have my men tie you and carry you. Your choice."

A woman about Peg's age with a baby in her arms raised a hand as if she were in school. "Lieutenant Doyle, is it?"

"Yes, ma'am?"

"You might want to hold off on that. You'll need your soldiers for more important matters."

"What matters, exactly?" James asked.

"Them," the woman said, pointing.

James turned.

The glow of the rising sun revealed that the circle of wagons had been encircled in turn by scores of warriors.

47

Panic spread like a prairie fire. Men swore and ran for their rifles and women cried out. Several of the smallest children caught the contagion of fear and burst into tears.

An older woman had her hands to her throat. "Look at them all. We don't stand a prayer."

James turned to Guttman. "You're their wagon boss. Calm them down. No one is to shoot unless I say." He moved to a gap between the prairie schooners so he could see the Indians better. "Damn."

The war party had swelled to over forty.

"There weren't that many before," Private Plover said. "Where did the others come from?"

"Who cares?" Private Howell said, feeding a cartridge into his carbine. "They're here and we're in for it."

The Indians were sitting their horses just out of rifle range. For them to come into the open was unheard of, and James was perplexed as to why.

The settlers scurried like rabbits. Women and children climbed into or under wagons while their menfolk took positions with their rifles. Guttman roved among them, bellowing for everyone to stay calm and keep their wits about them and for the men not to shoot.

A warrior in a breechclout gave his bow and quiver to another and approached with his empty hands out from his sides, guiding his animal by his legs alone.

"What do you reckon that's about, sir?" Private Howell said.

"I can pick him off if you want," Chester Gilliam offered. "Put a pea smack between his eyeballs."

"No." James gave his carbine and his revolver to Howell. "He wants to talk. I'll go meet him."

"Is that wise, sir?" Howell said.

"One of us has to and I'm the officer."

"How will you palaver?" Chester asked. "Do you speak Sioux or know sign?"

That gave James pause.

The wagon boss had heard them. "I know sign. I'll go with you." Guttman gave his rifle to Private Plover.

"Your six-gun and your knife, too," James said.

Guttman hesitated, then complied. "Let's go see what the red devil wants."

"You don't like Indians much, I take it."

"I hate them," Guttman said. "The Blackfeet killed a brother and a cousin of mine, both. Andy Jackson had it right. We need to round them all up and cage them like animals or wipe them out."

Had it not been for the fact that James had no way of communicating, he would have made the wagon boss stay with the wagons.

The warrior stopped midway and lowered his arms. Although within easy bullet range, he displayed no fear or anxiousness. He might have been a bronzed statue, he sat so still.

"I know that buck," Guttman said. "He's Sioux. Forget which band. Minniconjou, maybe. Or was it Sans Arc? Whites call him Broken Ear."

James understood why when they drew near and

stopped. The warrior's right ear had been mangled by a blow or a bullet.

Instead of covering it with his hair, the warrior wore his hair drawn back as if to show it off.

Broken Ear fixed them with a baleful glare. He ignored Guttman and said to James in English, "Bluecoat."

It was James's understanding that few Sioux spoke the white tongue. Most of the time the army relied on interpreters. "I am told that you are known as Broken Ear."

The warrior grunted and touched what was left of it with a hint of pride. "White dog do this. Me kill with knife. Take hair and hang in lodge. Take your hair. Hang in lodge with his."

"If you're trying to scare me, it won't work," James said.

"Me scare plenty quick," Broken Ear said.

"I'm Lieutenant James Doyle. Unless you break away and leave these people alone, there will be dire consequences."

Broken Ear scowled. "Use small words. Big words not go in head."

"Go, or more blood will be spilled."

"You say that like bad thing," Broken Ear said. "Me like spill white blood. Me like spill all white blood so there no more whites."

Guttman said something under his breath that James didn't catch.

"Want whites never come Lakota land," Broken Ear said. "Want Lakota land Lakotas."

"I don't blame you," James said.

"What?" Guttman said.

Broken Ear had lowered his arms. "You not blame? Then why you here? Why you come Lakota land?"

"It's not up to you or me," James said. "We can't change how things are."

"Whites go or Lakota kill."

"Be sensible," James said. "This is a war your people can't win. There are too many of us."

"More to kill."

"I was hoping you wanted to talk peace."

Broken Ear angrily slashed the air with his hand. "No peace ever, my people, your people."

Guttman swore and said, "This is a waste of our time, Lieutenant. Tell this red bastard to go to hell and we'll hunker down."

A crafty gleam came into Broken Ear's dark eyes. He gestured at the wagons. "Me let whites live if you give guns. All long guns. All guns with six-shots. Give those and we go."

Guttman laughed. "You're out of your mind, heathen."

"Quiet," James said. To Broken Ear he said, "You can't honestly expect us to hand over our weapons. It would put us at your mercy."

"Broken Ear keep word. Give guns, you live. Not give guns, all whites die."

"I'd like to see you try," Guttman rasped.

"You're not helping matters," James said.

"Whites think Lakota dumb," Broken Ear said scornfully. "Whites always trick Lakota. Me show you. Lakota smart, too. Broken Ear have good trick. Soon all you be broken."

"Big talk," Guttman said.

"Damn it to hell." James was at the end of his patience. "Shut up or go back." He appealed to Broken Ear one more time. "I speak for the whites now. I offer you the hand of peace if you will take it." He held out his.

Broken Ear's face betrayed his contempt. "Me not white. Me Lakota. Me put fear in whites plenty soon."

"Listen to reason," James said.

"Me done talk," Broken Ear announced, and wheeled his horse.

"Wait," James called, but the warrior made for his companions.

"I guess we told him," Guttman said.

48

James almost punched him. Pivoting on a heel, he returned to the wagons and reclaimed his weapons. A number of settlers had left their positions and wanted to know what the palaver had been about.

"Injun bluster," Guttman told them. "There's nothing to worry about."

As if to prove him right, the Sioux rode off to the east and were lost in the glare of the rising sun.

Several hours passed with the settlers in a state of nervous dread. An attack was looked for any moment, but the war party didn't reappear.

"What they waiting for?" a man loudly wondered. "Is this a trick to wear us down?"

"Maybe they went for more of their kind," another suggested. "Enough to wipe us out."

"That will do with talk like that," Guttman said gruffly. "There are women and children present."

"So?" said an older woman. "Do you think us so weak you must spare our feelings?"

James was outside the circle, leaning against a prairie schooner. He had made several circuits of the camp and not spied a single Indian anywhere.

"These folks sure do squabble a lot," Chester Gilliam commented.

"They're scared," Private Howell said, "and that makes 'em contrary."

Private Plover was nervously fingering his carbine. "I wish the Indians would do something. The suspense is eating at me to where I can barely think."

"Yankees have puny thinkers, anyhow," Private Howell said, laughing.

Plover wasn't amused. He turned to James. "Sir, how long before Captain Stoneman shows? I'll feel a lot better once he does."

So would James. By his reckoning, though, it wouldn't be until near sundown. "Seven or eight hours yet, Private."

"I hope I can stay awake that long, sir," Plover said. "I'm about dead on my feet."

"Go get some coffee."

"Me, too, sir?" Howell asked.

"All three of you, if you want."

James was left alone with his thoughts. He could use some coffee, too. He smothered a yawn and stretched and was leaning back when his shadow was joined by another. "What do you want?"

The wagon boss had a Winchester cradled in his left arm.

He was chewing a wad of tobacco and now he spat a dark gob, wiped his mouth with his sleeve, and squinted into the haze. "Someone should go on a scout to see if the redskins are still around."

"Don't let me stop you," James said.

"You're the army, not me," Guttman said. "It's your duty to protect these people."

"Don't tell me my job."

"Damn, you're prickly. But you know I'm right. Could

be the Sioux know your captain is coming. Could be they pulled off to ambush him. Did you think of that?"

Yes, James had, and the prospect troubled him. "They could be anywhere."

"There's only one way to be sure. I can't do it. These people are under my charge. I have to stay and look after them."

"You actually care what happens?"

"They pay me to care." Guttman spat again, and lowered his voice. "Between you and me, I wouldn't give a good damn for the whole lot if they didn't. I never have cared for people much."

"You cared enough to warn them about straying off the Oregon Trail."

"Cared, hell. I was thinking of my own hide." Guttman motioned at the plain and said sarcastically, "In case you ain't noticed, we're in the middle of Sioux country."

"Takes all kinds," James said.

"Yes, it does," Guttman agreed, and laughed. "You won't get my dander up, so don't bother trying. I'm not to blame for this fix. Dermit is. And you soldier boys, too, for not subduing the Sioux like you should."

"They don't subdue easily. Ask Custer."

"Everyone knows he was a glory hound. He got what he asked for." Guttman's cheek bulged with tobacco. "But he died doing his duty and that counts for something. Now how about you do yours and get out there and look for the damned Sioux?"

James remembered a time when he would have slugged someone for talking to him in that tone.

"Well? Nothing to say? Or is it you're yellow? You don't want to go for fear of being stuck with arrows? Must make your wife proud if you've got one, knowing she married a coward."

James hit him. He looped a right that smashed Guttman on the chin and knocked him against the wagon. Guttman dropped his rifle and his knees gave, and he grabbed at the schooner for support. Pulsing with fury, James punched him again, in the gut. Guttman doubled over. James was about to land a third blow when he got the better of his anger. He slowly lowered his arm.

"Don't ever mention my wife again, you son of a bitch."

Guttman waved a hand and sucked in breaths. "Like I said," he wheezed. "You're too damn prickly."

At that juncture Private Howell and Private Plover and Chester Gilliam returned. They looked from James to the wagon boss and back again.

"Did we miss somethin', Lieutenant?" Private Howell asked.

"This gent givin' you trouble?"

"Get your horses and bring mine," James commanded.

"Are we going somewhere, sir?" Private Plover asked.

"To look for the Sioux."

49

The prairie was an oven. The grass that had been so green during the wet months of early spring was now shading to the brown of summer and would stay brown until the fall.

James was in the lead. They had ridden for half an hour without any sign of their enemies. James was beginning to think that Broken Ear had indeed gone.

A killdeer cried. James saw it pretending to be hurt to draw them away from its mate and their nest. A hawk soared on high, and to the south antelope were clustered, watching warily and poised for flight.

James smiled. God help him, but he did so love the prairie. It was a vast ocean of life, at times sublime and beautiful, at other times savage and brutal. It was so unlike New York City, and Five Points. They were distinct worlds, the grime and greed and lusts of civilization contrasted with the picturesque splendor of the wilds. He wasn't poetical by nature, but when he gazed out over the rippling waves of grass shimmering bright in the golden light of the setting sun, he felt a stirring deep inside him, a sense of grandeur that he had never felt in Five Points.

Lost in his musing, James became aware that Chester Gilliam had come up next to him and was talking.

"—much farther we goin' to go, Lieutenant? Strikes me that if we ain't come across the redskins by now, we ain't liable to."

"I need to be sure," James said.

"Nothin' is ever certain where red devils are involved," Chester said. "They're unpredictable critters."

"They're people, like you and me."

"Not so, Lieutenant. Not so. They have their skin and we have ours and what's under our skins ain't the same as what's under theirs."

"They have organs just like ours," James said. "Stomach, hearts, livers, kidneys."

"Why, Lieutenant, are you joshin' me? That's not what I said and I suspect you know it. I was talkin' about natures, not organs. White folks have their natures and redskins have their own."

"Their natures are no different from ours."

"Not true, Lieutenant. Not true. They don't think like us. They don't feel like us. They crave blood more than we do, for one thing."

"Have you forgotten the Civil War?"

"That's not possible, seein' as how I was in it," Chester replied. "But that was for a cause. Redskins kill just to count coup."

"Or to keep from being forced off their lands."

"It sure is peculiar, you takin' up for them." Chester shook his head in disbelief.

James was scouring the ground. The tracks were plain enough; Broken Ear and the war party had continued on to the east and were miles away by now. He abruptly drew rein. "I guess you're right. This is far enough."

"Now you're talkin'," Chester said.

The privates were equally glad. Plover, in particular,

was so relieved he shouted for joy, then caught himself and looked sheepish.

"Sorry, sir."

The whole ride back James thought of Peg. He missed her more each day. They had been separated before, but this time she was with child and his feelings were stronger. He couldn't wait to take her in his arms again.

James wondered if he was being fair to her and their unborn child. Here he was, putting his life at risk. She could end up a widow, his child could end up fatherless. As if it were yesterday, he remembered the hardships his mother had faced. Did he want the same for Peg? He was still debating when they reached the wagon train.

Guttman and a dozen others came out to meet them. "Well?" the wagon boss asked.

"They're long gone," James said.

"Hallelujah!" Ezekiel cried.

"We can be on our way at last," another man said happily. "The Lord be praised."

"On to find our new homes!" declared a third.

"No." James burst their euphoria. "Nothing has changed. You will be escorted to Fort Sisseton."

"But the danger is past," Ezekiel said.

Another settler nodded. "We'll be perfectly fine on our own. And we've already been delayed long enough."

"As soon as Captain Stoneman arrives, we're heading for the fort," James reiterated. "Whether you want to or not."

Their smiles changed to frowns.

"This is damned unfair," Peter Dermit said. "But I'd expect no less from the likes of you."

James had nearly forgotten about him. "What are you doing out of your wagon? You were to stay there until I say differently."

"You weren't here," Dermit said, "and I refuse to be

treated like some sort of prisoner when all I did was speak my mind."

A few women were listening, among them the young woman with the baby. "Isn't that strange?" she said, half absently and in a low voice.

James gratefully turned his back on the men. "What is?" he asked.

"That," the young woman said, and nodded to the east.

In the distance dust was rising to the sky. A cloud so large, it lent the illusion of being a thunderhead, only the dust was brown and not the black of a storm cloud.

Others noticed and another woman cried, "My God! The hostiles are coming back."

James tried to distinguish shapes. There was too much dust for it to be Broken Ear and his war party. It couldn't be Captain Stoneman, either. It was too soon for Stoneman and there were too many.

"If they are they've brought a lot of friends," Guttman said.

"We'll be overrun," Dermit cried. "We have to get out of here."

"How far do you think you'd get in these heavy tortoises of yours?" Guttman countered. "They'd catch us before we went a mile."

"Anything is better than sitting here waiting to be butchered," Dermit said.

"Do you hear that?" the young woman with the baby asked, her head cocked.

"Hear what, Adeline?" Ezekiel said.

"That noise."

James heard it, too, a far-off rumbling.

"It's their horses," Guttman said.

"Doesn't sound like horses to me," Chester Gilliam mentioned.

It did not sound like horses to James. But he was mystified as to what it could be.

"By the Eternal," Ezekiel said, and took a step back in shock. "I know! I've never been west of the Mississippi River, but I by God know. The fiends! The vile heathen fiends. Only they would be so cruel."

"What are you babbling about?" Dermit snapped.

The truth dawned on James and a cold fist closed around his chest.

"It's buffalo!" Ezekiel cried. "The redskins are driving a herd of buffs down on our heads."

50

Disbelief sparked exclamations.

"Surely not!"

"It can't be!"

"How could they?"

James recalled the parting words of Broken Ear. "Soon all be broken," the renegade had said. Now it made sense.

From out of the dust rose the whoops and cries of the warriors driving the herd.

"What do we do?" Dermit cried in panic. "We can't just sit here. They'll stampede right over us."

"You run for your lives," Guttman said. "Hitch up your teams and get the hell out of here." He pushed several of the stunned settlers. "What are you standing around for? *Move*, damn you, or you're all undone."

James marked the dust cloud. The herd was a long way off yet.

"Can we delay the critters or turn them somehow, sir?" Private Howell asked. "Buy these folks time to harness up?"

"The four of us can't turn a tide of horns and hair," Chester said.

The settlers were dashing about like souls gone mad.

Women and children screamed. Men roared lusty oaths. Guttman was trying to keep them calm, and failing.

"We have to try," James said. "Bring the horses." Back when he was in Kansas, D Troop had come across a herd of cattle being driven to market. That evening the subject of cows and cowboys came up, and someone mentioned that a herd of stampeding cattle could be turned if it was done right. He wasn't a cowboy, but he would try.

"At a gallop," James urged when they were mounted. The dust cloud had expanded to monstrous proportions. In its depths dark forms moved. The rumbling was thunderous. He caught glimpses of horns and shaggy coats.

They were half a mile out from the train when they saw the buffalo clearly. There were hundreds if not thousands of the huge brutes, shoulder to brutish shoulder in a moving mass. The very ground trembled.

James drew rein.

"The four of us against all those?" Private Plover said, his eyes wide.

"We could charge 'em but I doubt they'd scatter," Private Howell joked.

"The three of us will charge them," James said, "while Mr. Gilliam sets the prairie on fire."

The Southerner touched a finger to his ear as if he wasn't sure he had heard right. "You want me to do what, now, Lieutenant?"

"The wind is right but there's not much of it," James said. "Get a fire going and it might do what we can't." He raised his reins. "We'll slow them if we can. Howell, Plover, you're with me."

The bison horde was terrible to behold. They poured across the prairie in a tidal wave of bobbing heads and rising and falling humps. Curved horns bristled like sabers. Their bellows and grunts and snorts created a discordant symphony.

James drew rein several hundred feet from the front ranks. He vaulted down, wrapped the reins around his wrist, and tucked the carbine to his shoulder. He recognized the futility but he took aim anyway. "Fire at will as soon as they are in range!" he commanded, and at the right moment, he banged off shot after shot at hairy beast after hairy beast.

Howell and Plover contributed lead of their own.

"It's having no effect, sir," Private Plover yelled, lowering his Springfield.

"It's like chuckin' peas," Howell said.

James turned to his horse. "Mount and make for the wagons." As he rose into the saddle, he caught sight of a warrior in the thick of the dust. What he wouldn't give for a shot at Broken Ear. Reining around, he galloped to the west with thunder in his ears. He caught up to Private Plover, who was whipping his reins like a man possessed.

Sudddenly Plover's horse squealed and crashed to the earth. Shattered bone ripped from a leg, gleaming white in the sun.

Plover was thrown clear and tumbled. Dazed but unhurt, he raised his arms imploringly. "I'm down! Help me!"

James was already hauling on his reins. Only now did he see the prairie dog burrows. He reached Plover's side, bent, and bodily swung the private on behind him. Another wrench on the reins and they were flying to the west.

Not just the ground but the air pulsed to the beat of thousands of heavy hooves. The roiling phalanx of mammoth monsters pounded implacably on.

Private Plover clung to James as if trying to climb inside his body and wailed for him to go faster, faster, faster.

Smoke rose ahead. Chester had done it; he had set the grass on fire. But the flames were small and extended in a line of no more than twenty or thirty yards. As a defense it was pitiful.

Private Howell overtook Chester and now both Southerners were racing toward the prairie schooners, many of which were in motion, the drivers frantically whipping their teams. Other settlers were yet hitching their animals with a haste born of desperation.

James reached the crackling flames. He figured to ride right through them as Private Howell had done. It didn't occur to him that his horse might be one of those that was deathly afraid of fire or that it would do what it did—namely, slide to a terror-spawned stop and then rise onto its back legs and rear.

James instinctively clung to the saddle and wasn't unhorsed. A squawk of fear rang in his ear and the pressure on his shoulders was gone, and he twisted to find that Private Plover had fallen off. Before he could reach down to pull Plover back up, his horse took several bounds to get clear of the fire.

James brought it to a stop, and wheeled.

Plover was on his feet. He had landed in the fire and now his coat was giving off smoke and flames of its own. He swatted at them, shrieking, "No! No! No!" Without looking where he was going, he ran—toward the stampeding buffalo.

"Plover! Stop!" James shouted, and went to go after him, but it was too late.

The buffalo were on them.

51

The fire didn't slow the herd at all.

Private Plover must have realized his mistake and glanced up. He shrieked as a horn hooked him in the chest. The bull that gored him tossed its huge head and Plover sailed over its hump and into the thick of the swarm.

James fled.

Private Howell and Chester Gilliam had swung to the south to try and get clear of the herd. The prairie schooners were scattering, but they were, as Guttman called them, tortoises on wheels, and much too slow. A few settlers were running off on foot, stragglers who had been left behind in the urgency of the exodus.

James was so intent on flying for his life that he almost didn't hear the squall of an infant.

Adeline wasn't in a wagon. She was hastening after a man on a prairie schooner and beseeching him to stop, but he didn't heed her plea.

James didn't have much of a lead on the buffalo. Fully aware that if his horse went down he would share Private Plover's fate, he reined to intercept her and shouted her name at the top of his lungs.

Adeline heard him. She had the presence of mind not to stop and instead, while still running, she flung up an arm for him to grab, her face a portrait of heartfelt appeal.

Half afraid he would tear the arm from its socket, James bent and grabbed and heaved. He got her and the baby over the saddle in front of him and shouted for her to hold on. They passed the wagon she had been chasing and the man on the seat glanced at them and said something.

James didn't hear what it was. He was holding on to Adeline and her child for dear life and slapping his legs against his horse.

"Dear God!" Adeline cried. She was looking back.

James glanced over his shoulder and witnessed a spectacular spectacle.

The buffalo had overtaken the slowest prairie schooner. Some broke to right and to left to avoid it, but the press of beasts from behind drove as many more into the rear of the wagon and into its wheels. The crash and rending of wood mixed with their bellows and cries. Some of the brutes went down and were trampled by their brethren. The back of the prairie schooner collapsed and dragged, possessions spilling pell-mell. Another instant and the whole wagon canted. The man in the seat saw that it was about to go over and leaped clear to save himself. But the buffalo had enveloped the entire wagon and his leap carried him into them. He screamed as he disappeared.

James rode for his life and that of Adeline and her baby.

Her pale face, streaked with tears, was turned up to him.

They overtook another prairie schooner. The man and woman on the seat were half turned and holding rifles. They fired and a couple of buffalo dropped, but then the rest were on them. The wagon was pushed broadside, seemed to bounce, and overturned. Hammering hooves reduced the man to pulp. The woman tried to scramble onto what was left of the box, but a horn sheared into her thigh and most of her dress, with her leg, was ripped from her body.

Ahead were three prairie schooners bunched together. James reined around them. On one was Peter Dermit, wielding a whip. Dermit was pasty with fear.

James could sense his horse was tiring. He had been told that buffalo could run for miles, and if that was the case, he would never see Peg again.

Out of nowhere a steep gully opened in their path. James wrenched on the reins, but his horse couldn't stop in time. It squealed and pitched headlong. James pushed against the saddle, pulling Adeline and her baby with him, and contrived to come down so that he bore the brunt of their fall. They rolled to a stop at the bottom, with James on top of her and the child.

Adeline screamed.

An upended prairie schooner had filled the sky above them.

It crashed down, the wagon wedging across the gully, the hickory bows that braced the canvas shattering like toothpicks, the canvas tearing and splitting at the seams. The grease bucket smashed within a few inches of James's neck. A brake block struck him in the leg. From out of the bed spilled clothes and utensils, tools and flour and blankets. Fighting the downpour, James pushed up just as a chest of drawers careened into his shoulder. He was thrown to his hands and knees.

The weight of the avalanche of effects was irresistible.

James and Adeline and the baby were buried.

For a harrowing minute James feared they would be

crushed or suffocate. But the rain of articles stopped. Propping his hands on either side of Adeline and the baby, he exerted all his strength. The press of weight shifted. He tried again, every muscle straining. The possessions moved but he still wasn't free. Once more he thrust upward and clothes and a pan and a saw went sliding away. His head and shoulders burst out and he sucked in air. Quickly, he shoved objects aside and cleared a space for Adeline.

They were in a pocket between the spilled possessions and the upended wagon. Above them the prairie schooner and the ground quaked to the passage of the buffalo. The gully was filled with a pungent reek. A cacophony of bellows assaulted their ears. Dust fell in fine particles like an artificial snow, fine yet thick, covering everything.

The baby was crying. Adeline held the child to her bosom and caressed and consoled it, her fright giving her face a ghostly pallor.

Suddenly the prairie schooner shuddered to the impact of a heavy body. A buffalo had fallen on top of it and was struggling to free itself. James saw a dark leg and a hoof kick at the shattered bed. He thought that maybe the buffalo would fall on top of them, but it broke out and ran on with the rest.

"God preserve us," Adeline breathed.

James could hardly hear her for the roar. The yips and whoops of the Sioux succeeded the thunder, and faded. He reasoned that most of the Indians were at the rear of the herd, goading them on, and he dared hope that the worst was over.

The din drifted west and a profound silence fell. Shafts of sunlight came through rents and breaks in the prairie schooner.

"We're not dead?" Adeline said in astonishment. She

coughed and swatted at the dust. Tears of joy welled in her eyes and she kissed and hugged her baby. "It's a miracle!"

"Not so loud," James cautioned. "There still might be hostiles about." He climbed on top of the pile and clambered onto a stove that lay on its side. Standing, he reached up. The wagon box had split in half. He carefully climbed through the break and crouched with his head below the gully's rim, listening. Someone was moaning, and there was a gurgling and thrashing.

James had lost his carbine. He drew his revolver and rose high enough to see over. To the west the stick figures of the hostiles trailed the dust cloud. All around, the prairie grass had been trampled to bits. Here and there lay dead buffalo. Here and there, also, were shattered prairie schooners, some on their sides, a few flat on their beds, one upside down. Dead horses lay near many of the wagons, and elsewhere. One that wasn't dead accounted for the gurgling and the thrashing.

James rose higher. Not much was left of the settlers who had been on those wagons. Pulped flesh and bones, mostly. One man was missing part of his face and his arm. A woman had somehow been torn nearly in half. Close by lay a body with the chest crushed flat and the legs turned in on themselves. The only part that was whole was the head; it was Peter Dermit, his mouth wide in the scream torn from his throat as he was pulverized.

"Lieutenant?" came a soft voice below.

James holstered the Colt. Bracing his legs, he bent and lowered his arms. It was the work of a few seconds to pull Adeline and her baby up beside him and then to steady her as together they climbed out. She straightened, took a step, and stopped.

"My God."

"I know," James said.

"What did we do to deserve this?"

James had no answer to that.

To the north were two wagons, intact. To the south was another, as well as two riders who were eagerly trotting toward them.

James wearily smiled and waved and Private Howell and Chester Gilliam waved back.

"Where's my husband?" Adeline said, walking in a slow circle. "Why didn't he stop when I was yelling to him?"

Again James held his own counsel.

"I don't see our wagon or him anywhere." Adeline moved around the gully, casting hopefully about.

James went with her.

"Oh!" Adeline stopped and put a hand to her throat. "There it is."

The prairie schooner was a loss, the canvas in tatters, the wheels busted, the bed splintered. What little was left of an arm and a hand poked from under the rubble.

Adeline sank to her knees and sobbed.

James put his hand on her shoulder. "I'm sorry, ma'am," he said. "I truly am."

She wept without sound, her head hung in despair, the baby strangely quiet in her arms.

James respectfully walked off a few yards.

The surviving prairie schooners were heading back, too.

Presently Howell and the Southerner drew rein and Howell beamed with glee.

"We'd given you up for a goner, sir. It's a delight to see you breathin', if you don't mind my sayin' so."

James gestured at Adeline and Howell sobered.

"Sorry, sir. I wasn't thinkin'."

Chester Gilliam surveyed the carnage. "I never saw the like in all my born days. Hellfire, I never imagined the like of any of this."

"Where's Plover?" Private Howell asked.

James shook his head.

"Damn," Howell said. "For a Yankee he was almost all right. Timid, but then Yankees ain't naturally got as much grit as us boys from south of the Mason-Dixon."

"I'm a Yankee, Private," James said.

Howell coughed. "I stand corrected, sir."

Chester was staring to the west. "You know, if those redskins take it into their heads to finish what those buffs started—"

"I had the same thought," James said. "Go hurry those wagons along."

Private Howell nodded and rode to the south. Gilliam headed to the north.

James turned to the gully. He walked along the rim until he saw a tail sticking from under the box. It took some doing to work down and under to his horse. He tried to remove the saddle, but there wasn't enough space. He did manage to get his saddlebags off, and his canteen. He was about to climb out when his knee bumped something sticking out of the riot of effects: a hardwood stock. He pulled and wriggled and pulled some more, not knowing if it was his carbine or the settler's rifle, and finally worked it free. "Someone up there likes me," he said, and patted the Springfield.

By the time James clambered from the gully, the three prairie schooners had arrived.

One of them belonged to Ezekiel. "You made it," the old man said with a sad smile.

"Barely," James said.

Ezekiel stared at the bodies and the ruin. "I almost feel guilty to be breathing. A lot of those folks were my friends." He peered about. "You didn't see what happened to our wagon boss, did you?"

James shook his head.

"I did," Private Howell said. "He tried to outrun the buffalo, but his horse wasn't fast enough."

"Just as well," Ezekiel said. "The truth be told, I never liked the man much."

"We have to get out of here," James said. "Ezekiel, any objection to having Adeline and the baby up there with you?"

"Be glad for the company."

"Private Howell, I'll need your horse. You can ride on one of the wagons—"

"Beggin' your pardon," Chester broke in. "But why don't you use my animal? I don't mind ridin' with Zeke, here, and the lady."

"I'll take you up on that," James said. "I'll go fetch her."

"What's your hurry, son?" Ezekiel asked.

"He's worried the hostiles will return," Chester said.

"You are, Lieutenant?"

"I sure as hell am," James said.

52

For more than a mile the prairie schooners clattered and creaked. Their slow pace rubbed at James's nerves. He rode at the rear with Private Howell.

"No sign of them yet, sir."

"Don't jinx us," James said, only partly in jest.

"Even if the redskins do come back," Howell said, "maybe they won't see our tracks and think we perished with the folks in those wagons."

James made no comment on the prospect of the Indians failing to notice the ruts of the three schooners that led away from the slay ground. The only surprise was that it was taking Broken Ear so long to come after them. Rubbing his sore neck, he glanced back for the hundredth time. "I told you not to jinx us."

A knot of riders were in the distance. As yet they were too far away to identify, but they were coming from the west; it could only be the hostiles.

Just then Chester Gilliam poked his head around the canvas of the lead wagon and hollered, "Lieutenant! Get up here right quick! We have company."

"More Injuns?" Private Howell said.

James hurried to the front. Ezekiel had brought his

schooner to a stop. Off to the east were more riders, only these were in a column and not bunched together.

"It's the captain!" Howell cried in delight. "They got here sooner than we reckoned."

James shifted in the saddle. The Indians and Captain Stoneman were about the same distance from the prairie schooners. It was likely that as yet, neither was aware of the other. An idea came to him, and he immediately put it into execution. "Private Howell, ride like hell to the captain. Tell him that the hostiles are almost on us and for him to come on fast but as quietly as he can."

"Quietly, sir?"

"No bugle. No shouting. Speed is everything. Off you go now."

Puzzled but dutiful, Howell galloped off.

James reined toward the prairie schooner. "Ezekiel, I need you and the others to turn your wagons. Line them up from north to south so that you're between the hostiles and our relief."

"Whatever for?" the old man asked. Then his eyes lit and he jerked as if he'd been slapped, and he laughed. "Oh. I'm savvy. So the redskins won't see the soldier-boys until it's too late."

"It's worth a try."

The settlers in the other wagons weren't as eager, but they obeyed. James had everyone climb down and get under the schooners. He dismounted on the west side and stood with his carbine in his hands.

"Awful risky," Chester said, "usin' us as bait. What if the hostiles reach us before your captain does?"

"We keep them busy," James said.

"Are all officers like you?"

"In what way?"

"You must have been born with grit in your veins."

"I'll take that as a compliment."

"Good. Because it is." Chester nodded. "I've done made up my mind. I make it through this, I'm sure enough enlistin'."

The war party was a lot closer. Broken Ear was out in front, whooping and waving a rifle over his head.

"They think they have us," Chester said.

"Get under a wagon."

"Not if you don't."

One of the warriors fired and lead smacked into the schooner behind them. An arrow whizzed into the canvas. All the hostiles were yelling and yipping with savage glee. As whites would say, the Indians thought they had the survivors dead to rights.

James raised his Springfield. He aimed and held his breath to steady the carbine. Ignoring more slugs and arrows, he stroked the trigger.

Eighty feet out, Broken Ear went rigid. Blood spurted from the hole in his throat and he dropped his rifle and pitched from his warhorse.

James dived under the schooner. Shafts and bullets smacked the wood like hail. Ezekiel and the other settlers were firing.

He aimed and banged off another shot.

The war party broke to either side to encircle the prairie schooner.

They were met by waves of blue. Carbines crackling like firecrackers, the troopers tore into the surprised renegades. The Indians were caught completely off guard. At such close quarters the soldiers made nearly every shot tell and a third of the hostiles fell in the initial seconds. A mad chaos ensued, with the warriors more intent on escape than counting coup. The fight became a rout.

Captain Stoneman wasn't about to let any get away. Roaring commands, he gave chase.

Just like that it was over. Dead and dying warriors lay by the score. A few figures wore blue.

Sergeant Strake and half a dozen troopers were moving among the prone forms, finishing off any with red skin that moved.

James slid from under the prairie schooner. He was about to go to Strake when Chester Gilliam said his name.

The Southerner sat propped against a wheel, blood trickling from his mouth, two arrows sticking from his body.

"No," James said. Kneeling, he saw at a glance that it was hopeless. Either wound was mortal. It was a wonder the Southerner was still alive.

Chester coughed and more blood flowed. "Looks as how I won't be enlistin', after all."

"I'm sorry."

"Not your fault, now, is it?" Chester grinned. "I should've skittered under the wagon when you did, but I was a mite slow."

"You would have made a fine trooper."

"Thank you." Chester's eyelids drooped, but he forced them open. "You see Howell, tell him for me that he's right. Not all Yankees are worthless." He chuckled, and was gone.

53

James stood in the doorway to their bedroom in the quiet stillness of dawn and watched the rhythmic rise and fall of her bosom as she slept. The first blush of light wreathed their pink curtains, lending her face a rosy glow. She was beautiful, the most beautiful sight he ever set eyes on. That so beautiful a woman cared for him was a miracle of life beyond his fathoming.

James felt an ache in his chest. The ache was as deep as his marrow, a hurt like no other, a hurt of pleasure and not pain. He'd never felt anything like it. Not with the wild girls in Five Points. Not with the fallen doves in St. Louis.

Peg stirred something inside him that he'd never realized was there. Maybe it took a woman like her to bring it out of him. Maybe that was what love was about. Real love, the kind that endured, the kind that filled a heart to bursting with the potency of raw need.

James quietly removed his hat and set it on the chest of drawers. He sat on the edge of the bed and tugged his boots off and set them aside. He undid his belt, started to unbutton his uniform, and stopped. Easing onto his side, he turned. Her back was to him. He snuggled against her and placed an arm across her belly. She wasn't showing yet. It would be a while.

A lump formed in his throat and he had to swallow. He moved her hair and kissed the nape of her neck.

"James?"

He hadn't meant to wake her and stayed still thinking she would go back to sleep.

"James?" Peg said again. She stirred and looked dreamily over her shoulder and a smile lit her whole face. "Why don't you say something?"

"I've missed you."

"I've missed you, too."

James kissed her and put his nose to her hair and breathed deep of her scent. It was one of the most perfect moments of his life.

"How did the patrol go?"

"Fine."

"Did you meet up with any hostiles? The other patrols are already back and they didn't see sign of any."

"We saw a few," James said.

"Tell me all about it."

James ran a finger along her ear. "There's not much to tell."

Peg slid her hand from under the blankets and touched his lips. "You're saying there was no danger?"

"No more than I expected," James said. Which was the truth, as far as it went. He would elaborate only if she pressed him, and fortunately, she didn't.

"Good. I was so worried." Peg rolled over and pressed her cheek to his chest. "It's so nice to have you home." She sniffed a few times and laughed. "Even if you do smell like your horse."

James almost told her that his horse was dead but caught himself in time.

"The first thing you need is a bath."

"The first thing I need is to sleep here by your side for a while."

"I would love that," she said.

James stroked her hair. "Are you happy, Peg?"

She looked at him. "What kind of question is that? Of course I am."

"Say the word and I'll give up the army and be a store clerk or do whatever other kind of work I can find."

"What in the world are you talking about? I'd never want you to give up army life."

"I'm just saying that if you did, I would."

Peg shifted and peered into his eyes. "Oh. I understand."

She playfully rubbed his chin. "You felt guilty leaving me alone. But no, I don't want you to give up what you love most in this world." She grinned. "Next to me, of course."

"There is nothing on this earth I love more than you," James confessed.

"Goodness, you get romantic when you are away." Peg paused. "But why did you ask? Do you want to muster out and move back East?"

"Not this bluecoat," James said. He wearily sank his head onto a pillow and closed his eyes. He was tired, so very tired.

"The East isn't my home anymore. The West is."

"The West forever," Peg said.

"Forever," James Marion Doyle echoed.

They fell asleep in each other's arms.

54

The baby came into the world squalling. James wanted to name it Randall in honor of his father, and Peg said she didn't mind so long as they named their first daughter after her mother.

They stayed at Fort Sisseton until the army closed it. After a short spell at Fort Leavenworth, James was assigned to Fort Yellowstone.

The Indian Wars, as the newspapers dubbed them, slowly wound down. Tribe after tribe was subdued by the overwhelming force the whites brought to bear on the "Indian problem."

The mighty Comanches, the stalwart Cheyenne, the determined Sioux, all were brought to bay. Even the bands many considered the most fiercely independent of all, the Apaches, were eventually forced onto reservations.

James had one more encounter with the red man. He had been at Fort Yellowstone for two years. By then he had made captain.

His duties, compared to the wild and perilous days at Fort Sisseton, were mild. The troopers were there to safeguard the newly created national park from vandals and to enforce its game laws.

On a routine patrol in the fall, James was deep in the geyser country. It had been so long since he had seen an Indian, let alone fought one, that when he climbed to the crest of a timbered ridge and beheld an Indian seated cross-legged on a flat boulder, he was as surprised as the young troopers who were with him. He ordered a halt and dismounted. His sergeant wanted to go with him, but James climbed onto the boulder alone and sat facing the apparition.

James had never learned to tell the tribes apart as well as the scouts could. He didn't know if the man before him was Cheyenne or Sioux or Blackfoot or what.

The warrior was old. Wrinkles formed crags of his loose flesh. His buckskins hung in folds to his skin-and-bones body and were worn thin from long use. His moccasins were fit to fall apart. He looked at James with tired eyes and spoke so softly that James had to perk his ears to catch his words. "White man."

"Indian," James said. "To which tribe do you belong?"

"Does it matter?"

"Eh?" James said, surprised by the question. Most warriors took pride in their people.

"Does it matter?" the old warrior said again. "To your kind we are all the same. We are animals to be driven onto land we do not want to live on and made to live as you live even though we do not want to live as you do."

"You speak the white tongue good," James said.

"That surprises you, does it? An Indian who can use the white tongue as well as his own? I learned it many winters before you were born from a white man who came to our land to trap beaver. He was a good man. He had a good heart."

"How are you known?" James asked.

"Does it matter?" the old warrior again rejoined.

"If I ask you what you are doing here, will you say the same thing?"

The suggestion of a smile touched the wizened old-ster's lips. "I have come here to die."

"Here?" James said in considerable surprise. To his knowledge no tribe had lived in that immediate area.

The old warrior raised his gaze to the magnificent vista of forest and snowcapped peaks and a bright blue lake. "I have always loved what you whites call Yellow-stone. I came here often when I was young to hunt and to seek visions."

"Where is your family? Your friends?"

"Dead and dead."

"Your tribe?"

"On the reservation where your people put them," the old warrior said.

"So you left it to come here? Are you aware that any Indian caught off a reservation is to be taken back to it?"

The warrior looked at him. "I am old, bluecoat. I am not stupid."

"Yet you came anyway?"

Bowing his head, the old man sighed. "Because he has many guns, and because there are more of him than there are of us, the white man can tell us where to live and how to live. He can tell us what we must eat and make us go to his schools so he can tell us how to think." The old warrior raised his head and his voice. "But he will not tell me where to die."

"I'm not supposed to let you," James said.

"Even this the whites would deny me," the old man said sadly.

"I have my orders."

"Then shoot me."

"What?"

The old warrior placed a gnarled hand on the hilt of a knife on his hip. "I will attack you. Shoot me so I can die where I want to die."

"It means that much to you?"

"I am here," the old man said.

A gust of wind brought a chill to the air. James pulled his coat about him and said, "It will be winter soon."

"I will be dead before the first snow."

"Would you like some water? Or anything to eat?"

"Do your orders say to feed me before you drag me off?" the warrior asked.

"The only thing that might drag you off is a bear," James said.

The old man was quiet awhile. "I thank you, bluecoat. You are the second white man I have known to have a good heart."

"A lot of whites have good hearts."

"If they do they hide it well."

James grinned. "At least tell me your name."

"I am Eagle Soaring. My days here are finished. I go to the next world happy to be done with this one."

Rising, James stared to turn, and stopped. "I never wanted to fight your kind. I never wanted to kill any of you. I did it to protect others."

"You have counted many coup?"

"I guess you could say that."

The crags on the old man's face deepened. "We are warriors, you and I. Once there were many of us, but now there are few. Our time is over. My people and yours will plant seeds and sell goods and drink whiskey and our ways will be forgotten."

"There will always be a need for warriors," James said.

"Will there?" the old man said. His chin sank to his chest and he closed his eyes. "I am tired, friend. Leave me. It will not be long."

James climbed down and accepted his reins from the sergeant. "Mount up."

"What about the Indian, sir?"

"What Indian?"

James made it a point to return by the same route. The old warrior was gone, nor could James find any trace of where he had gotten to. Off into the forest, James imagined, to die far from anywhere, all alone. James wished his spirit a peaceful rest.

55

The turn of the century came and went.

James retired from the military, and they bought a house in the foothills near Denver. From his front porch he could sit and see far out over the prairie he so loved.

Why he took it into his head to visit New York one last time, he would never know. Peg was curious to see his old haunts, but there was nothing to show her. Five Points had been razed. His old neighborhood had ceased to exist. In its place were prosperous businesses and homes. So much had changed, he had trouble finding the street he had lived on. Where his tenement had been now stood a bakery.

The slum was no more, but the poor were still there. Most had moved to the Lower East Side, existing in the same squalor as before.

The old gangs had gone the way of Five Points.

It was as if none of it had ever been. James stood at the intersection of Worth and Baxter and reflected that his life and that old warrior's had more in common than he thought.

Peg passed on to her reward before he did. She was eighty-three when she succumbed. He was at her bedside, holding her hand, and after she had breathed her last, he buried his face in the blankets and cried.

James outlived her by another seven years. His two sons and two daughters had eighteen grandchildren between them, and his last days were spent in the company of loved ones.

Then, on a warm evening in the spring, he was on his porch in his rocking chair, sipping coffee, when the pain struck. He dropped the cup and clutched at his chest. He tried to rise, but his legs wouldn't work. Sinking back, he felt the pain lessen. His oldest daughter was supposed to visit in an hour and he thought that if he sat there quietly, he would recover and she could get him to a doctor.

Then his chest seemed to explode. His last sight was of the prairie, golden in the glow of the setting sun. He felt as if part of him was flying toward it.

"A writer in the tradition of Louis L'Amour
and Zane Grey!"
—*Huntsville Times*

National Bestselling Author

RALPH COMPTON

AUTUMN OF THE GUN
THE KILLING SEASON
THE DAWN OF FURY
BULLET CREEK
RIO LARGO
DEADWOOD GULCH
A WOLF IN THE FOLD
TRAIL TO COTTONWOOD FALLS
BLUFF CITY
THE BLOODY TRAIL
SHADOW OF THE GUN
DEATH OF A BAD MAN
RIDE THE HARD TRAIL
BLOOD ON THE GALLOWS
BULLET FOR A BAD MAN
THE CONVICT TRAIL
RAWHIDE FLAT
OUTLAW'S RECKONING
THE BORDER EMPIRE
THE MAN FROM NOWHERE
SIXGUNS AND DOUBLE EAGLES
BOUNTY HUNTER
FATAL JUSTICE
STRYKER'S REVENGE
DEATH OF A HANGMAN
NORTH TO THE SALT FORK
DEATH RIDES A CHESTNUT MARE
RUSTED TIN
THE BURNING RANGE
WHISKEY RIVER

**Available wherever books are sold or at
penguin.com**

S543-110310

No other series packs this much heat!

THE TRAILSMAN